Lucía's hand shot ▮▮▮▮
curled around the ▮▮▮

For a long moment all she did was look at him, her bright brown eyes ablaze with curiosity. "No one's ever spoken to me like you do, either."

"Oh?" Leo blinked. "Is that a good—"

Lucía surged up on her tiptoes, her face so close to Leo's that her breath ghosted over him when she said, "I like it. And I would like it even more if you kissed me."

With more enthusiasm than grace, or even skill, he kissed her.

It was too glorious for words. Her lips were like silk, or velvet, or one of the expensive fabrics at Don Enrique's store that Leo always longed to touch. She tasted sweet—a little like the dessert they'd just had, but mostly a heady, complex flavor that was all her own.

The sound of her name being called from the terrace was like waking up.

"Lucía! We're leaving!"

Author Note

The thing about side characters is that however lightly you try to sketch them, sometimes they spring into full color in a way you never intended them to. That was what happened with Leo, who first appeared in *Compromised into a Scandalous Marriage*, and Lucía, whose sister is the heroine of *Alliance with His Stolen Heiress*.

At first I wasn't sure what their story would entail, but when I came across a news clipping from the early twentieth century that detailed a case against a man who was claiming recompense after his warehouse full of goods had burned down—only for a witness to prove that there was nothing in it—I knew that was the kernel I needed to put Leo and Lucía into a situation that would test their resolve to stay away from each other.

I have always loved a second chance romance, and I hope that you will feel the same way about Lucía and Leo's story!

LYDIA
SAN ANDRES

The Return of
His Caribbean Heiress

HARLEQUIN
HISTORICAL

HISTORICAL™

Recycling programs
for this product may
not exist in your area.

ISBN-13: 978-1-335-59597-3

The Return of His Caribbean Heiress

Copyright © 2024 by Lydia San Andres

For questions and comments about the quality of this book,
please contact us at CustomerService@Harlequin.com.

Harlequin Enterprises ULC
22 Adelaide St. West, 41st Floor
Toronto, Ontario M5H 4E3, Canada
www.Harlequin.com

Printed in U.S.A.

Lydia San Andres lives and writes in the tropics, where she can be found reading and making excuses to stay out of the sun. Lydia would love to hear from her readers, and you can visit her at lydiasanandres.com or follow her on Instagram, Twitter and TikTok @lydiaallthetime.

Books by Lydia San Andres

Harlequin Historical

Compromised into a Scandalous Marriage
Alliance with His Stolen Heiress
The Return of His Caribbean Heiress

Look out for more books from Lydia San Andres coming soon.

Visit the Author Profile page at Harlequin.com.

To K and G, the two puppies who kept insisting that I pet them instead of typing. I would have finished this book much faster without you, but it wouldn't have been nearly as much fun.

Prologue

San Pedro de Macorís, 1905

Eighteen-year-old Leandro Díaz was a poet, and therefore, well versed in all the intricacies of love. He didn't know he had been wrong about all of it until love walloped him between the shoulder blades one bright summer day.

To be fair, it was a ball that struck him first. It wasn't until he twisted around to look reprovingly at the little boy he'd assumed was the culprit that Leo came face-to-face with the most beautiful girl he had ever seen. And it hit him again—love. The sudden, desperate, breathtaking kind he had only ever read about.

Everything around him seemed to go still. The shouts of the children playing behind them quieted, and the conversation coming from the group sitting in Paulina de Linares's terrace was suddenly no more than a hushed murmur. Leo couldn't even feel the breeze, which just a moment before had been moving briskly through the leaf-heavy branches of the mango tree.

It was as if the world had come to a complete stop—

and when its movement resumed, it was at a slightly different pace than before.

In a white dress bedecked with lace-edged ruffles, the girl looked like one of the clouds scudding across the sky behind her, though of course that simile was all wrong. He ought to be comparing the sparkle in her eyes to the stars above, or her lips to budding roses. Or maybe that was too trite…

He was so busy composing a poem in his head that it took him a moment or two to realize that she was talking to him.

"Are you all right?" she asked.

Concern was evident in every line of her delicately angular features, and it only grew more pronounced when Leo found himself too tongue-tied to reply immediately.

His first impression of Lucía Troncoso was quickly followed by even more favorable second and third impressions. Although one wouldn't have guessed it from looking at her pristine dress, she'd been playing ball with four rambunctious little boys. After making sure that Leo hadn't been grievously injured by the throw, she coaxed him into joining the game. Truth be told, it wouldn't have taken much persuading. Leo may have been more adept with a pen than he was with a bat, but he was as fond of the boys as if they were his own younger brothers, and he had always loved running around with them.

And it didn't hurt that joining in the game gave him the excuse to look at Lucía as she dashed from one side of the lawn to the other, ruffles aflutter.

They didn't have the opportunity to play for long—the sun was high in the sky and the air was redolent with the scent of the Moorish rice and pork chops that were being prepared for lunch. Whether by the grace of the fates or the artful intervention of his hostess, Leo was seated next to her at the table. Her nearness left him even more breathless than all the running had.

Then her fingers brushed his as she passed him the *tostones* and Leo was rendered almost delirious.

He tucked into the mound of rice on his plate with an enthusiasm that surprised him. Weren't people supposed to lose their appetites when they were in love? Leo was ravenous, and not just for the crisp salad with its tangy vinaigrette or the figs in syrup they were served for dessert. He drank in every single word that fell from her lips. He shivered at every bright peal of laughter and every sparkling sidelong glance she gave him whenever she said something impish.

It wasn't until the rest of the gathering had settled drowsily into rocking chairs with their demitasses of strong, sweet, aromatic coffee that she took the initiative and asked him to go for a stroll. Their path took them around the shadier part of the garden and the brick-bordered flower beds, bursting with periwinkle flowers in delicate blue clusters. On an impulse, Leo bent to snap off a spray, which he presented to Lucía with a flourish.

Her answering smile was made of the same stuff as cooling breezes and refreshing drinks, lighter and sweeter than the lemonade he had been sipping earlier. One of her front teeth was ever so slightly crooked, and the sight of it hit him like another blow, this one to the chest.

"You're sweet," she observed, tucking the blossoms into her hair, which had been braided into a coronet. "No one's ever given me flowers before."

"How can that be possible?" The question popped out before Leo had a chance to think them through. "I should think you'd had entire gardens dropped at your feet in celebration of your beauty." He came to an abrupt stop, suddenly stricken that she'd find his compliment insincere as some people did when his words came out overly ornamented. "You really are, you know. Beautiful. In a way that transcends your features, as if what one sees is your soul shining through."

Her soul, and what looked like an excess of feeling that intrigued him.

They had wound around the mango tree and were momentarily hidden from view behind its thick trunk. Leo took a hasty step backward, mindful that Lucía's older sister and brother-in-law must be watching out for her from the terrace. Before he could get too far, Lucía's hand shot out and her fingers curled around the front of Leo's shirt, tugging gently until he was once again behind the mango tree.

For a long moment all she did was look at him, her bright brown eyes ablaze with curiosity. "No one's ever spoken to me like you do, either."

"Oh?" Leo blinked. "Is that a good—"

Lucía surged up on her tiptoes, her face so close to Leo's that her breath ghosted over him when she said, "I like it. And I would like it even more if you kissed me. Would you?"

Leo jerked his head into a nod. With more enthusiasm than grace, or even skill, he kissed her.

It was too glorious for words. Her lips were like silk, or velvet, or one of the expensive fabrics at Don Enrique's store that Leo always longed to touch when he went in to buy ink and pencils. She tasted sweet—a little like the dessert they'd just had, but mostly a heady, complex flavor that was all her own.

The hand that had been clutching his shirt drifted down to his forearm, and he had to restrain a shiver as her fingers came into contact with the bare skin below the sleeve he had rolled up to his elbow. He didn't dare touch her. Didn't dare do anything but stand there, drawing in long drafts of air as he grazed her lips with his, over and over again.

If everything around him had gone still when he'd first laid eyes on her, the entire world fell away when he kissed her. Leo had never felt like this, as if he was in a daze—or a dream.

The sound of her name being called from the terrace was like waking up.

"Lucía! We're leaving!"

Lucía's grip tightened on his arm, her teeth closing gently on his lower lip.

Then, like a girl out of one of Perrault's stories would upon hearing the clocks strike midnight, she broke away from him and hurried to her waiting family. Only she was no penniless scullery maid—she was an heiress, and so far beyond Leo's reach that he knew dreaming about her was as useless and foolish as trying to climb a ladder to the moon.

And yet dream he did.

It was all Leo could do to wait for midmorning the next day. He had bathed and dressed by the time the sun started peeking over the horizon, and he checked his watch so frequently that his mother made a remark about him wearing out the silver plating.

As soon as the hour hand had shifted over to ten, he

seized his hat and jacket and strode out of the house, checking his pace only because he didn't intend to arrive at Lucía's house covered in perspiration.

His steps slowed further when he rounded the corner. The house where she lived with her sister and brother-in-law was so large it was daunting, its neatly manicured grounds sprawling from one end of the street to the other. A large, columned terrace wrapped around the front and side of the house, and the main door was easily more than twice his height.

Unlatching the wrought iron gate, Leo stepped through and resolutely marched up the front steps, where a woman in a dark dress was watering a spray of orchids that sprouted from a ceramic pot.

"Buenos días," he said politely. "Is Lucía home, by any chance?"

"Lucía?" the woman echoed, straightening the watering can. "You just missed them. Their ship sailed half an hour ago."

"Sailed?" Leo's heart began to pound. "Sailed where?"

"Why, to Europe," the woman said, eyebrows raised as if the answer should have been obvious. Her voice gentled, likely at the flicker in his expression.

"Europe," Leo repeated the word as if he'd never heard it before. "I didn't know they— When are they expected back?"

Sympathy. It was sympathy in the woman's tone when she said, "Not for several years, at least."

Chapter One

Five years later

After five years in Vienna, Lucía Troncoso had returned to San Pedro with more than twice the number of trunks she had set off with.

"No need to unpack that one," she told one of her sister's two housemaids as the young woman reached for the clasp on the smallest. As well as the matching burgundy leather valise, the trunk was stuffed with sheet music, which Lucía didn't anticipate needing anytime soon.

Holding her violin case by its handle, Lucía contemplated shoving it into the back of her wooden wardrobe, half of which was already occupied with the dresses the other young woman had just unpacked. The prospect of seeing the case every time she got dressed made her reconsider. A better spot for it would be the on top of the wardrobe, against the wall, where it would be hidden from view by her smaller pieces of luggage.

Lucía hooked her foot around a three-legged stool and awkwardly pulled it into position in preparation for clambering atop it.

"Why don't you let me help you with that?" one of the housemaids said gently, taking the violin case from Lucía and lightly hopping onto the stool herself. She set the case upright on top of the wardrobe, in a way that would be all too visible from the bed, even with every valise Lucía owned piled in front of it.

Biting her lip, Lucía tried not to frown. "Thank you," she said, choosing to leave it for the moment. She could always move it later.

The girl dipped her head into a nod. "We can finish the rest of the unpacking if you want to join your sister on the terrace."

For all the suggestion had been delicately worded, Lucía knew what it truly meant—she was in the way.

She paused for a second to survey her bedroom. The tall, lofty windows with their wooden shutters were framed by the lace curtains she had purchased in Brussels. Her bed had been made with a quilted satin coverlet and matching pillows, underneath which peeked white linens edged with delicate floral embroidery. On the antique vanity were her cosmetics and perfumes and the porcelain figurines she had collected.

All that was truly left to unpack were the few dresses remaining in the last trunk.

It was just as well. The flurry of their return to San Pedro had worn thin after two days of unpacking trunks and sorting through luggage, and Lucía was craving a trifle more excitement than could be found even among the folds of her most cherished frocks.

Excitement—and something sweet.

She ventured into the kitchen with the intent of making a Sacher torte with some of the apricot jam they had brought with them in carefully padded crates, only for the cook to hurry in from where she had been taking a well-deserved rest before starting dinner.

"You'll ruin your lovely clothes," she told Lucía, eyeing the eggs and flour on the table. "Just tell me what to do and I'll have it ready for you in an instant."

Lucía glanced down at the white shirtwaist and pale, fawn-colored skirt she had picked out that morning. Neither garment was particularly elegant or expensive, but they were fairly new, as was the brown crocodile belt cinching her waist. It had been polished to a high gleam, and its brass buckle echoed the hints of gold in Lucía's earrings and the thin bracelet that encircled her left wrist.

She and Amalia had gone to Paris the previous winter to order their wardrobes for the warmer seasons—which here could be worn year-round—and even their simplest outfits were modishly cut and well trimmed.

Forcing herself to smile, Lucía closed the drawer she had been rummaging around in and recited the recipe she had learned by heart. Then she made her escape.

Or tried to.

"Where are you going?" someone asked as Lucía reached the front door.

The voice belonged to Lucía's elder sister, Amalia. Lucía took a step back to peer around the large potted palm that had hidden Amalia from view.

There were a staggering number of rooms in this house, but Amalia hadn't settled on which one she wanted to use for her study, so the lovely secretary that had once belonged to their mother was currently residing in the front room, within view of the door.

Amalia's husband had spent the few weeks immediately following their marriage teaching her the finer points of estate management, and though Amalia had insisted that Lucía learn as well, she had shouldered most of the work of managing the lands and properties left to them by their father. Their uncle had taken charge of it all for years, keeping them both on a tight leash—financially *and* socially—until Amalia had driven him out of their lives.

Lucía was still a little in awe of their drastically changed circumstances, but Amalia had taken to the new challenge like she had been born to it. And, well, maybe she was.

Though she hadn't yet begun to show, pregnancy—and the long journey—had daubed shadows under Amalia's eyes. Visibly suppressing a yawn, she set her pen down next to the ledger she had been studying. "Why don't you take someone with you, dear? We're not in Vienna anymore, you know."

Lucía resisted the urge to roll her eyes. "I'm two months away from my twenty-third birthday, Amalia. I hardly need a nursemaid to take me on a walk," she said, a trifle more heatedly than she meant to. "It's not like I'm going to be snatched by a bandit and taken halfway around the island."

"I'm sure one would oblige you, if you asked nicely," Amalia replied swiftly.

Deft though she might be at concealing her expression, her eyebrows winged up enough to let Lucía know her outburst had startled her. Lucía felt immediately ashamed.

"I'm sorry," she told her sister, pushing back the brim of her hat. As a concession to Amalia's concern, she undid the clasp on her bracelet and dropped it beside the open ledger. "I've been out of sorts all day. I really do need to get some fresh air before I turn into an outright monster."

"You could never be a monster," Amalia said, grinning. "You're far too pretty."

So everyone else claimed. Lucía was too pretty, too sweet, too *fabulously wealthy*, to quote one of the girls she had befriended in Vienna. The girl's breathy whispers had made the rounds with surprising swiftness, and before the hour was over, half the academy had heard about the exotic—their word, not hers—heiress from the tropics.

The rest had found out before the second hour was up.

Lucía sighed. It was truly a ridiculous problem to have, and that it bothered her as much as it did always made her feel a little foolish.

It had rained earlier that day, and though the streets were filled with puddles, the bright blue sky had a freshly washed quality to it. The weather was slightly too warm for even the summer clothes Lucía had worn abroad. She'd have to remember to wear shorter sleeves tomorrow, and for however long it took to grow used to the tropical heat again…

She still craved dessert, but mindful of how unseemly it was considered for a young woman—or any woman at all—to sit alone at a restaurant or café, she headed instead for Don Enrique's store.

It only took a couple of minutes after arriving at the store for Lucía to wish she hadn't left the house.

The two clerks, who couldn't have been older than eighteen or nineteen, weren't making much of an effort to hide their admiration for Lucía as they all but shoved each other aside in their haste to show her the best Don Enrique had to offer. It was embarrassing and faintly exasperating—Lucía was no stranger to being the center of attention, though to her eternal dismay, it was rarely due to something she had accomplished instead of who she was.

As she'd strolled into the store, she'd heard someone whispering, "That's one of the Troncoso heiresses." Lucía didn't know how much the residents of San Pedro knew about what had happened five years before, when her uncle whisked Lucía clear across the island to marry her off to a man who wouldn't have been out of place as the dastardly villain in a Puccini opera. Accompanied by the man who was now her husband, Amalia had hared off after them and had actually interrupted the wedding by riding a horse right into the church, brandishing an unloaded pistol.

Maybe Lucía should write an opera of her own.

Whatever the townspeople had heard about the debacle, it was clear that Lucía and Amalia's long absence had only inflamed their curiosity. Uncomfortably aware of their gazes on her, Lucía chose a box of candied pineapple almost at random. She reached for her handbag— and realized a second later that she had left it behind in her haste to leave the house.

Her face felt so warm that Lucía couldn't help but be grateful that her skin was too dark to show a blush. "I forgot my handbag at home," she said, half wishing she hadn't come into the store. "I'll just go and fetch it and—"

"You can have it on credit," one of the boys said quickly.

The other one took half a step forward. "Please, allow me to make a gift of it."

As his companion turned to give him a furious glare, Lucía tried to intervene. "I appreciate the offer, but—"

Her protest was drowned out as one of the boys lunged at the other one. The second boy sidestepped his would-be attacker, leading the boy to stumble over a small barrel and crash directly into a neatly arranged tower of canned goods.

If there was a single person left in the store whose attention hadn't been drawn by the squabble, the metallic clatter fixed that. Every pair of eyes in the store was now directed their way.

Lucía's cheeks felt like they were about to burst into flames.

"Thank you for all your help." She raised her voice, though she couldn't be sure the clerks heard her over their bickering.

Without waiting to see if they had heard her, she began hurrying away, her chin tucked in and her gaze firm on the floor. She was almost at the door when she looked up.

And there he was. Leandro Díaz.

The two of them had corresponded for more than a year after meeting at Paulina de Linares's one bright summer day. In the years since his letters had abruptly stopped, Lucía had sometimes wondered if Leo had really been as handsome as her memory insisted he was. She let her gaze linger on him as she tried to reconcile the man before her with the boy she had once known. If anything, he was even more handsome than she remembered.

He was much broader through the shoulders than he had been at eighteen, and he carried himself with a confidence that Lucía found highly appealing. He was also much better dressed than the last time she had seen him, in a lightweight black suit that had been perfectly tailored to accommodate the breadth of his shoulders and a crisply ironed shirt that didn't gape at the wrists or collar. The hint of a silver watch chain, lustrous but not showy, peeked out from his waistcoat pocket.

He looked prosperous—like he had thrived without her.

Her gaze skipped to his face.

He saw her. She knew he did. He was standing so still he looked like a bronze statue, his eyes just wide enough for her to see a thin rim of white around his dark irises.

Her lips parted, already starting to curl into a smile as she took a step toward him.

She could have sworn that a smile had started to form on his lips, too. Which made it all the more inexplicable when he turned on his heel and went the other way.

Leo's heart was hammering inside his chest.

Lucía Troncoso, here in San Pedro. For years now, she had existed only in the hazy memories that unspooled across his mind just before he awoke in the mornings. Seeing her face for the first time in five years had been a sharp joy, shards of it splintering inside him. Or maybe that was just his lungs burning from lack of oxygen as the very sight of her had rendered him unable to draw in a proper breath.

One glimpse of her and he felt unsteady, as if his entire life had been knocked askew by the sight of her face.

He lengthened his stride. Two more steps would take him right out of the store—and her presence.

He hadn't heard a word about her coming back. But then, how would he? He was working more often than not, and though he'd dined with Sebastian and Paulina the previous Sunday, he had never told them about his correspondence with the girl he had kissed under their mango tree.

"Leo!"

Briefly, he considered not stopping. Four or five more steps and he could take refuge inside the bank and pretend he had business there for however long it took for her to desist and return to wherever she had come from.

One look at her, and all the hunger and yearning he had long since smothered had once again flared to life inside his chest, as if not even a day had passed since she had thrown her ball between his shoulder blades.

But they had. A great number of days had passed, and Leo was supposed to be not just older, but wiser, too. Less prone to falling in love at the merest suggestion of a smile. Less willing to follow every curve of a woman's lips wherever they may lead him, even if it was over a cliff.

"Leandro Díaz."

Her voice was like his morning hot chocolate, its sweetness kept from being overwhelming by a hint of spice. She hadn't raised it—hadn't needed to. The very sound of it sent another jolt through Leo, one that made his step falter.

He forced in a deep breath. Then he made himself stop, just beside the bank's tall wooden door.

When he turned to face her, his first thought was that between her dark brown skin and the white shirt and light brown skirt she was wearing, she even looked like a cup of hot chocolate. A delicate, expensive, porcelain one, the kind he had never been able to afford.

"Oh," he said, as if he had only just noticed her, and

stretched his lips into a blandly polite smile. "Lucía. Pleasure to see you."

Her own smile, which had been leagues more genuine than his, flickered like a guttering candle. Looking a little uncertain, she placed her hands on her hips.

"Is that all you have to say for yourself?"

"All I have time for at the moment," he returned with a calm he didn't feel as he tried not to look down at the dark, slim fingers bracketing the slight swell of her hips. "I'm expected at the office. And the bank."

He tore his gaze away from her hips and met her eyes.

And, well. That was a mistake. One of the many he had made since he'd first met her.

He had once compared the sparkle in her eyes to stars. The thought struck him as childish now. Not because they weren't luminous, but because the light in them was far more incandescent than the cold, pale, distant glow of any celestial body.

The splinters burrowed deeper into the tender flesh of his chest.

"I won't take up too much of your time," she was saying. "I just wanted to ask you to pass on a message to your mother."

His *mother*? Before her headaches had grown debilitating, his mother had been a midwife.

Leo's heart didn't stop, but it did feel like it seized as his gaze darted to Lucía's trim midsection.

"For my sister," Lucía clarified. A dimple—*the* dimple, the one he had dreamed about for months—appeared next to her mouth. "It's her first, and I know it would do her a world of good if she had someone to talk to. Someone with experience in those matters, who could guide her as a mother would."

"No," Leo said shortly.

"No?" She tilted her head, making her gold earrings catch the light. "I don't mean to inconvenience her. I was just wondering if she could look in on Amalia every now and then. I'd be happy to—"

Before she could complete the sentence—or her offer of payment—Leo interjected, "I won't have my mother bothered."

He knew he sounded unfriendly and hard. He meant to. And it wasn't entirely for Lucía's benefit. He was desperately worried about his mother. Though four years had passed since she had taken sick, she hadn't quite recovered, and Leo felt like he was waging a daily war as he tried to keep her from taking on too much and risking a relapse. He could have said as much to Lucía, but it wasn't her business.

Her eyes narrowed. "Do you always speak for her, or is she allowed to make her own decisions?" she asked, her voice snapping with spice. "Maybe I ought to go speak with her directly."

Leo felt another jolt run through him, this one markedly less agreeable.

Of all the entitled things to say…

Over the course of their correspondence, Leo had never gotten the sense that Lucía was spoiled. But he knew better than anyone just how much a letter, no matter how heartfelt, could conceal about its writer's life and character. After all, hadn't he written her scores of missives in which he made no mention of the long, sleepless nights he spent hunched over ledgers or the panic that gripped him whenever his mother had one of her spells?

Finding out that Lucía was just another spoiled heiress shouldn't have been such a disappointment. But it did feel like the last remnants of what had once been his most cherished dream had crumpled to ash and were being swept away in the warm breeze.

"I don't know how people conduct themselves in fine society, but accosting someone in the street to make demands of them and insisting that people attend to you without so much as inquiring over their health or spirits is just about the most selfish thing I've ever witnessed. Not everybody is sitting around waiting for the opportunity to serve you. I'll be damned if I let my mother be plagued by a demanding, spoiled heiress."

His words brought a suspicious shine into her eyes, though her voice sounded steady enough when she said, "I'm not spoiled."

"Then, you're thoughtless," he snapped, and immediately felt like a brute.

"At least I'm not intentionally rude," she returned.

Leo drew in a shallow breath. "Allow me to say it in terms you'll understand—I have no wish to further this acquaintance. Have a good day, *señorita*."

And then he really was going to turn around and leave before he said something he'd have cause to regret—only she halted him again.

"Leo," she said quietly.

That was all she said, just his name, and yet he felt like an unstable building after its foundations had been rocked by an earthquake. He met her gaze squarely, feeling his irritation melt away. His shoulders, which had been tense and tight, eased a fraction as he let out a breath.

It was all about to come pouring out. Everything he had carefully kept out of his letters. All the heartbreak and anxiety and panic that he had lived through since the last time he had laid eyes on her sweet, frank, open face.

Every instance in which he had wished with a fierceness that bordered on desperation that he could confide in her without feeling like he was laying his burdens on her dainty shoulders.

Every moment spent dreaming about what it would feel like to have her in his arms. To trace the curve of her earlobe with his fingertip and follow the line of her neck, all the way down to the prim little collar of her lace blouse.

But he only got as far as "Lucía, I—" before he was interrupted by a young woman in a plain cotton dress.

Leo shifted to one side of the narrow sidewalk, though he wasn't really blocking the entrance to the bank, before realizing that the girl wasn't going inside—she had come for Lucía.

"Your sister sent me." She held up a large, furled umbrella, glancing from Lucía to Leo with evident curiosity. "It looks like it's about to start raining again and she didn't want you getting wet."

"It's fine," Lucía told her, clearly embarrassed. "I'll be fine. You needn't wait for me."

"I was given instructions, miss. I wouldn't want to get in trouble with Doña Amalia."

Lucía's brow knit with obvious frustration, but after a quick glance at Leo, she gave the girl a nod. "We'll go in a second."

The girl retreated down the sidewalk, where she stood clasping the umbrella by its ivory handle and politely turning her gaze toward the bustle of afternoon traffic outside Don Enrique's store.

Maybe Lucía wasn't spoiled. But she was certainly

coddled and overindulged, enjoying the kind of security Leo had barely allowed himself to dream of. Whatever happened during her sister's confinement, she would never have to count coins or go without just to ensure they had money for a doctor or medicine if they needed it.

A profound weariness washed over Leo. The dreams he'd once had about Lucía, and meeting her again, and telling her all he'd ever felt for her, were only that—dreams. They had no place in reality. And Leo no longer had time for useless dreams.

"You must excuse me," he said with chilly politeness, having finally regained his senses. It was a damned good thing the girl had come when she did—spilling his thoughts to Lucía may have brought him some momentary relief, but nothing good would have come out of it. "I'm expected back at the mill."

And then he did leave, and Lucía said nothing to stop him.

Leo didn't go to the mill. His pace was so clipped that he walked all the way to the docks in half the time it should have taken him, his heart thundering as if someone were after him. The thick cover of clouds overhead shielded him from the punishing afternoon sun, but the air was so humid with incipient rain that he could feel drops of perspiration beading across his forehead.

Even this late into the day, the frantic bustle of the docks hadn't slowed. San Pedro had one of the busiest ports in the island, from which the sugar that was produced in the region—as well as the tobacco and cigars brought in by locomotive from land-bound Santiago—was shipped to other countries. Plenty of passenger steamers stopped there, too, though it was more common to see fast cargo schooners, like the one that was pulling into the wharf as Leo neared the wooden, single-story buildings lined neatly across from the rippling water. Docked just beyond it was the *Caridad*, the schooner Leo had come to see.

At the age of eighteen, Leo finished his schooling and began working for Sebastian Linares as the bookkeeper at the latter's sugar mill. He had quickly realized the mill would save a great deal in costs if it manufactured its own sacks. Sebastian had agreed. Taking on Leo as a partner, he had purchased a factory. Now Leo was hoping to apply the same logic to distribution.

A great deal of the sugar produced here was taken north to New York in Norwegian steamers. Investing in a ship of his own was a risk—all investments were, in their own way—which was why Leo was taking pains to hammer out any uncertainties before the sale was finalized. Currently, the main uncertainty was the state of the ship's interior, which Leo had yet to tour. Ignacio Vargas, an importer of luxury goods and the current owner of the schooner, had promised to take him inside—seconds before he was called away unexpectedly. A second attempt at a visit had been similarly cut short. But Leo was nothing if not persistent, and the attractive price he and Vargas had settled on made Leo as reluctant to call off the sale as he was determined to get inside, once and for all.

A long line of sailors was unloading wooden crates from a cart and carrying them up the lowered gangplank, perspiration streaming down their faces with the effort. Each of the crates, Leo noticed, was being opened and ostentatiously inspected by a man in a rusty suit before the sailors holding it were allowed to proceed. Frowning slightly, he strode the length of the quay and tried to calculate if the ship was riding lower in the water than the last time he'd seen it. The *Caridad* wasn't supposed to be taking on more cargo, not if it was going to be passing into his ownership in two days.

He had just reached the bottom of the gangplank when his progress came to an abrupt halt at the appearance of a man in a cap and rolled-up sleeves, brown skin weathered by decades of exposure to the sun. He wasn't a large man, but the way he held his shoulders made Leo think of the bulwarks on a Colonial-era fort.

Leo extended his hand. *"Buenos días, señor.* I'm Leandro Díaz. I'm in the process of purchasing this ship from Ignacio Vargas. I spoke with him earlier this week about taking a look at the hold."

"I'm the first mate," the man said, though he looked more like a guard than anything. He glanced down at Leo's proffered hand without making a move to shake it. "Now's not a good time. We've just received some very valuable cargo and we're under strict orders to not let anyone inside."

The self-important little man at the top of the gangplank was certainly not taking pains to hide it. If the cargo really was as valuable as all that, Leo would think they'd all be more discreet.

He slid his hand in his pocket. "I'm sure that if I speak with Vargas—"

"He's out of town for the next fortnight. And we set sail in two days' time."

Leo swore under his breath. "But I'm meant to be signing the papers the day after tomorrow. Vargas assured me that I would be able to have a look inside before then."

The man spread his hands. "I wouldn't know about that. You'll have to speak with him when he returns."

His tone was final—and very similar to the way Leo's old schoolmaster used to sound just before he lost his patience. There was precious little chance that this man would work out his frustrations via a ruler to the palm, however, so Leo retreated.

All the same, he'd be sending word to Vargas, wherever he was.

Fueled by frustration, Leo reached the center of town in minutes. The slate gray sky was beginning to darken behind the round, turret-like corner of the Morey building. Leo followed a cart that was rumbling down Calle Duarte, absorbed in calculations. Taking a chance on Vargas's schooner meant risking less of his and Sebastian's money. But wouldn't it be more prudent to purchase a ship from someone more trustworthy, even if they ended up paying a little more?

It wasn't until he had reached the next cross street that his footsteps slowed. Without having quite realized it, he had walked, not to his own home, but to the two-story house on the corner of Duarte and La Esperanza. It was empty, as it had been for years, the shutters on all four doors behind the elegantly curved balustrades and stately columns of the porch shut tight.

The house Leo had grown up in hadn't even had a proper floor, just hard-packed dirt. And while the house Leo currently lived in with his mother had tile running all through it, he was convinced that his convalescing mother would grow stronger in high-ceilinged rooms with plenty of tall windows to let in the sunshine.

This wasn't the first time that Leo had stood there, staring at the house as he imagined what life would be like within its walls, and it likely wouldn't be the last. But maybe, one day, if this new venture proved as profitable as he was convinced it would be, he would do more than stare at it.

If everything went according to plan, Leo would be purchasing this house before the end of the year.

Chapter Two

"**P**aulina agreed to help me, but she's not much further along than I am and we're both so *exhausted* all the time. Still, I never thought I would find refurbishing a house so interesting. Did you know that—Lucía? *Lucía*."

Amalia's voice, colored with amused exasperation, finally cut through Lucía's abstraction. A little guiltily, she turned to her sister. They were sitting in their plushly upholstered carriage as it rolled along Calle del Comercio on its way to Paulina de Linares's home. While Lucía had been occupied being humiliated in front of Leo, Amalia's friend had sent a note to the house telling them that she was hosting a welcome-back party for them the next evening.

Outside the carriage's windows, San Pedro sped by in a streak of brightly lit houses and electric street lamps, made all the brighter by the full moon above. The sky had long since grown dark, and it held no trace of the rainclouds that had gathered the day before. Not a single drop had fallen as Lucía followed the umbrella-bearing housemaid, seething all the way.

She couldn't fault Amalia for wanting to keep her

safe, especially after everything they'd been through with their uncle. But Lucía was so tired of being treated as though she was made out of spun sugar. She wouldn't have melted if she'd been caught in a downpour—the worst that could have happened was that her shoes would have gotten muddy and her hat ruined.

And for Amalia's overprotectiveness to have been revealed in front of Leo…

San Pedro wasn't all that big, as towns went, and unless he had moved elsewhere, Lucía had known it was only a matter of time before they ran into each other. But whenever Lucía had pictured the moment—and she'd thought about it often enough, those first weeks after his letters had stopped coming—she'd always imagined herself in a devastating gown, tossing off a string of witticisms to the delight of her many, *many* admirers…

The Leo she had once known would have chuckled with her at Amalia's overprotectiveness. Or better yet, offered to walk her home himself. If the rain *had* fallen, maybe they would have strolled through the raindrops while he recited one of the extravagant number of verses he had memorized. Maybe they would have laughed as they took refuge under some picturesque overhang, only for their laughter to fade as their eyes met and their lips were drawn inexorably together…

Or maybe, the poet Lucía had gotten to know had been nothing more than a character crafted out of ink and paper, and his true self was the one she had met the day before.

Amalia was frowning at Lucía. "What in the world has gotten into you? I've never seen you so distracted."

"Nothing," Lucía said quickly. "Just…a headache."

"Well, which is it? Nothing, or a headache. Or…"

Amalia's features took on a shrewd look. "Or a certain handsome young man with beautiful penmanship?"

Lucía felt a pang as she remembered how Amalia and Julian would tease Lucía mercilessly whenever a letter from Leo arrived and Lucía would hurry into her bedroom to sigh over each word in private. It had taken only a few weeks after the letters stopped arriving for them to stop asking about her beau and start exchanging worried glances when they thought Lucía wasn't looking.

"Nothing," Lucía said, more firmly this time.

The coachman opened the carriage door and Lucía alighted first, hovering behind him as he handed Amalia down. The sisters took a moment to adjust their evening gowns—Amalia's a black silk, Lucía's a gauzy rose, spangled with beads and paired with a matching bandeau—then they swept inside the Linares's pale yellow home.

Almost large enough to rival the house where Lucía lived with Amalia and Julian, it boasted a spacious terrace for the Linares's frequent parties—there seemed to be nothing that Paulina enjoyed more than being surrounded with friends and family.

The last time Lucía had been in the house was the day before they'd left for Europe. The day she'd met Leo.

Biting her lip, she gazed around the beautifully decorated front room. Paulina did have a knack for pulling together furnishings and decorations that made a house look both opulent and comfortable. Tonight, the well-made furniture she had selected for her own home was glowing with polish in the light of dozens of silk lanterns. The staircase and most of the doorways Lucía could spot from the entrance were festooned with garlands of greenery, while every surface held arrangements of cascading ferns and sweet-smelling roses.

It was no wonder that so many San Pedro residents had started seeking out her help for decorating their homes—according to Amalia, Paulina had turned a pastime into a thriving business. Lucía couldn't help but wonder if she could have done that with her music. Maybe she would have been able to, once upon a time. She'd never know now.

All three of the tall, arched doors at the far end of the room were open to the terrace that ran the length of the house. The soft strains of a *danza* filtered in from that direction, a sweet melody that made even the chatter produced by the Linares's many guests sound like it was part of the song.

Lucía followed Amalia farther into the room, her steps slowing as she felt numerous pairs of eyes descending on them. In the days after her uncle's abduction of her came to light, the gossip papers had run almost daily pieces on her and Amalia. But that was five years ago. Hadn't everyone moved on to fresher gossip by now? Or had their return reignited the flames?

Catching the eye of a woman who had just turned to whisper something to her companion, Lucía almost turned on her heel and walked out. She was kept by doing so by Amalia's reassuring hand on her elbow, and by Paulina's husband, Sebastian, who beckoned to them from several feet away.

Sebastian drew her closer for the customary kiss on the cheek. He was one of those people who gave the impression of being a column or a pillar—partly because of his height and the solidity of his stance, but mostly because he was the steadiest person Lucía had ever met. "Lucía, Amalia, what a pleasure it is to see you both after so long."

Lucía tilted up her face to receive his warm greeting, then stepped back with a polite smile already arranged on her lips as she waited for Sebastian to introduce the two men flanking him.

The smile vanished almost at once, as she caught sight of a familiar face.

Leo. Looking glorious in a crisp, black evening suit.

"You remember Eduardo Martinez, don't you?" Sebastian asked. "And this is Leandro Díaz."

"We've met, remember?" Leo told Sebastian, at the same time that Lucía said, "Good to see you again."

The day before, she had noticed how much Leo's thin frame had filled out. Now she had time to take in the details—mainly, the way his broad shoulders and powerful legs looked in his exquisitely tailored suit, this one paired with a starched shirt that made his burnished brown skin look as luscious as toffee.

For the space of a second, Lucía wondered what it would be like to run the tip of her tongue along his firm jaw, tasting him as if he really were made out of something sweet. Until a glimpse of his expression made her crash back into reality.

Leo didn't look happy to see her. He didn't even look moderately pleased to see her. If anything, his expression conveyed the sort of enthusiasm most people reserved for things that had to be scraped from the sole of their shoes.

How flattering.

Blissfully unaware of the awkwardness crackling between them, Sebastian excused himself to greet a new arrival. As he vanished into the crowd, Lucía tried to calculate how long she had to wait before she could make her own escape without appearing too rude.

It was clear that Leo and Eduardo had been in the middle of a conversation—and just as clear that Leo didn't welcome the interruption. Eduardo, however, accepted their presence with friendly ease and politely tried to draw Lucía and Amalia into the conversation.

"How long have you been back?" he asked curiously, flagging down a waiter who had just been passing by with a silver tray full of champagne coupes. He handed Lucía and Amalia each a sparkling, faceted crystal wineglass that caught and refracted the warm glow cast by Paulina's lanterns.

Tiny jewels made out of light danced over them all and Lucía couldn't help darting a glance at Leo, who looked momentarily entranced. Then his lips thinned as he pressed them together and shifted his gaze toward Eduardo.

"Only a few days," Lucía told Eduardo, taking a sip of the bubbly liquid. "We're still getting our bearings."

"How are you settling back into town? I imagine it must seem quite dull indeed after you've had a taste of the world."

"Not entirely. It's a comfort to be in familiar surroundings," Lucía replied. "Not to mention, trying to keep up with friendships over the transatlantic post can be frustrating at times. We didn't learn that Sebastian and Paulina's little girl had been born until well over four months after their letter was posted."

Leo's contribution to the conversation came in the form of a grunt.

"Yes," Lucía added airily. "The mail can be *so* unreliable."

Leo didn't react at all to the barb, but Lucía caught her sister burying a smile behind her champagne. Next to her, Eduardo had embarked on a story about how he and a group of friends from Puerto Rico had grown so weary of corresponding that he'd invited them all to visit.

"I've shown them around San Pedro for the past week, and tomorrow, we'll set off for Santo Domingo, to stay with my grandfather for a fortnight or so." Eduardo paused, eyebrows rising as if he'd been struck by a sudden thought. "It's very short notice, as we planned to leave just after sunrise, but wouldn't you like to join us? One of the young ladies has brought her mother along to chaperone and keep us all in line, so you needn't worry about any impropriety. We're sailing in one of the old man's boats."

Boats? If Lucía's memory served correctly, Eduardo's grandfather owned an entire fleet of ships.

"Does your family still have the *Leonor*?" Amalia asked. "I remember being wretchedly jealous of everyone who was allowed to spend Saturday afternoons on deck with you and your cousins."

Fearful of any outside influence—and of losing control over Lucía and Amalia—their uncle rarely let them socialize outside his presence. In spite of his many prohibitions, Lucía had managed to befriend a group of young women her age. She'd been eager to reconnect with them now that she was back, but the reception she and Amalia had gotten as they'd entered the party was making her reconsider her eagerness.

"We'll have to rectify that soon," Eduardo said gallantly. "We'll take the *Leonor* out on a jaunt to make up for all the frolics you missed. You too, Díaz. I know you've a great deal of work, but surely, even you can spare a few days."

"I'm afraid I won't be able to get away anytime soon,"

Leo said, and cleared his throat. "Though if you'll be at the port tomorrow, I might impose on you for a favor. I'm in the process of purchasing a schooner and—"

"Oh?" Lucía couldn't help interrupting. "You no longer work at the mill?"

Leo flicked a glance in her direction. "I've been running operations there for the past two years. But Sebastian and I are partners on another venture—we recently began manufacturing sacks for the sugar made at the mill, and we've been exploring the possibility of taking care of the shipping ourselves."

"Another one of your great ideas?" Eduardo asked, and Lucía detected the admiration in his tone when he added, "All it takes is a single glance at a ledger for Leo to know exactly how to increase profits without cutting salaries, as so many are all too eager to do."

Amalia raised her eyebrows. "That's certainly a useful talent. Maybe you ought to come take a look at *my* ledgers."

Lucía suppressed a wince, thinking of how her request for his mother's help had offended Leo the day before. But all Leo did was give Amalia a polite, though noncommittal nod—which Amalia didn't appear to notice as her attention was captured by a tall, dark-haired man standing by the door.

"Julian's arrived," she said, a smile spreading not just over her lips but her entire expression, and hurried off toward her husband.

Eduardo nodded toward the reuniting pair. "Almost makes a bachelor wish for a change in his marital status."

Leo made a sound in the back of his throat that did not quite sound like agreement. "Eduardo, about the schooner—"

But Eduardo was being pulled aside by a very pretty girl in a rustling violet crepe. The apology he threw them over his shoulder was belied by the interested curl of his lips as he followed the girl out to the terrace.

Leo's jaw tensed, and Lucía couldn't keep her eyes off the hard line it made. It was odd, having gotten to know someone through letters. Where once she would have said that she knew him as well as she knew herself, she was beginning to realize that there was a wealth of details that she'd missed—like the way he ground his teeth when he was frustrated and how his dark brown eyes gained new depths and complexity when out of the sunshine.

It made her wonder what else she had missed.

"Leo," she began, trying to screw up her courage to ask all the things she needed to know.

Leo's gaze shifted behind her. "Will you excuse me? There's someone I need to have a word with."

He didn't wait for her answer. For the second time in as many days, Leo walked away from her, leaving Lucía in a turmoil.

She twirled her wineglass by the stem, watching the refracted light dance on her beaded dress. When she glanced up again, it was to see half a dozen pairs of eyes directed her way. Her face heated. How many of the whispers she could hear under the music were about her?

Lucía looked again at Leo's retreating back. Was that why he had stopped writing? Because he'd heard of everything that had happened to her right before they met and he no longer wished to pursue their acquaintance? Or had he done it because he'd gotten to know her and found that he didn't like whatever lay beneath the surface? Was that what he'd been about to say the day before, when he'd followed the sound of her name with a pause that held the weight of years?

Lucía set the glass on a low table. Without meeting anybody's gaze, she hurried after Leo.

She deserved some answers, once and for all.

Leo should have waited for the next day to pay a visit to the schooner.

Prowling around the docks wasn't entirely safe at the best of times, much less in the dark of night. It was foolish—more than that, it was imprudent. And Leo hadn't gotten this far by being imprudent.

He'd meant to discuss Vargas and the schooner with Eduardo, who had all but grown up aboard the many ships owned by his family's company. But then Lucía had arrived, looking like something out of a dream in a gauzy confection that sparkled in the lantern light, and all thoughts had flown out of Leo's head.

It was damned inconvenient, especially since he had already committed to the purchase. Leo couldn't have said what was making him so hesitant, since he knew very little about ships other than they weren't supposed to be called *boats*. Over the years, though, he'd learned to trust his instincts when it came to business matters—and his instincts were all but screaming at him to find a way out of the deal.

Sidestepping one of the many potholes in his path, he gazed at the *Caridad*, careful to keep out of sight of whoever was guarding the ship. From the outside, at least, it seemed sound enough. The Caribbean Sea behind it was a stretch of impenetrable darkness, distinguishable from the sky only by the shimmering ripple made by the waves as they caught the bright moonlight.

Leo crept closer. Maybe he could talk to the guard, persuade him to let him aboard—if the cargo really was as valuable as Leo had been led to believe, then it was all likely locked in the hold. What harm would there be in letting him explore other parts of the ship?

The gangplank was still lowered. Leo didn't have enough experience to know if this was normal or not. Approaching it cautiously, he glanced toward the crude wooden-and-rush chair that had been placed between the gangplank and the ropes.

It was empty. There was no guard. Not down here, in any case—they must have all been on deck, or perhaps down in the hold.

A sudden noise had Leo glancing back sharply. Before his mind fully finished registering that what he'd heard had not been the heavy footfalls of a man but the soft pad of dancing slippers, he had already spun around, using the momentum to walk right into his pursuer and seize him by the collar.

Only…the young woman he was holding wasn't wearing a collar but an evening gown with gauzy fabric wrapped around her shoulders that tore easily under his hand.

Leo heard a sharp, furious intake of breath. Then she frowned up at him, and moonlight shone full on her features.

Where her sister was beautiful in a wild, windblown way, Lucía had a quiet, reserved kind of beauty, the kind that lived in the slight arch of an eyebrow and the almost imperceptible deepening of the dimple on the corner of her mouth and the parted fullness of her lips.

He'd written sonnets about those lips.

Well, one sonnet. And then he'd torn it up, unsatisfied

with how insufficient the entirety of the Spanish language was when it came to the challenge of describing her sweetness, or the impishness of her charms.

"What the devil are you doing here?" he asked Lucía in a furious whisper, instinctively moving toward the wooden warehouse opposite the ship to avoid being overheard by anyone on the deck of the *Caridad*.

Lucía let go of her ripped sleeve. "You and I have a great deal to talk about."

"So you thought you would follow me? This is hardly the place for a conversation."

"You won't speak to me on the street," Lucía pointed out. "Or at friends' houses. What does that leave me?"

"I would have thought with the message that I don't want to speak with you at all."

That was unpardonably rude, but all Lucía did was smile. "There, a little bit of progress. Now all you have to do is tell me why."

Why indeed. Leo turned away, feeling his throat tighten. He had almost slipped up once, and he didn't mean to let it happen again. Resolutely, he began marching away.

"Where are you going?"

"To escort you home. You can't think I'd allow you to hang around the docks in the dead of night. Your sister would have my hide."

"*Allow* me?"

Her voice vibrated with outrage, and when Leo glanced back, her expression was a marriage of determination and stubbornness. He couldn't help but notice that she didn't look the slightest bit apprehensive at being alone with a man on the docks this late into the night—one more indication of just how sheltered she was.

"I won't go anywhere until you talk to me."

"What the devil," he said evenly, "is wrong with you?"

"Not a single thing," she said, raising her chin. "Though *you* certainly wouldn't know that. You stopped writing to me, Leo, without a single word of explanation. When our paths finally cross again, you can hardly bring yourself to look at me—and when you do, it's only to treat me with abysmal discourtesy."

The words burst out of her in a torrent, as if they had been held back for so long that they could no longer be contained. Leo was intimately acquainted with the feeling. Her brows were tightly knitted together, but her voice wavered with genuine hurt.

When they had first met, that sunny day in Sebastian Linares's garden, he had seen a similar hurt lurking behind the sparkles in her eyes. An abundance of feeling, he'd called it then. It had taken him months to realize it was sadness he'd seen, and he'd never quite mustered up the courage to ask her about it.

Something—or someone—had hurt her once. And here Leo was, hurting her again. Or still, by the sounds of it.

If only he could tell her how much he had hurt himself with his decision to stop corresponding with her. But he was not as eager to reopen old wounds as she seemed to be.

"What is it that you want from me?" he asked wearily.

Lucía gazed at him. "Answers. I want to know why you stopped writing. And I want to know why you're so angry with me."

"I'm not angry with you." He was worried—about his mother, about whether the purchase of the schooner would turn out to be a costly mistake. But someone like Lucía, who had never needed to strive for anything, could hardly hope to understand.

Leo's pulse began to pound in his ears, sending urgency through him with every beat until he could no longer hear the water lapping at the ship's hull. The *zafra* would begin soon, and once the sugarcane was harvested and processed, there would be precious little time before the sacks of refined sugar had to be on their way to Europe.

Only when the sugar had been unloaded on those frigid shores and the ship returned with the profits would Leo have enough funds to buy the house.

"I don't have time for you—or for your demands. I'd appreciate it if you would *allow me* to escort you home so that I can get on with my business."

"Is that all you care about now? Your business?"

"It's all I can afford to care about," he said roughly, feeling his racing pulse confirm the truth of that statement.

A warm, salty breeze rose from the water, making the dainty, shimmering fabric of her ripped sleeve flutter over her bodice and graze the swell of her breasts. Leo had to wipe his hand against the leg of his trousers in an attempt to relieve himself of the memory of the tiny beads pressing against his palm—and the soft skin beneath it.

He glanced away from her. "I'd just as soon not take you home looking so…disheveled. Here. Have my handkerchief. Maybe you can fashion a…" Extracting the linen square from his pocket, he held it out to her. "A fastening or something."

Lucía pushed his hand away. "Keep it. You might

need it—to cover up the large, gaping hole where your heart used to be."

She started to step away, but Leo stopped her suddenly, seizing her by the wrist with a hissed, *"Wait."*

Lucía's response was a look that should have withered him on the spot. "And what exactly would you like me to wait for?"

"Be quiet," Leo told her, dropping his own voice. "I think I hear something."

He tugged her farther into the shadows of the warehouse, scanning the area around the schooner. And then he heard it again. Footsteps. And this time, not the light, swift ones made by dancing slippers—this was the heavy tread of multiple pairs of boots coming from the deck of the *Caridad*. Had the sound been accompanied by the raucous laughter and catcalls of sailors out for an evening's entertainment, it wouldn't have felt quite so sinister.

But these footsteps were quiet, precise, as if the men they belonged to were doing their best to go unnoticed.

Chapter Three

Lucía's affront dissolved into pure fear the moment she heard the footsteps. There were voices, too, though they were pitched so low they were almost imperceptible, leaving little doubt as to the clandestine nature of the men's errand.

Moving slowly within the shadows, as if he were a shadow himself, Leo stepped in front of her, so close that his lapels brushed the fluttering scrap of fabric that had begun the evening as her sleeve.

She tilted her head up in silent inquiry, a moment before she realized that he was blocking her from view with his body. Or, rather, with his black suit. The beads on her dress, made to catch the light, had all but turned her into a beacon.

At the thought, a fine tremor ran through her. Leo instantly gathered her close, one arm around her waist and his large, warm hand at the back of her head. Something about his touch, or maybe the faint scent of his cologne, transported her to the past. Her response was as startling as it was visceral, her knees almost giving out under the sudden onrush of emotion. How many nights had she lain awake beneath her silk, quilted coverlet, longing to be wrapped in his embrace?

Lucía had to remind herself that there was nothing romantic in the gesture—he must have been worried that her trembling would make the beads sparkle more noticeably. And if anyone did spot them, looking like a trysting couple might help them avoid suspicion.

But as she pressed her forehead against his hard chest, so close she could hear the solid thump of his heartbeat under his starched shirt, she couldn't help but feel a faint stirring.

Without really meaning to, she burrowed against him, taking deep, steadying breaths until she felt calm enough to think. Every shred of reason she possessed told her they ought to run—get out of the warehouse's shadow and as far away from these men as possible.

"We have to get out of here," she murmured, rising on her tiptoes to speak as close to his ear as possible.

A pause, then his head jerked in agreement. "But we have to wait until they're gone."

Lucía risked a glance over his shoulder. Carrying heavy-looking crates, the men were stealing along the ship's lowered gangplank, silent but quick, and so sure-footed that she was instantly convinced they had done this kind of thing before. Only one of the men kept his arm free of crates, and that was because he was holding a pistol instead.

They had come prepared for violence.

"They're armed," she whispered. "Do you think there were guards aboard the ship?"

"I hope not," Leo said grimly.

"Maybe we should—"

The man with the pistol came to an abrupt halt halfway down the gangplank, moving his head as if he were scenting the air like a bloodhound. Lucía forced herself to freeze, her limbs tensing so tightly that they began to ache.

She was still on tiptoe, and her calves were protesting the effort. She didn't dare lower herself to the ground, though, not until the man was no longer looking their way. Her hand closed convulsively around Leo's forearm—and just when she thought she couldn't hold on any longer, the man turned away and quickly followed the rest of the thieves down to the wharf, where they disappeared among the shadows cast by the moored ships.

Letting out a sigh of relief, Lucía began to lower her heels. Then her leg cramped, and she found herself pitching to the ground, stifling a cry. Leo seized her before she could fall, grasping her tightly around her waist.

After yearning for him for so long, it felt faintly ridiculous that she should find herself wrapped in his arms twice in a single night. And that, considering the situation they were in, her body would react so strongly to the sensation.

Then again, maybe it wasn't a reaction to his touch, but a manifestation of her fear or of the gripping urgency to hurry away from this place and lock her door and slip under her satin covers and pretend that none of this had happened.

"Are you all right?"

She could feel his breath against her skin, as soft as a caress and as warm as the breeze rising from the water. It made her breathless—as did the thought of his strong hands massaging the cramp out of her leg.

She made the mistake of glancing up. What she saw in his expression made her lips part. Could it be— Did he—

"Your leg," Leo said in a low but clearly impatient voice, the faint glimmer in his eyes gone with a blink. It must have been a trick of the light. "Can you stand? If there are more men in the hold, we ought to get away from here before they come out."

Dipping her head into a quick nod, Lucía cautiously tried to rest her weight on her leg again. Luckily, this time it held. The second he had made certain that she could stand on her own, Leo released her as quickly as if he'd been scalded.

Lucía wrapped her arms around herself. "I'm all right now."

Leo cast a quick backward look at the ship, not bothering to answer. No one was visible on deck, and if there were any guards inside, they hadn't sounded the alarm. Lucía shivered, trying not to think of why that was so.

"It doesn't seem like they left behind a lookout," Leo said after a moment. "But just in case, be as quiet as you can, and stick to the shadows wherever possible. Come on."

He began to steal back the way they had come, the only way to reach the street from where they stood. Though there was nothing Lucía wanted more than to rush after him, she couldn't help but glance back toward the ship. There was no one on the lowered gangplank, or on the deck, who she could see, but the thought of stepping out of the warehouse's protective shadows made her uneasy.

Leo glanced back at her, looking impatient. "What's the matter?"

"Should we go and see if anyone was aboard? If there were guards or crew, they might be injured…"

Leo studied the wooden ramp as if he were considering it, then shook his head. "There's not a lot either of us could do in that case. We'd better report the robbery to the Civil Guard and let them deal with it."

Lucía wanted to argue—but she was more eager to leave this place without being spotted than to prove herself right. Biting her lip, she nodded. She started to surge forward again, so tightly wound that she almost forgot herself and screamed out loud when a hand landed on her shoulder.

It was Leo's, and he was looking at her with the steadfastness she had once believed was the hallmark of his character.

"Don't worry," he said softly. "I won't let anything happen to you. I promise you that."

He meant to offer her comfort, but all he had done was make Lucía's heartache feel as raw as it had those few weeks when she'd realized that he never meant to reply to her last letter.

She must have paused for too long, because he let his hand drop to his side. "Let's go."

Deprived of the warmth of Leo's hand, her shoulder felt colder than it should have in the balmy night.

They had hurried past another warehouse and had almost reached the street when it was Leo's turn to pause. He must have heard something—a cough, perhaps, or some soft noise—that made him turn back.

Her pulse racing, Lucía peered into the darkness. "What? What is it?"

"I just… I thought I saw…" He shook his head, looking troubled. "Nothing. It must have been a trick of the light."

Ignacio Vargas was out of town on business.

Leo reminded himself of what the *Caridad*'s first

mate had told him as he and Lucía hurried away from the warehouses and the wharf. He couldn't have seen the ship's owner—he couldn't even be sure that what he had spied in the shadows was a person. As he'd told Lucía, it could have just been a trick of the light.

After all, if Vargas really were around, he would never stand back and let his precious cargo be stolen. Unless...

Leo had to shake his head to dispel the thought. Being around Lucía—and inhaling her sweet scent as she stood pressed up against him—must have addled him more than he'd realized if he was leaping to such ridiculous conclusions.

He couldn't be altogether sorry that she had come after him. If it hadn't been for her, he'd have likely surprised the thieves onboard, and it would have been much harder—if not impossible—to escape their notice. By delaying him, she'd probably saved him from having a club smashed over his head.

Or worse.

Leo pushed the thought out of his mind—they were well on their way to safety now, though he did regret her involvement. He glanced toward Lucía, half expecting her to be overcome by what they had just witnessed.

Instead, she was frowning. And slowing down. "Where are you going?" she demanded as he turned into a well-lit street that would lead them to the genteel neighborhoods at the center of town. "The barracks are this way!"

"Do you really think I would take someone like you into a *cuartel*?" he asked tightly. "I'll take you home first, and then I'll go fetch the guardsmen."

She gaped at him, coming to a full stop. "Take me

home first? Someone's ship was just robbed, and heaven only knows what happened to whoever was in it."

That would have been Leo's first thought, if his pre-occupation with delivering Lucía safely home hadn't crowded out everything else.

"Those men were armed," he told her, not bothering to inject any kind of gentleness into his tone. "Whoever was in that hold is surely dead, and I'll be damned if I let you end up that way just because you—"

"The more time you waste arguing with me, the like-lier it is that they'll get away."

Before he could get another word in, she began marching away at a furious clip, leaving Leo with no option but to grimly chase after her.

Leo would be impressed with her tenaciousness if it weren't putting him in a difficult situation. What the devil would he say to a *cuartel* full of guardsmen to explain why he had been perfectly positioned to watch the ship of a business acquaintance being robbed? At the very least, they'd suspect him of something untoward.

"No, what I need to do is get you home, where you'll be safe," he snapped, catching up to her with several long strides. "And where your reputation won't be risked if anyone knows that you've been wandering around the docks late at night, with a man—and a torn dress!"

Lucía glanced down at her sleeve and bit her lip. "I'll wait outside or hide somewhere while you fetch the guardsmen."

Exasperation surged through Leo. "I'm not putting you in danger. I don't care if they steal the ship itself."

"Well, I do. I refuse to let some poor man's property get stolen just because you insist on treating me like something that should be kept on a high shelf, wrapped in cotton batting."

"Trust me, there's nothing poor about Ignacio Vargas. He can afford losing whatever's in the hold of that ship."

At that, she did pause. "Ignacio Vargas? I don't think he can afford much of anything right now."

"What do you mean?"

"That I heard my sister's husband mention him just yesterday. I wasn't paying much attention, but I distinctly heard him say something about Vargas being in tight circumstances. He has been going around town making reckless promises to whoever gives him a loan."

That must have been why he was offering the ship at such a low price. And why he'd taken on another cargo trip after he'd already told Leo he could have the ship. What he couldn't understand was why the man hadn't ordered his people to be more circumspect about it. After the way they'd flaunted the cargo the day before, it was no wonder they had gotten robbed.

The businessman in Leo was shrewdly calculating how much less he could persuade Vargas to accept for the ship. But his conscience didn't let him get too far.

"All right," he said reluctantly. "We'll go get the guardsmen first. Just…keep your face turned away. The last thing I need right now is for someone to accuse me of trying to compromise you."

That was how Sebastian had gotten snared into marriage. And though that had ultimately worked out, Leo was under no illusions that the same would happen for him. Not with this spoiled, thoughtless heiress who was determined to play the hero, regardless of the cost to her person or her reputation.

They made it to the barracks without incident, though

it took Leo a few minutes to persuade the handful of guardsmen there to lay down their cards and bottles of rum. Then, tucking Lucía's hand firmly through the crook of his arm and scowling as he tried to shield her from the men's sidelong looks, he led them to the docks.

The sky was growing lighter over the steeply pitched roofs of the warehouses. Leo frowned. He had left Sebastian's party before the clock had struck midnight. And he was reasonably sure that he and Lucía had spent less than a quarter of an hour hidden in the shadows of the warehouse.

A gasp drew his attention to the woman beside him a fraction of a second before the wind turned and breeze swept over them, carrying with it an unmistakable scent.

Smoke.

Putting on a burst of speed, he and Lucía and the pack of guardsmen turned into the wharf, just in time to see that the orange glow in the horizon was not, in fact, due to the approach of dawn.

The *Caridad* had gone up in flames.

Leo was finding it hard to breathe, and it wasn't just because the air was thick with smoke.

He was never altogether comfortable with fire, ever since an explosion at the sugar mill cost his father his life. He'd tried to exorcise his discomfort by writing long, tortured poems about it, but from the way his lungs were struggling to perform their most basic function, it was clear that Leo had never really outgrown the panic that gripped him whenever he saw flames higher than those on the tip of a match.

To make matters worse, it was obvious that Lucía had noticed. How could she fail to, when her hand was still tucked between his elbow and rib cage and she could probably feel his ineffectual attempts at drawing breath?

Dimly, he recalled one of the poems he had once sent her, some nonsense about heroism in the face of a conflagration. Another one of the many ways in which he hadn't been completely truthful with her.

Silhouetted against the fire was a small group of men, one of whom was gesticulating wildly, waving a handful of papers in the air as he said something that Leo couldn't quite hear over the roar of the flames.

One of the guardsmen broke off from the group and ran off, shouting something about fetching the firefighters, though Leo was sure that would prove unnecessary—the blaze would be more than visible from the firehouse's high tower. It wouldn't surprise him if they were already on their way.

The thought steadied him, at least enough for him to realize that Lucía's hand was still tucked into the crook of his elbow. Hastily, he released her.

She glanced up at him, her large, concerned eyes reflecting the blaze in front of them. "Leo, are you—"

"I'm fine," Leo snapped, more harshly than he'd intended.

Lucía, who clearly never knew when to quit, started to say something else. Leo hardly heard her. The man who'd been shouting turned, and as the orange glow caught his features, Leo recognized the owner of the *Caridad*.

It hadn't been a trick of the light, after all.

Vargas really was here.

And he looked furious as he told the man facing him, who Leo vaguely remembered as being some sort of customs authority, "There was a fortune inside that hold.

More than ten thousand pesos worth of merchandise. You inspected it yourself yesterday—I have your signature right here."

The customs inspector said something that was too low for Leo to hear, but his distress was evident in his furrowed brow. He raised his hands in an appeasing gesture, which Vargas met with another bellow.

"This did not happen by chance—whoever did this is most certainly trying to ruin my business. I demand that you find whoever's responsible. Someone will be held accountable for this loss, even if that person is you."

Suddenly, all of the pieces were falling together. The ostentatious display as the crates were loaded onto the ship, which no one at the docks could have failed to notice. The robbery, which likely hadn't been a robbery at all. Vargas must have never meant to sell Leo the ship—or maybe he had, until a better opportunity had presented itself. With an inventory of goods that had been signed by the customs inspector, he could claim a hefty insurance payout. Heftier than anything Leo might have paid him for the ship itself. And since by now, the crates must have been stashed somewhere to sell at his leisure…

The only question was, if Leo had seen Vargas earlier—had Vargas seen him too? Did he know that Leo had witnessed the crates being taken off the ship?

A sickening wave spread over Leo just as Vargas turned and saw him. Surprise passed briefly over the other man's features—even if he had spotted Leo before, he clearly hadn't expected him to return. A moment later, Vargas's finger rose into the air and he pointed directly at the spot where Leo and Lucía were still standing.

"There he is!" Vargas shouted furiously. "That's the man who set my ship on fire!"

"What the devil did you just say?"

Vargas stalked forward, and in the flickering glow of the flames, Leo couldn't fail to notice his calculating expression.

"This man is a business rival," Vargas told the uniformed official. "He's had some sort of grudge against me for years and he's clearly the one responsible for this confounded mess."

Denying Vargas's lies was sure to be a waste of breath. Still, Leo couldn't help but try. He drew himself up and squared his shoulders. He wouldn't have been able to summon Vargas's kind of angry, arrogant posturing if his entire existence depended on it. All he had on his side was the truth, and his reputation as an honorable man—two things that had never been enough to avert trouble, not when pitted against money and influence.

Leo wasn't naive. He knew how things worked here. He'd seen himself how the well-connected—or those who were prone to smoothing their path with well-placed bribes—could get away with largely anything they wanted. It didn't matter that he'd tried to do the right thing. It didn't matter that Lucía was a witness to his innocence.

He looked past Vargas to address the customs inspector himself. "I've done nothing except fetch the guardsmen to lend their assistance in what I believed was a rob—"

His mistake became evident almost immediately. The robbery. Vargas *had* seen him, and that was why he was so eager to frame Leo.

If Leo and Lucía were the only witnesses to his fraud, that meant...

It meant that they were both in danger.

Leo took a half step in front of Lucía, his mind racing. He had to get her home. Her family had all the wealth and influence that Leo lacked, and they would be able to protect her far better than he could.

Vargas and the customs inspector were closing in, though, and Leo couldn't be sure who the guardsmen would listen to if it came to a dispute. He didn't mean to wait to find out. "I have no motive to damage your property, Vargas, and no desire to listen to more baseless accusations. If you'll excuse me, I'm taking the young lady home."

"You mean your accomplice?" Vargas swept his gaze over Lucía with a nasty sneer as he took in her torn sleeve, eliciting an indignant sound from her. "Or your—"

Leo cut him off, taking another step forward. "I'd advise you to think very carefully about what you're about to say."

Dropping Lucía's family name might help, but it would also expose her to unwelcome scrutiny when word got out that she'd been seen alone with a man late at night. And at the docks, no less. It wasn't just the danger to her person that Leo had to shield her from.

Vargas abandoned his disparagement of Lucía's character for what Leo believed to be the ace in his sleeve. Turning to the customs officer with the smug air of a man who is convinced of his own victory, he said, "General Canó is a personal friend of mine. He'll agree with me that this scoundrel needs to be apprehended at once." At the flicker in the custom inspector's expression, he added, "I'll have someone run to get the general if I have to, but I doubt he would take kindly to being roused out of his bed so late at night."

The Commander of Arms was the highest military authority in the province, aside from Governor de los Santos. Hearing his name made Leo's blood run cold.

"Send the Civil Guard to fetch me at home in the morning, if you must," he told Vargas, projecting as much confidence as he could as he started to step away. "But I'm done with this matter tonight."

"Can't you see he's trying to get away?" Vargas asked the customs official impatiently. "What the devil are you waiting for? Seize the scoundrel before he can escape!"

Looking apologetic, the customs inspector gestured to the guardsman who'd been standing beside Leo. The uniformed man sprang into instant action, swinging aside the rifle he wore on a strap and grabbing Leo by both arms.

A sudden rattle filled the air, and in the flickering glow of the flames, everyone was suddenly and momentarily startled as the fire brigade's horse-drawn wagon rolled into view. While half a dozen men wielding axes and buckets leaped out, Leo saw his opportunity.

He wrenched away from the guardsman and lunged for Lucía's hand. Gripping it tight, he issued one low, terse command. "Run!"

Chapter Four

Lucía ran.

Faster and farther than she ever had, propelled by the true panic she had glimpsed on Leo's face. The diaphanous skirts of her evening gown whipped and tangled around her legs. Without sparing a thought for propriety, she grabbed a handful and hitched them up, gasping as panic snatched her breath away.

The blood rushing in her ears was so loud that she couldn't hear their pursuers, and she didn't dare look back to see how close they were. She concentrated on staying as close to Leo as she could without slamming into barrels or tripping over heavy coils of rope.

It wasn't until he grasped her arm and pulled her into the shadow cast by two large ships that she realized how far away the guardsmen still were—the firefighters' cart must have slowed them considerably.

Leo was peering cautiously around a barrel when Lucía noticed the name on the ship to their right. She tugged on the back of Leo's jacket.

"The *Leonor*," she whispered. "Eduardo's ship. We can hide in there."

Leo's only response was a terse nod.

The *Leonor* was much smaller than the burning sloop whose garish orange light still illuminated the night sky, but she was still a sizable ship. It took a boost from Leo for Lucía to manage to haul herself on board. The muscles on her leg, strained from running, made their protest known. Her calf seized, making her stumble, and Lucía spilled onto the deck on her hands and feet.

Leo swung himself after her—much more athletically than she had—and was reaching to help her up when a series of footsteps beat a quick tattoo on the planks of the wharf below. Their eyes met for one panic-fueled instant before Lucía flattened herself on the deck's rough planks.

Leo landed on top of her. It wasn't until several seconds went by without his shifting aside that Lucía realized that he was covering the shimmer of her dress with his dark suit, as he had before. He seemed to be bearing most of his weight on his forearms, which were braced on either side of her. Though his body didn't actually touch hers, she imagined she could hear his heartbeat pulsing through her. It was a moment before she realized that it was her own racing heartbeat that she was hearing.

A deep breath—or maybe it was the ship's gentle rocking—made her chest brush against his. Lucía's gaze skipped to Leo's, and the breath turned into a quiet gasp when she saw that he was looking back, his gaze full of smoldering intensity. She was filled with the sudden desire to arch her back and pull him down to meet her.

As if he could hear her thoughts, Leo's lips parted. Lucía tilted her head, bringing her mouth a fraction closer to his. Everything seemed to fall away—the fire, still lightening the sky above them; the man's accusation and the nasty way his gaze had raked over her torn dress; the guardsmen; even Lucía's own annoyance with Leo.

Everything fell away, except the burning desire to kiss him.

Leo shifted. Lucía held her breath, gazing at him expectantly, but all he did was turn his head.

"They're gone," he said.

Sure enough, the loud pounding of footsteps had receded into the distance, along with the guardsmen's shouts. Leo wasted no time in lifting his body off hers. Holding out a hand, he helped her to her feet and muttered something about getting out of view.

She was still breathing hard when Leo found the door to the staircase and led her below deck, into a pitch-black corridor. It was narrow enough that she could touch both of the paneled walls with her fingertips as they inched along.

"Quiet," Leo cautioned. "I'd just as soon not awaken the crew until Eduardo gets here."

Lucía nodded, realizing belatedly that he couldn't see her in the darkness. Her trailing fingers brushed against something cold and hard—a doorknob. It opened under her hand when she turned it, and she let out a breath of relief as she let herself inside.

The cabin was dominated by a wooden bed built into the far wall. In the moonlight that filtered past the half-closed curtains, Lucía was able to make out an armchair and several other bulky pieces of furniture before the gleam of a brass sconce caught her eye. She began reaching for it, then thought better of turning on any lights that could be seen from the outside.

Instead, she perched on the armchair, trying not to glance over at the very large bed.

Leo went to the porthole. Twitching the curtain side, he gazed down at the wharf below. "I think we're safe," he said after a long while. Before Lucía could relax, he added, "For now, at least. I don't think anyone saw us climb on board, and they won't dare search *this* ship without express permission from someone in Eduardo's family."

Lucía nodded, well aware of the deference with which the island's more prosperous families were treated. Not only was their word law, their property was close to sacred.

Surreptitiously, she eased off her slippers under her long skirt and wiggled her stockinged toes. Her calf was cramping again, hard enough that she hid a wince as she stretched out the leg.

"What—" Lucía forced herself to draw in a deep breath through her nose, then let it out slowly through parted lips, the way she used to when she was called upon to perform in front of others. When she tried to speak again, her voice was markedly steadier. "Were you planning to explain to me why we ran instead of telling that man to go to the devil for falsely accusing you of a crime?"

Leo was little more than a silhouette outlined in moonlight, but she could hear the tightness in his voice when he said, "I didn't set the fire, if that's what you mean."

"I gathered that much," she said tartly. "You haven't been out of my sight from the moment you left Paulina and Sebastian's party, and I can attest to that. Why not say as much?"

"Because I didn't wish to involve you any further, or expose you to scandal when word got out that you and I had left the party together and gone to the docks, of all places."

He turned around but stayed by the window, crossing his arms as he leaned against a desk or a table. Lucía couldn't make out the details in the dim light, but she caught the moonlight gleaming on the curves of a bottle on its surface.

"And in any case," Leo continued, "what we witnessed wasn't a robbery, at least I don't think so. If Vargas is in as much financial trouble as you say, enough about it must have gotten out that he's having trouble securing a loan. If that's the case, and if he needs the money badly enough, it's not far-fetched to think that he might have turned to fraud."

"Fraud? So all that merchandise he was shouting about wasn't on the ship after all?"

"Oh, I've no doubt it was—I myself saw it being taken aboard yesterday. Me, and half of San Pedro. It seems obvious now that they meant for everyone to see it, so as to have many witnesses, but at the time, it didn't occur to me to wonder if there was a reason for such an obvious display. The men we thought were robbing the ship must have been hired to take everything out discreetly so that none of it was lost to the fire."

"Well, Vargas won't get away with it," Lucía said, with far more confidence than she felt. "Not with accusing you. Eduardo will help us get home safely. And then—"

"He'll do what he can," Leo said. "But Vargas is a very well-connected man. And until I know exactly what he's planning, I'd just as soon keep my head down."

"We can't stay here forever," Lucía pointed out. "Eduardo did say last night that he was taking his visitors to Santo Domingo this morning."

"He might have a stowaway."

"You don't want to stay and try to clear your name?"

"And risk being hauled in front of a magistrate who's made some sort of deal with Vargas? Have you been gone for so long that you've forgotten how things work here? Or do you just not have any common sense?"

"Maybe I don't," she said, tossing her head. "Or maybe I just don't like to believe the worst of everyone."

"The man tried to frame me," Leo bit out. "I can believe whatever the hell I want of him."

"Fair enough. What I don't understand is why he'd do that."

He shrugged. "Because we saw the crates being taken off the ship. Because we made things convenient by showing up at the right time. Either way, I can't stay in town. As for you…"

His gaze lingered speculatively on her, and she felt her heart begin to drum inside her chest.

"As for me?"

Leo shrugged again and scraped a hand over the back of his slicked-back hair. "I'm sure that your sister and her husband can protect you."

For most of her life, Lucía had kept her head down to avoid her uncle's wrath, letting Amalia be the object of it instead. Lucía was far too old for that now.

"But would I be able to protect them?" Lucía bit her lip, releasing it only to add, "Amalia's only four months along, and she's already exhausted with all her work and the long journey. To bring this kind of trouble to her doorstep…"

Her sister was almost thirty, which everyone said was

a trifle old to be having her first child, and the doctor in Vienna had cautioned them all against causing her any unnecessary stress. Julian would be more than capable of helping, but Lucía knew that he and Amalia kept very little from each other. And if Vargas were to decide to make a nuisance of himself, there wasn't much she and Julian would be able to do to prevent Amalia from finding out.

"No," she said, shaking her head. "I don't think I should go home, either."

Her words almost rang in the silence of the cabin. Although part of her wanted to pretend she hadn't said them out loud, another part of her was experiencing a rush of excitement. Escaping the tedium of being gossiped about—or worse, fawned over—by making herself an outlaw had not exactly been in her plans. But now that it had happened, why not seize the moment?

Lucía was so absorbed in her thoughts that she hadn't realized how long the silence had stretched until Leo broke it. "Blast it, Lucía, I'm sorry."

"Sorry?" she echoed, blinking into the dimness separating them.

Leo must have reined in whatever impulse had driven the apology out of him, because his next words came out sounding stiff and formal, as if his real self were retreating behind a mask of bland politeness. "I have to apologize for dragging you into this predicament. You wouldn't be here if it weren't for me."

"Not entirely. I did decide to chase after you," Lucía pointed out. "Though I wouldn't have had to if you hadn't been so infuriating. In any case, you're stuck with me now."

His eyes narrowed. "You seem to think this is some

kind of adventure. Then again, maybe it is—for you. But I don't have a rich and well-connected family to get me out of this. If Vargas persuades a magistrate that I had cause enough to set his ship on fire—"

Leo pressed his lips together in a gesture that, unfortunately, was becoming all too familiar to Lucía.

"We're fugitives from the law," she informed him. "We're fleeing from our homes and our families. I realize you'd much rather I beat the floor with my fists or wail at the heavens, but I'd just as soon make the best of things."

Hoisting herself to her feet with help from the chair's padded arms, she hobbled over to the table Leo was still leaning against.

"Where are you going?" he asked warily as she approached.

"To have a drink."

She couldn't really read the label on the bottle she had seen, but a quick sniff told her it was rum. The best quality, of course.

"Were you limping? Did you hurt yourself?"

"It's nothing," Lucía said. There were no glasses to be seen, so she unstoppered the bottle and took a swift gulp of the eye-searing liquid within. "A cramp in my leg, that's all."

To her annoyance, she belied her own words when she set her foot down and almost lost her balance. She reached for the table to steady herself and found Leo instead.

"You're in pain."

"I'll be fine." Lucía said, and drowned her rising exasperation in another sip of rum.

"Will you be fine if we're discovered and you're forced

to run again?" Leo asked, and Lucía answered with a scowl. Leo's lips rose at the corners. "I thought so."

"Well, I don't hear you volunteering to massage the cramp away," she snapped. Even with the rum making its fiery way along her body, Lucía knew immediately she shouldn't have said it. For one, she'd be damned if she'd do anything to make him see her as helpless or coddled. For another, the notion had introduced a new tension to an environment that was already fraught.

Leo went stock-still. "I'm not."

"Good, because I don't need you to."

She'd been clutching the edge of the table to keep her balance. Releasing it, Lucía tried to flounce away—but all she did was hobble back to the armchair, where she only narrowly managed to catch herself as another cramp tightened her calf. She huffed out a breath, losing her fight to keep the rum from sloshing out of the bottle as she sank into the upholstered seat.

"Oh, for—" Leo detached himself from the table and went to kneel in front of her. "Which leg is it?"

"The right one," Lucía said automatically. "Do you even know what to do?"

He raised an eyebrow. "I'm no doctor, but I think I can figure it out."

Lucía grabbed a handful of her skirts. It would be scandalous of her to lift them, even an inch. But wasn't she living with the consequences of scandal, when it hadn't even been of her own making?

Defiantly, she raised her hem to her knee, baring her pale rose stockings.

There was enough light in the cabin for her to see the amusement playing over Leo's features as he glanced down at her stockinged toes. He didn't say anything, though, just placed her foot on his hip and briskly began to knead her calf with his strong fingers.

Lucía gripped the chair's arm so tightly her fingertips began to ache. For all that Leo seemed to be an expert in schooling his voice and his expression to show nothing more than cold courtesy, it was obvious he couldn't do the same with his hands. The tenderness in his touch confused her—was it possible to touch someone with such soft regard if you didn't care for them?

His fingers glided over the silk of her stockings, making tingles dance up her leg and over her thighs. Lucía couldn't hold back a gasp. It was a soft exhalation, almost inaudible against the sound of the waves breaking against the side of the ship, but Leo looked up at her.

"Did that hurt?"

"I—just a little," Lucía lied. "It's all right, though—keep going."

It made her breathless to think that she could have spent years enjoying this. If she hadn't left. If he hadn't stopped writing. If somehow they'd found a way to come together in spite of all the obstacles in their path. She'd be lying if she said she hadn't thought about Leo over the years as she lay awake at night, her imagination growing bolder and bolder as she pictured the way he might drag his lips over the curve of her shoulder, or perhaps even her knee…

Her breath was coming faster. It wasn't just the knot on her leg that was loosening under his careful ministrations, it was her entire body. She could feel her limbs growing delightfully languid as he massaged the soreness away with long, even strokes that felt like caresses.

"Leo," she breathed out.

He paused immediately, lifting his gaze to her face. "Yes?"

Throat tightening, she glanced away from his expectant face. "How long until dawn, do you think?"

"Hours," he said softly.

It couldn't come fast enough.

The list of foolish things Leo had done that night had grown by another item. Being in Lucía's presence really did make him witless. Why else would he have voluntarily suggested doing something so unsettlingly intimate?

The first brush of her body against his, back at the docks, had shocked him into breathlessness. He had inhaled deliberately deeply before reaching for her leg, but he needn't have bothered. It wasn't his breath that was failing him now—it was his ability to think of anything other than the startling heat of her skin beneath the sheer weave of her silk stockings. They were high enough that they disappeared under her dress, the hem of which she had lifted until it grazed her knees.

His gaze snagged on the ribbon trailing down her calf, and his mouth went so dry so suddenly that he had to avert his eyes.

Lucía was wearing a set of earrings and necklace that were made out of lustrous red stones, the latter fashioned into a pendant that looked more expensive than the damned ship they were on. The central stone, bigger than his fingernail, was suspended from a bow twisted out of some metal that was probably white gold, not silver. The pendant spilled over her collarbone, so low it brushed the edge of her bodice, the stone moving gently with her every inhalation. Though she barely moved, except to draw in breath, her jewelry and beaded dress caught the light and made her shimmer. Like a mirage.

Leo's gaze traveled over her and he amended his comparison. Nestled in the plush armchair with her spangled evening gown bunched around her, she looked like a debauched princess as she watched him from behind her long, curling lashes. Just enough moonlight came into the cabin for Leo to see the gleam of her eyes as they followed the movement of his hands.

He could have very happily gone the rest of his life without having touched her—and without hearing those soft little hitches in her breath whenever his thumbs probed a particularly sensitive spot.

Leo gritted his teeth. Tempting as it would otherwise be to think about following the line of those stockings all the way up her thighs, first with his hands and then with his lips, he didn't have the luxury of giving into that kind of fantasy. Not about Lucía, and definitely not while he was still occupied with—

A low, breathy moan pushed past her lips. Leo's fingers, which had just brushed the underside of her knee, went still. Lucía froze, too, her forehead creased with mortification.

"Does your leg feel better?"

She gave him a curt little nod. "I could run away from any number of false accusations."

Releasing her, Leo pushed away from the armchair. "With any luck, there won't be any more of those. Not tonight."

If she was a princess, or even a mirage, what did that make him? Other than extraordinarily foolish.

He had done his level best to stay away from her, and

here he was, stuck with her. Worse than that, responsible for her.

Stifling a sigh, Leo sat back, propped up against the side of the bed's thick wooden frame, his forearms resting on his raised knees. It was terrifying how quickly his life had fallen apart. One moment he'd been poised on the verge of success. The next? He'd made an enemy of a very powerful man, been forced to abandon his business—and to leave his mother to fend for herself.

Thinking of her made his stomach clench with anxiousness. He had made an arrangement with a neighbor to keep his mother company during the day, as well as do the cooking and some light cleaning. It had been difficult to persuade her to stay long enough for Leo to stop by Sebastian and Paulina's party, which he'd only done because of his need to discuss the ship with Eduardo. The older woman had her own family to look after, and though he doubted that she would leave his mother alone overnight, what would happen when he didn't arrive in the morning?

Leo should have hired a damned team of nurses and housemaids, like he'd meant to, not given in to his mother's insistence that she could take care of herself. She still wasn't steady on her feet, never mind well enough to cook for herself. Her eagerness to do so was mostly stubbornness, though Leo suspected that it also stemmed from her reluctance to let Leo spend any more money on her after all those costly hospital and doctor bills.

He'd tried to tell her that none of that mattered, that he made a good living now, and that as soon as his latest investments started to pay off, he'd be very well off indeed, but she'd still been worried. His mother, Leo knew, had never quite gotten over those hard, lean years after his father had died. She was still meticulous about every *peso* she spent, though the allowance he gave her was more than twice what he used to make as a bookkeeper at the mill.

If he didn't get out of this mess and find a way to get home quickly, she was bound to do something even more foolish than what he'd just done.

Leo scrubbed a hand over his face, then held out a hand. "Pass me the rum."

"I should warn you—it tastes foul." Lucía gave a little shudder, her eyelids at half-mast. "But then, I only like dessert wines. I suppose you think that's to be expected of a spoiled heiress like myself."

Leo took a measured sip of rum to keep from answering. There was nothing foul about the rum, of course. Its flavor was smooth and complex—and it did little to douse the waves of desire still coursing through him.

He gazed at the bottle, forcing himself to turn his thoughts to other matters. Like the fact that rum was made out of sugarcane. There was an idea. How likely was it that Sebastian would agree to open a distillery? Maybe he wouldn't even have to get his partner's approval—with the arrival of his and Paulina's third child, Sebastian had grown adamant about spending more time at home. He'd gone so far as to turn the sugar mill into a cooperative, from which every one of the people employed there could profit. The factory for manufacturing sacks was still a private enterprise, and a rum distillery would likely be one, too. Leo could handle it himself.

So if Leo ever did manage to purchase a ship, he could turn his hand to exporting rum as well as sugar— molasses, too—why not?—and make an even tidier profit. Which might mean not just purchasing the house on the corner of Calle Duarte, but also a second home on the northern coast for his mother to convalesce in…

Lucía's voice broke into his thoughts. "Back at the ship, before Vargas saw you—you looked as if you were about to keel over." Leo didn't know if it was the rum that was making her so blunt, or if she was always so direct and he just hadn't been around her long enough to find out. "Was the ship really that important to you?"

"It was important. But…" Leo sighed and handed her the bottle. Maybe her question had caught him off guard—or maybe he had drunk more than was advisable. Either way, he found himself offering her an explanation. "My father died in an accident at the mill when I was fifteen."

"I remember you saying so."

"I don't think I ever said exactly what happened." Leo averted his eyes as Lucía lifted her feet up onto the chair's cushion, adjusting her skirt until her legs were properly covered. "It was just before Sebastian Linares bought the mill, back when it was still owned by Paulina's brother. Antonio didn't care much about keeping the equipment in good working order—all he cared about was profits, though from what I've heard, he didn't seem to have much of an idea of how to increase those. Part of the machinery overheated, causing an explosion. The mill caught fire and my father…"

Leo drew in a deep breath. So many years had passed since he'd seen his father being carried out of the burning mill, but the image was one he would never forget.

"My father was caught in it. He lived only for a day or two after. I've been…uncomfortable around fires ever since then."

"I'm so sorry," Lucía murmured. The bottle tipped in her hand, and Leo caught it before it fell. "I didn't know."

Leo lifted his shoulders into a shrug. "I never told you."

"Why didn't you?"

"Why would I have?" he countered. "There wasn't much space for reality in those pretty letters we sent each other."

She stared at him. "Was it *all* fiction?"

Leo looked down at the bottle in his hands. "I'd rather not talk about it. All of that is over and done with."

For once, she seemed to be about to leave well enough alone. But if Leo thought that meant she would abandon all attempt at conversation altogether, he was mistaken. "You're different, you know," she said. "Harder. Sharper."

He didn't think she meant it as a compliment, but he took it that way. Unlike the pampered Señorita Troncoso, he knew just how necessary it was to create a hard shell between himself and the world.

He hadn't lived an easy life, and if the price for survival—his mother's and his own—was becoming hard and sharp, he would pay it twice over. He was not the man he used to be, and he'd only ever been thankful for that.

"I don't think I like it."

"Fortunately for me," he replied lightly, "I don't give a damn what you like or don't like."

"The words every girl loves to hear." She wrapped her arms around her midsection. "If only we could tell society the same thing."

"You have nothing to worry about—if worse comes to worst, I'll do right by you." In response to her uncomprehending gaze, he spoke out loud the words that had been clanging inside his head from the moment he saw her standing at the docks. "I'll marry you."

Her eyes narrowed, and her puzzled expression was replaced with one of pure haughtiness. "We just interrupted a robbery in progress, were accused of arson, ran away from the authorities, and someone thinking you have compromised me is the worst thing that could happen? You're the one who doesn't need to worry—I wouldn't marry you if the entirety of San Pedro caught us in bed together."

It served him right for trying to do the right thing.

She scrambled to her feet and spun around, but there was really nowhere to go unless she chose to leave the small cabin. Unable to hold back a chuckle, Leo watched as she let out a little huff and dropped back into the cushioned armchair.

"A man might be offended, having his proposal thrown in his face like that," he said, laughing again to show her how little it bothered him.

"That wasn't a proposal," she said stiffly.

"I suppose you would know."

"What is that supposed to mean?"

Leo took another swig of rum. She hadn't asked for the bottle back, and it was just as well, because he wasn't inclined to relinquish it. If the past half hour had been any indication, he would need every drop in it just to get through the night. "Just that I'm sure half the men in Europe were falling over themselves to propose all sorts of things to you."

He'd tortured himself by picturing her in glittering balls, dripping with jewels even more expensive than the ones she was wearing now, two dozen of her conquests elbowing each other out of the way for the privilege of handing her a dropped handkerchief.

"No one ever has," Lucía said, looking away. When she turned back to him a moment later, her eyes were like finely honed daggers. "I thought I'd come back to find you married. What happened? Couldn't find a woman perfect enough to satisfy you?"

His hands were shaking, ever so slightly. Leo drained the last of the rum, absently rubbing his open palm on the side of his trouser leg in a vain attempt to erase the memory of her touch.

"On the contrary," he lied. "There's been too many to choose just one."

"Well, I'm glad you've been having such an agreeable time."

Maybe he was reading too much into the tone of her voice, but it sounded as though the words *without me* hung suspended in the air between them.

Leo wouldn't have called the past few years agreeable, exactly. He'd stumbled through them in a haze of exhaustion and ambition, spending countless evenings hunched over ledgers or nodding off in stiff chairs, with the bitter scent of the hospital in his nostrils. He hadn't been the one going to balls.

"I'm surprised that you care," he said after a few moments had passed.

"I don't," she snapped.

Leo layered his tone with the thinnest layer of sarcasm. "I can see that."

She opened her mouth, as if to continue arguing. Leo interrupted her before she could say another word. "You shouldn't care. Not about me."

"I'd really appreciate it if you would stop telling me what I'm supposed to feel or how I'm supposed to act."

"I would if you acted like a sensible person. What in the world possessed you to sneak after me?"

"I didn't sneak," she protested. "And I wouldn't have had to follow you if you'd just *talked* to me."

"You and I have nothing to talk about," Leo said, imbuing his voice with as much finality as he could muster. "It wasn't as if you and I had any kind of understanding— we were nothing more than correspondents. And in any case…the past should be left in the past. The sooner you accept that, the less painful the next several days will be."

Chapter Five

Had it not been for the rum, Lucía was doubtful that she would have slept a wink. As it was, she must have fallen asleep at some point in their wait for Eduardo, because she jerked awake just as the sky outside the porthole was beginning to lighten with the approach of dawn.

Lucía wasn't an early riser at the best of times, and this morning was decidedly not that. Her mouth was dry and her temples were throbbing with the aftereffects of all the rum she'd consumed the night before—almost a quarter of the bottle before Leo had taken it upon himself to finish it.

If he had been in any way affected by the rum, it hadn't shown. Not last night. This morning was another story, however. Leo sat sprawled in the armchair she had vacated only a short time before, having finally talked herself into curling up in a corner of the large bed. The skin under his eyes was shadowed with exhaustion.

As insufferable as he was, Lucía couldn't help feeling a pang of sympathy for him. He had lost a great deal last night, and he was clearly torn up about having to leave San Pedro. She'd thought at the time that maybe

Eduardo would have some alternative solution for them, but the long night had disabused her of that notion. Leo wouldn't have spent all this time with her if there had been any possible alternative.

She was cautiously sitting up when she heard it again—the sound that had awoken her.

"Someone's coming," she whispered, hesitating for a second before prodding Leo's arm with her finger.

He rose to his feet in a single fluid movement, as awake and composed as if he hadn't been sleeping after all, merely resting his eyes. A split second later, the door to the cabin opened and Eduardo burst inside.

Or started to. Looking understandably startled, he came to a sudden halt in the doorway when he caught sight of Leo. "What the devil?"

His gaze landed on Lucía—or, more specifically, her torn dress and her disheveled hair. His eyes narrowing in fury, Eduardo turned to Leo, repeating, "What the devil?" in tones that conveyed more outrage than the surprise he had shown with his first exclamation.

Leo held his ground, though Eduardo looked like he was seconds away from striking him. Lucía rushed to intervene.

"I'm all right," she said. "Nothing happened. But we do need your help."

She began to explain what had happened, as well as what Leo suspected. Out of the corner of her eye, she saw Leo lean against the desk as he had the night before, his arms crossed. He didn't add a word to her hurried explanation.

Eduardo was looking more concerned by the second. "The *Caridad*? That ship was barely seaworthy—she took a great deal of damage in last year's hurricane. Vargas doesn't have much in the way of scruples if he was willing to sell it for as much as a peso." His expression tightened with suspicion. "Speaking of Vargas, when I got here he was insisting that all the ships be searched before they're allowed to leave the harbor. I had no idea the two of you were the cause."

"You believe us, don't you?" Lucía asked anxiously.

"I do," Eduardo reassured her, and though Leo didn't move, Lucía thought she saw some of the tension leave the rigid cast of his shoulders. "And I agree that you should both leave San Pedro, at least until the matter can be sorted out. It won't be too hard to hide you among my guests. Come with me to my grandfather's house, and I'll make sure to put all his resources at your disposal. But first—" He turned to Lucía. "Are you sure this is what you want?"

"It is," she said firmly.

To his credit, Eduardo didn't question her decision. All he did was nod and say, "We'll tell my guests that I invited you last night and that you decided to accept at the last minute. There are two women in the party who will serve as chaperones—your sister would have my hide if there's the merest hint of impropriety in the whole thing."

"Speaking of my sister. Is there time to get a message to Amalia and Julian? They'll panic if they can't find me." She winced. "They must already be panicking."

She knew it for a fact, since it had already happened once before—Amalia had arrived home to find that Lucía had been taken halfway across the island. And this time, Lucía wouldn't have the chance to leave a note behind the mirror frame telling Amalia where she had gone.

Leo cleared his throat. "I'd like to send a note, too."

Eduardo nodded. "Of course. There's paper and ink in the desk over there. I'll fetch you both something to wear, too, so that my guests don't suspect anything. Fortunately, my cousins are in the habit of leaving behind several changes of clothing in the other cabin, in case of travel mishaps. I'm sure there'll be something suitable in there for both of you."

"They won't mind?" Leo asked.

Eduardo shook his head. "In the case of my youngest cousin, she'd probably be thrilled to know that she'd be helping a pair of outlaws."

Leo cringed at the word, but Lucía surged forward, reaching for Eduardo's hand. She clasped it warmly between both of her own as she gave him her most heartfelt thanks.

"Just remember that when your sister tries to have me murdered," Eduardo said. "Which is what'll happen when she finds out I helped you."

Lucía tilted her head, grinning. "Are you scared of Amalia?"

The men exchanged glances.

"Who isn't?" Leo said.

The three of them smiled, and Lucía felt some of the anxiety drain out of the room. At the sound of a voice outside the cabin, however, Eduardo bustled into action.

"Go ahead and write your notes," he said, striding to the door. "I'll be back as soon as I've had a word with the captain."

Leo wasted no time in jerking open the desk drawers. There was a tidy sheaf of writing paper inside, as well as a pen and a small pot of ink. He offered them to Lucía first, who dashed off a note that she hoped wouldn't worry or infuriate her sister too much. Blowing on the ink to help it dry faster, she passed Leo the pen.

He deliberated for much longer than she had, braced against the desktop with his left arm while the fingers of his right hand curled around the pen as if they'd never held one before. Lucía couldn't help but let her eyes linger on them as she remembered how those dexterous fingers had made her toes curl a scant few hours before. The mere memory made her body feel as though it was twinkling as brightly as her beaded dress.

The heat of his gaze recalled her attention to the task at hand. Flustered, and hoping not to show it, Lucía asked tartly, "What's the matter? Have you been struck again with the disease that makes you unable to write letters?"

His jaw tightened. For a long moment, she thought that he wouldn't answer. She saw his fingers flexing on the wooden desktop, the muscles in his arms taut with the strain of holding him up. Then he set down the pen and sighed.

"It's my mother. I can't leave her alone," he said reluctantly. "She has dizzy spells, and her caretaker can only stay with her for a few hours each day. The last time I left her alone, she burned her hand trying to cook. I tried to hire a nurse, but…"

Understanding dawned on Lucía. Was that why he'd been so short with her when she had tried to solicit his mother's help?

"Amalia would be more than happy to look in on her—or have her stay at the house, if that suits her better." Lucía took the pen again to add a postscript to her note, trying not to notice the way he twitched away when her fingers brushed his. "You can count on her to take care of your mother's needs, whatever they may be."

For what felt like the first time in years, Leo's eyes met hers squarely. "Thank you."

It felt like a truce, or at the very least, the beginning of one.

Feeling unaccountably flustered, Lucía waved a dismissive hand in the air. "No need to thank me," she said briskly. "I know the two of them will appreciate having someone to complain to about us."

Eduardo returned as Leo was finishing his note, and led her to another of the ship's five staterooms. Lucía was pleased to discover that there was water in the jug by the washstand, as well as a fresh cake of scented soap, fresh linen towels and a comb.

And there were indeed plenty of clothes in the trunk he'd mentioned, including a navy skirt and a white blouse with dark blue trim. The fit wasn't perfect, particularly in the skirt, which was just a touch too loose on Lucía's waist, but a narrow leather belt helped her cinch it tight.

It didn't take long to put herself to rights. By the time she emerged onto the deck, the messenger with her and Leo's notes had been dispatched, Eduardo had gone down to speak personally to the guardsmen and the customs inspector, and the visitors from abroad were beginning to board.

Lucía settled herself into a deck chair and reached for one of the several folded newspapers pinned under a paperweight—it would hide her face, in a pinch. She was just in time. Hardly a minute had passed before half a dozen guardsmen were on the deck and striding past a deckhand in a flat cap who was diligently mopping the floorboards.

Leading the way was the man she now knew as Ignacio Vargas.

"She was wearing a pink dress," Lucía heard Vargas say as she tried not to make it too obvious that she was hiding behind the newspaper. "Torn, I think—Díaz is a blackguard as well as an arsonist."

Lucía was so enraged at the thought that Vargas was using her to accuse Leo of yet another thing he hadn't done that she almost tossed the newspaper aside and leaped up to confront him. Almost—for all her protestations, Lucía found she wasn't quite brave enough to do such a thing.

And in any case, she wasn't altogether certain of how much help that would be. Vargas had already claimed she was Leo's accomplice.

She glanced away from Vargas and the guardsmen, trying to appear unconcerned as well as inconspicuous. The men were milling around, getting footprints all over the polished deck, and—

Where the devil was Leo?

The newspaper's thin pages crinkled under her fingers as she scanned the people on deck. She hadn't seen him come up from below, had she?

"Search the ship," Vargas commanded.

The customs official looked put out at having his authority usurped, but he waved irritably at the guardsmen, who sprang to follow Vargas's order.

Leo would have had the sense to find a hiding spot. Eduardo had helped them get rid of the clothes they'd both worn throughout the night—Lucía had no idea if

he'd tossed them overboard or shoved them into a fire.
There should be nothing down below to give them away,
and Eduardo's normally pleasant expression had shifted
into a frown so forbidding that neither Vargas nor the
customs official looked inclined to start examining the
faces of his guests.

Still, when the guardsmen returned to the deck
empty-handed, Lucía's breath came out in an explosive
little gasp that she managed to hide with a rattle of the
newspaper.

"Are you satisfied?" Eduardo asked Vargas coldly.
"Or do you want to continue wasting my guests' time?"

Vargas looked like he wanted to argue, but the customs official was clearly finished with the matter.
Apologizing profusely for the intrusion, he herded the
guardsmen out of the boat.

Lucía lowered the newspaper, her fingers shaking as
she smoothed out the creases she had clutched into it.
She drew in a deep breath—which turned into a gasp
of choked laughter when the sailor with the mop turned
and she saw Leo's face peeking out from beneath the
brim of his cap.

Eduardo must have given the captain the order to set
off, because the ship began to stir underfoot. The hum
of the engines, far quieter than the powerful roar of the
steamers Lucía had been on, grew in volume and intensity as the ship began to pull away from shore.

They'd really done it. They'd gotten away.

Lucía's relief made her almost giddy. She tried standing at the railing with her face turned up toward the sun,
but it was simply too impossible to keep still as San
Pedro grew farther and farther away.

She bounded away and began prowling the deck,

looking at all the details she had been too rushed and scared to notice when she and Leo had first come aboard the ship.

The *Leonor* was nothing like the grand transatlantic steamers that had taken her and Amalia and Julian to Europe. It was much smaller, for one. But it was no less luxurious. Like the cabin she and Leo had spent the night in, the furnishings on the deck held a comfortable, understated elegance that would not have been out of place in someone's home.

They included a table long enough to accommodate the unexpected arrivals, on which a pair of waiters in white jackets were setting up a lavish traditional breakfast. Remembering how many hours it had been since her last meal, Lucía tried not to stare at the mound of *mangú* in one heavy porcelain serving bowl, topped with thinly sliced red onions that she knew would be tangy with vinegar. On the platter beside it were more than a dozen fried eggs, their edges crisp and their yolks as sunny as the band in Lucía's hat. There were sausages, too, and gleaming slices of avocado dusted with grains of salt, and silver pots, which, Lucía discovered as the group took their seats around the table, held plenty of coffee and hot chocolate.

Whether by accident or design, Leo had ended up on her left. The way the sleeve of her borrowed dress brushed against his as she reached for her hot chocolate reminded her of the day they had met.

Trying to ignore the pang that went through her, she looked instead toward Eduardo, who was rising from his seat at the head of the table.

"Amigos míos," he said, holding his cup of *café con leche* aloft. "As you all know, I'm not one for long

speeches. I can only say that I hope today marks the beginning of the kind of journey we will hold in our hearts and our minds for years to come. To friendship! *Salud!*"

At the conclusion of Eduardo's speech, everyone around the table clinked their coffee cups together. Lucía slid a finger through the delicate porcelain loop of hers and quirked an eyebrow at Leo.

His expression was blank as he touched his cup to hers. Lucía opened her mouth to ask why he wasn't overjoyed at having gotten away, but the white-skinned young woman to her right was trying to get her attention, her own cup in the air. Lucía obliged her with gentle tap, noticing as she did the unmistakable curiosity in the other woman's expression.

Lucía's gaze skipped to her plate, anxiety making her stomach clench. There was only ever one reason why someone looked at her like that—they had found out who she was and were seconds away from asking her things they would never ask anyone else, all for the purpose of indulging in idle gossip with their friends later.

Setting down her cup, Lucía braced herself for the onslaught.

But all the woman said was, "It's such a pleasure to meet more of Eduardo's friends, Miss Robles."

The musical lilt in her voice reminded Lucía that Eduardo's visitors had recently arrived from Puerto Rico. They wouldn't have heard all the gossip about the Troncoso heiresses. And even if they had…

A slow smile spread over Lucía's lips.

Even if they had, Eduardo had introduced her as Luz Robles and Leo as José Delgado. His guests had no way of knowing who they really were.

Under her uncle's command, Lucía had been meek,

obedient Lucía. In Vienna, the exotic heiress. In San Pedro, someone scandalous to whisper about. Here in the open seas, the ship under her feet heading toward a city she didn't know and whose inhabitants didn't know her, she could be…anything she wanted.

"Call me Luz," Lucía said, and clinked her cup against the woman's again.

As exhausted as she was, a thrum of excitement was starting to race through her, similar to the one she had felt when she'd ridden the *Riesenrad* for the first time. The dangling carriage had swept upward, and Lucía's breath had caught as the Ferris wheel performed its first revolution. Gliding into the air, taking in the dramatic view—first of the Prater and then of the city itself—Lucía had felt the thrilling rush of possibility.

Only this time…this time was different. *She* was different.

Leo shifted beside her, his sleeve grazing her arm as he reached for his water glass. Behind him, the coastline was speeding by.

Lucía didn't have the answers she had set out to find the night before. But she had something better—the promise of a fresh beginning. This time, she knew better than to repeat the mistakes of the past.

The house looked like a small palace to Leo.

He had known that Eduardo's family was extraordinarily wealthy. He just hadn't realized what that implied. It was no wonder he had agreed so readily to let Leo and Lucía tag along—there must have been more than a dozen rooms in his grandfather's house, and enough staff to make two unexpected arrivals seem inconsequential.

Behind them, several manservants were already hoisting the luggage out of the large cart that had followed them from the port, while two younger housemaids in starched caps and aprons greeted the new arrivals with trays of glasses full of juice.

"This is passion fruit, *señor*," Leo heard one of the girls say. "Lime on the other tray."

The clinking of ice against fine crystal followed their path through a sitting room furnished with valuable antiques. Leo trailed after the group as Eduardo led them to a gracious, high-ceilinged sitting room where side tables full of cut flowers and potted plants had been arranged among damasked sofas and chairs with needlepoint panels or ornate carvings along their backs.

The white-painted shutters that made up most of one wall folded into each other in a style similar to that of the fans the women were using to stir the lazy breeze. Beyond the shutters was a terrace, and beyond that were extensive lush gardens, the end of which Leo couldn't see from where he stood.

The sun was too high and hot overhead for anyone to venture out there, much less Leo, since the cap he wore offered far less protection against the broiling sun than his regular hat would.

He felt ridiculous with his shoulders straining the seams of his sailor's garb—none of the clothes Eduardo's male relatives had left in the ship had been wide enough to accommodate his back and shoulders, which had grown bulky over the years.

More than the clothes, though, it was being at someone else's mercy that made him uncomfortable. Eduardo was a damned good friend for helping them through this. Leo was aware of how lucky it was that Lucía had spotted his ship. Without his aid, Leo would be scrambling through the wilderness at the mercy of the hot tropical sun, struggling to provide food and shelter for a woman who slept on feather mattresses, swathed in silk.

Still, when all was said and done, Leo had never enjoyed being dependent on the kindness of others, even when he counted them as friends. He couldn't even write a letter to his bank in order to have some of his funds transferred to the Santo Domingo branch without risking being discovered. Sending a telegram to his office to have his correspondence forwarded was, of course, entirely out of the question. The prospect of leaving his work unattended for however many days or weeks it took to sort out this mess made his shoulders tight with tension.

But Leo had never been the type to dwell on his own misfortunes.

Trying his best to shake off his anxiety, he went to pay his respects to Eduardo's grandfather. He had met the older man only once before, in San Pedro, but they were soon deep in conversation. Don Amable, an amateur botanist when he wasn't busy being a shipping magnate, grew voluble as he told Leo all about the plants he was propagating on one side of the terrace.

Eduardo's visitors were a lively bunch. As well as the young woman Lucía had befriended on the ship, who was traveling with her mother, there were four rowdy young men who had been introduced as the Fajardo brothers, each one with names reminiscent of Renaissance painters.

They had congregated on the other side of the terrace, and Leo couldn't help but be relieved at the reprieve from having to answer their well-intentioned questions about who he was and what he did for a living and whether he was acquainted with the Puerto Rican industrialist they had been staying with while in San Pedro.

He had fended off their friendly curiosity with as much good grace as he could muster. It wasn't the dishonesty of their ruse that bothered him—concealing his and Lucía's identities was plainly necessary if Eduardo's plan was to work.

There'd been a time when he would have given anything to be anyone other than himself. Over the years, he'd achieved just that. He was no longer a penniless poet who kept the books at a sugar mill in order to feed his ailing mother. He was a businessman now, a well-respected one.

And in any case, the more he mingled, the bigger the risk that someone would discover that he was not in fact José Delgado—or worse, his real identity.

With every polite inquiry that Eduardo's visitors sent his way, Leo found himself growing more and more withdrawn. Lucía was far less reticent. She had fallen into the group as if she had known them for years rather than a few short hours, and was even now flitting from person to person like a butterfly.

She had struck up a friendship with one of Eduardo's visitors, a young woman who'd been introduced by Eduardo as a photographer named Cristina.

The two young women were both in high spirits, laughing with Eduardo's other friends about all the amusements their host had planned for them. Not one to spoil anyone's fun, Leo didn't tell Lucía that neither of them would be able to take part in any of the excursions, since leaving the house meant risking being recognized. This island was damnably small, its population always eager to engage in friendly gossip. He could come across someone completely unacquainted with Vargas, who'd only to tell an acquaintance or two about having seen Leo in Santo Domingo for the information to get back to the ship's owner.

Until the threat posed by Vargas was contained, they were effectively housebound.

The second time he caught himself stealing a glance at her, the reason why came to him in a sudden flash of insight—he was drinking in the details. After their first meeting, their communication had been conducted solely through letters, so he'd never had the opportunity to notice things like the arch of her eyebrows or the way she moved her hands when she talked, her slender fingers fluttering as if she was trying to coax music out of the air.

They'd had so little time together, he only had a few hours' worth of memories to stem the tide of his yearning. It hadn't been enough. Centuries of her, Leo suspected, wouldn't have been enough, either.

It was a good thing that he had found a way to move past all that.

Still, his gaze insisted on returning to the group every few minutes. Surrounded by four admiring young men, who, judging from her peals of laughter, all seemed to be exceptionally witty conversationalists, she looked radiant.

It struck him again how much more petite she was than he had remembered. In his daydreams, she had been tall and stately. There was something delicate about her in reality, a fragility in the lines of her slender neck and the slim wrists and forearms that were left bare by her short-sleeved blouse.

Eduardo's cousin's clothes suited her. They were far

plainer than the extravagantly ruffled or beaded ensembles he had seen her wear, and the clean lines accentuated her willowy figure. In a plain straw hat and no jewelry, she almost looked like a different person.

The only problem was, she seemed to be *acting* like a different person, too.

Not that Leo was overly concerned with what Lucía was doing—it was only that she was making it damned hard for anyone to ignore her antics.

Leo wasn't quite close enough to hear the conversation, only the bursts of laughter that drifted his way, so he couldn't have said what exactly led to Lucía tossing her head and holding out her hand to one of the young men. When he took it, she pulled him into a wild dance along the length of the terrace, her distinctive laugh trailing after them as they careened right into a high-backed wicker chair.

She had taken off her hat upon their arrival and replaced it with a flower that had fallen from one of the many pots on the terrace. As she righted herself, the wind tugged it out of her hair. Instead of letting it flutter away in the breeze, Lucía lunged for the red petals, the tip of one shoe on the lip of a large clay pot that was on the floor of the terrace, her entire body outstretched as she reached for the flower.

Her foot slipped.

Before his mind quite registered what he was doing, and with a speed he wouldn't have guessed himself capable of, Leo crossed the terrace with several lunges of his own and grabbed her before she went tumbling over the railing and into the flower bed below.

His arm locked around her waist—in his frantic desire to keep her from smashing into the railing, he drew her a little too forcefully against his chest. The faint tang of salt on her skin flooded his senses as he clasped her to him, breathing hard.

He had forgotten about all the other people in the terrace. Maybe it was for their benefit that Lucía let out another exuberant laugh and exclaimed, "My hero!"

Her words were met with a round of applause. Under the cover of the noise, Lucía brought her face closer to him to say, "You can let go of me now. Unless you're trying to take liberties with me, in which case I suggest waiting for a more appropriate time."

Leo released her so abruptly that she wobbled on her feet. "What the devil is wrong with you?"

"Nothing that couldn't be cured by a little—" She cut herself off as she turned around to face him. Her gaze softened a little as she saw his expression. "I'm fine, Leo. Calm down—nothing happened."

Nothing happened?

His stomach felt like it was filled with the shards of ice that had clinked in his juice. And his heart… His heart was a runaway locomotive that was about to speed right over the edge of a cliff.

The housemaids that had greeted them at the door had begun circulating around the room with trays of *pastelitos* and fried plantain that had been molded into cups and filled with shredded beef. This caused enough of a distraction that Leo was able to draw Lucía aside without exciting comment from the gathering.

"You could have gone over the railing—or through it," he told her furiously, the harshness in his tone amplified by the storm raging inside his chest. "And broken an arm or a leg—or your head—or seriously injured yourself."

"Lucky for me you're so fast and strong," she said, fluttering her eyelashes at him.

She may have meant it as a joke, but Leo was failing to see the humor in the situation. "You're not acting like yourself."

Lucía lifted her chin, apparently unconcerned with how the near fall had disheveled her hair. "How would you know? It's been a long time since you knew me."

She wasn't wrong. But something about the way she said it made Leo want to challenge her. "I wasn't aware you had changed so much."

"Well, I have. And you'd know that if you hadn't decided you were too busy for our correspondence."

There she went again, demanding much more from him than he was prepared to give.

She was wrong, too. But Leo wouldn't waste his breath correcting her.

"I can't say I'm sorry I declined to continue our acquaintance. Clearly, it was the right thing to do," he snapped, and strode back to Eduardo's grandfather.

Chapter Six

Traveling always took so much out of Lucía. She was so tired by the time the group finally went to bed that she crashed into sleep almost as soon as her head hit the pillow. It wasn't until the morning—late the next morning, judging by the warmth of the sunshine flooding past the half-open shutters—that she was able to look around the bedroom that had been prepared for her by the accommodating housekeeper.

A demilune table with lovely legs had been placed between the bedroom's two tall windows. Next to it was an armchair upholstered in a rose print that matched the small arrangement of pale pink roses on the table. When Lucía scrambled out of bed and poked her head out one of the tall windows, expecting more roses, she found jasmine growing up a trellis instead.

The window overlooked the magnificent garden she had glimpsed from the terrace the day before. The vast stretches of lawn and the brick-paved pathways were all empty, save for the gently waving plants that bordered them, among them clusters of red-and-pink ginger flowers that rose taller than any Lucía had ever seen.

Lovelier than the gardens was the warm, salty ocean breeze that blew in through the shutters, ruffling her unbound hair. Lucía stood at the window for a long moment, letting her eyes drift shut as the scent of the ocean and the roses wafted over her.

It couldn't have been more than a minute or two, but when she opened her eyes again, Leo was standing on the path below, looking up at her. He must have found some proper clothes to borrow, because he wore a black suit and even a black-banded Panama hat.

And Lucía was in her nightclothes.

She remembered it with a jolt—the freshly laundered nightdress she had found folded at the foot of the bed was a very pretty affair of delicate white lawn decorated with thin bands of lace. It was sleeveless, and long enough that the hem brushed her ankles. And it must have also been fairly sheer with the sun shining full on her.

Even so, her first instinct was not to cover herself, or withdraw from the window. It was inexplicable, and she wouldn't have been able to formulate an answer if asked why, but all Lucía wanted was to lean over and call out to Leo and...

And what?

How exactly did she think Leo would react if she did call out to him? By climbing the trellis like the fervent lover in some opera and proclaiming his undying love to her? Taking her into his arms and kisssing his way down her throat and neck until she trembled with desire?

Leo hadn't moved. He was as frozen as if he had been turned into a statue—one hewn from bronze and obsidian, as beautiful as any she had seen in a museum. She had never seen what lay underneath his shirt, but her fingers curled against the window frame with the memory of the hard planes of his chest and the finely sculpted ridges of his abdomen.

From the moment they had met for the second time, Leo had looked at her with nothing more than a mixture of cool indifference and annoyance. Now, however, as he stared boldly up at her from the garden, she could have sworn that what she saw in his gaze was something close to hunger.

And it matched the desire coiling deep inside her, a more intense echo of what she had felt when he'd massaged her leg—or when he'd caught her in his arm the day before, and an exaggerated attempt at flirting had been her only defense against the sudden onrush of feelings.

A warm gust of wind drifted over her, as soft as a caress. Though she was standing in a patch of sunshine, Lucía couldn't help but shiver. It should have been impossible to perceive at a distance, but Leo started as suddenly as if she had shouted—or as if she had actually leaned out the window and let her nightgown slip provocatively down her shoulder.

But as daring and bold and even wicked as she felt she could be in her guise of Luz Robles, without really fearing that the gossips in San Pedro would get wind of her behavior, Lucía couldn't quite bring herself to forget that the man standing below was the one who had shattered her heart.

Her heart pounding, she reached for the shutters and pulled them firmly closed.

Over the course of a regular morning, by the time the clock struck ten, Leo would have already walked half the town, running errands for his mother, ridden on horseback to the mill, gone on a long trek through the sugarcane fields to assure himself that everything was in order, and bounded half a dozen times up and down the rickety wooden stairs that led to his office.

He never missed an opportunity to take up a machete and work alongside the cutters for a few minutes. At first because he'd found it a good way to take his mind off Lucía, and then when he no longer needed distraction, because the labor had become appealing in its own right. He'd be lying if he said that he didn't also like the respect it earned him from the cane cutters, some of whom used to know his father—and the muscles that came with it, visible proof that he was no longer the young poet who did nothing more strenuous than hold a pen.

It was no surprise that the morning after their arrival in Santo Domingo, he had found himself in desperate need of exercise. Since leaving the property wasn't really an option, he had turned toward the garden instead. And what a mistake that was.

The garden was beautiful enough in the mellow glow of late morning. Red paving bricks wound a circuitous path around leafy *níspero* trees bursting with pale brown fruit, flower beds crowded with ferns and tall sprays of yellow flowers, and even a small man-made pond bordered with more bricks, inside of which swam several large fish. Leo stood there for a long moment, watching how the flash of their scales mimicked the movement of the sun on the water.

Making a mental note to bring some bread crumbs on his next walk—and some dried corn for the little brown birds flitting from one vine-tangled branch to another—Leo strode around the thick trunk of a mango tree before turning back toward the house.

He came to a sudden halt.

Lucía was leaning out a window, framed by unpainted wooden shutters as if waiting to be captured in a photograph. Tiny yellow butterflies flittered around the sprays of jasmine growing outside her window.

The light that shone through the leaves of the garden was shining through her nightdress, too, silhouetting her slight curves. Her eyes were closed, her lips ever so slightly turned up, and Leo...

Leo felt as if he had been turned into stone.

He didn't know how long he stood there, rooted to the spot, unable to tear his gaze away. Long enough for her eyes to flutter open. Long enough for her to notice him.

She didn't move. And Leo knew he should—he had to.

He remained standing there for the space of one breath, and then another, gazing at her as she gazed at him. And then, when the moment between them had stretched so far that Leo half thought he would blink and find that a century had passed like in a fairy tale, he finally managed to wrench himself away.

It was a good thing this house was the size of a small palace, because he was definitely going to have to stay away from Lucía. Standing there looking up at her, it had become all too clear to him that he couldn't trust his own mind to keep from conjuring up little daydreams about what it would be like to glide his fingertips over the smooth brown skin of her collarbone or explore the side of her neck with his lips until she smiled as softly as she'd been smiling before she'd opened her eyes and seen him...

The sight of her made him want to hope—worse than that, *dream*.

And Leo knew all too well that hoping and dreaming

were merely the first steps in a long journey that led to certain disappointment.

He walked until his stomach begged him for sustenance, hoping to drive the image from his mind. Neither the physical exertion nor the broiling sun was a match for the vivid picture of Lucía in that diaphanous nightgown, so after several paths around the plant-bordered path, Leo went back into the house. He'd intended to find a newspaper and retreat with it to some unpopulated corner where he could be alone with his troubled—or troubling—thoughts. But one of the many uniformed housemaids intercepted him and pointed to the staircase as she told him that breakfast was being laid upstairs.

Leo followed the murmur of conversation to a long, shady balcony where a pair of stone urns overflowing with glossy-leaved philodendrons and trailing pothos flanked a table big enough for a dozen chairs. Place settings had already been laid out at each seat, though only half of them were occupied.

Eduardo greeted him with a hearty wave as soon as he stepped onto the terra-cotta tiles. "Breakfasts are informal here," he said, gesturing to the covered platters on the long sideboard. "Help yourself and sit wherever you like. There are newspapers, too, if you're so inclined."

Leo murmured his own greeting, his gaze skipping over the people gathered at the sideboard and the table until it landed on Lucía, who was chatting with her new friend, a bowl of cubed papaya and pineapple on the embroidered tablecloth in front of her. Behind her, the Caribbean Sea was a sliver of bright blue on the horizon—a more glorious backdrop than the one in the photograph of her that had been printed in a local magazine a year or two before.

She looked far more beautiful here, with her hands in constant motion and a streak of sunlight gilding her curls. Leo couldn't help but think that she wore light well, whether she was limned in moonlight or crowned with sunshine—or bathing in it, her nightdress turned to liquid gold wherever the sun touched it.

At least she was fully dressed now, in a blouse that buttoned up to the neck and sleeves that ended at her elbows in sharply pressed cuffs.

Before he could notice any more details about her dress or her person, Leo turned to the sideboard and began piling fried eggs onto a cream-colored plate. He was pulling out a chair on the other side of the table from Lucía when one of Eduardo's friends turned to their host and remarked, "You haven't shared what's on our itinerary for today."

Eduardo took a sip of his coffee before answering. "I've a long excursion planned for tomorrow, so today I thought I'd keep things simple—a walk around Plaza Colón, followed by a tour of the cathedral and lunch at a nearby restaurant. There are some picturesque places where we might stop for an hour or two, for those who'd like to sketch some views. Or photograph them," he added, nodding toward Cristina.

A murmur of approval greeted his words. Even Lucía lit up, as if she didn't remember—or hadn't realized— that neither she nor Leo was setting so much as a toe outside the house for the duration of their stay.

He glanced at her again, and his muscles tensed as it became clear that she hadn't.

Eduardo was too busy chatting with Cristina's mother to notice Lucía's excitement, so it fell to Leo to say something.

"Are you well enough for an outing, Lu—Luz?" he asked, and silently cursed the momentary slip. It was a good thing she'd chosen a name so similar to her own. "You did say you were feeling a little unwell."

Lucía received his words with a frown. Of course. She was a spoiled heiress and probably too accustomed to getting her own way.

She raised her chin in what looked like defiance, but she must have thought better of it because after a few moments, she nodded.

"That's right," she said, giving their host an apologetic smile. "I'm afraid I have had some headaches. Would you mind if I stayed behind?"

Before Eduardo could answer, Cristina said, with deep concern, "Mamá and I will stay with you, of course."

"Or I could," one of the young men said quickly. "I'd be more than happy to keep you company."

Leo watched from behind his newspaper as Lucía acknowledged her new friends' offers with a wave of her hand. "Please don't worry about me," she said, adding as she turned to Cristina, "I know how eager you have been to try out your new photographic equipment. I wouldn't want to rob you of the opportunity."

"I don't mind." The lie was made obvious by the way Cristina's brow furrowed. "Mamá and I could use a rest and—"

"I'll stay with her," Leo said, not bothering to look up from his newspaper.

A brief silence greeted his words, then Cristina tried again. "But—"

This time, it was Lucía who forestalled her protest. "I'd be pleased to have your company." She paused for a moment before adding, with a slight emphasis, "José."

"Well, that's settled," Eduardo said cheerfully, and added something about Leo resting a fictional injury before skillfully guiding the conversation toward a different subject.

From the way Lucía's friend and her mother darted glances at each other, hiding their smiles behind their cups of coffee, it was clear that they shared the assumption that Leo and Lucía had contrived to spend the day together. Better they should invent some sort of romance between them than they suspect the truth.

It wasn't until the group had left and silence descended on the balcony that Leo realized just how daunted he was by the prospect of spending the entire day alone with Lucía. So much for staying away from her.

Returning his plate to the sideboard, he took the newspapers that had been left folded beside the coffeepot and carried them back to the seat he had just vacated. A cursory glance through the first one didn't reveal anything out of the ordinary, but there was small notice about the *Caridad* in the second one. Leo flipped back the pages to read the newspaper's name. *Boletín del Comercio*—a Santo Domingo paper that was circulated widely through the island's biggest cities.

The piece was a short one. It only took up about three or four centimeters on a page that was crowded with shipping tables and advertisements for Tomas Sanlley's photography gallery and Pepsin Digestive Elixir. Within those few square centimeters of newsprint, his name stood out starkly. Vargas wasn't just going forward with his accusation—he was so serious about framing Leo that he must have sent a telegraph to the paper's editors in Santo Domingo to ensure it would be printed quickly.

He could only be grateful that Lucía's name hadn't

appeared alongside his. While the piece did mention that Leo had been aided by a female accomplice, it didn't include anything that could potentially identify her. Whether that was because Vargas hadn't gotten a good look at her or because he'd merely chosen to keep that information out of the papers, Leo didn't know.

By now, the authorities throughout the island would have been notified and would likely be on the lookout for them both. But that wasn't the only reason why Leo could feel his stomach sinking. It wasn't just merchants who read *Boletín del Comercio*. There was little doubt in his mind that gossip and speculation had already begun spreading throughout San Pedro. And as concerned as he should have been about the damage to his reputation among other businessmen, who he'd taken pains to cultivate so that everyone thought of him as upstanding and honest, all he could think about was what the one thing he had failed to consider on that long night they'd spent on Eduardo's ship—what his friends and family would think when they heard Leo was being accused of arson.

And of fleeing town with an heiress.

He preferred to think that no one who knew him would believe it. And yet he and Lucía had disappeared at the same time. For anyone who knew their history— what little there was of it—there could be no question in their minds that he and Lucía had run off together.

Leo thought back to what he'd told Lucía on the ship, about being willing to marry her should the need arise. He'd meant it—but he hadn't quite realized how likely it was that he might be called to act upon his promise.

Or how terrifying he would find the prospect.

Chapter Seven

Without a fun little outing to fill up the day, Lucía wasn't entirely sure how to pass the hours until the others returned. Even after escaping her uncle's clutches, her life in Vienna had been structured around her lessons at the Academy and her own punishing practice schedule. She'd never really had the freedom to while away an entire day.

She tried chatting with the maids as they cleared the table, but they all had their own work to do. Eduardo hadn't left much in the way of reading material, save for a handful of newspapers and two illustrated magazines she had already flipped through. And Leo seemed to be determined to keep his nose buried in his newspaper. He had been staring at that morning's edition of the *Boletín del Comercio* for a tediously long time, as if to avoid having to make conversation with Lucía—or even look at her. Ironic, after the way he'd looked his fill earlier that morning.

Her skin prickled pleasurably at the memory, and she couldn't help but let her own gaze roam over him.

Eduardo was taller than Leo by a handful of centimeters, and lean where Leo was stocky. His cousins seemed to share his build, because the linen suit that Leo had borrowed from one of them was a shade too tight through the broad expanse of his chest and shoulders. Lucía watched the seams in his jacket strain to the point of bursting as he reached for the coffeepot.

"You can take it off, you know," she said.

He froze. "Excuse me?"

"Your jacket. You're clearly uncomfortable in it. It's just the two of us, and it's so hot here." Being Luz Robles, however temporarily, seemed to be giving Lucía the courage to say things she wouldn't have dared to as herself. "Not to mention the fact that you saw me in dishabille—it would be only fair to return the favor."

Leo's jaw tightened. Instead of responding to her impertinent remark, he returned his gaze to the paper in his hands and glowered down at whatever he was reading. Probably an engrossing account of how many barrels of sugar had been exported that month, or detailed inventories of… Well, Lucía didn't know enough about business to guess what he could be reading, but she could be sure that it was boring.

Still pretending to ignore her, Leo took a sip of his coffee—and grimaced, swallowing though he looked like he wanted to sputter it out all over the potted orchids that had replaced the remains of breakfast on the center of the long table. Lucía hid a smile and held out the silver sugar canister. She was only three seats away, but as he reached for it, the unmistakable sound of tearing fabric filled the air between them.

"You might want to reconsider my suggestion," Lucía said, tilting her head. "Unless you want to repay Eduardo's kindness by reducing his cousin's wardrobe to rags."

Leo muttered out a curse and tossed the newspaper aside. His attempt at peeling off the jacket was so unsuccessful, though, that Lucía found herself bursting into a fit of giggles as she stood to help him.

"Hold still," she commanded, grasping the jacket by the neck and trying to tug it down over his arms.

Leo craned his neck to look at her. "You're making it worse."

"Is that how you speak to everyone who's trying to help you?"

"Helping me?" Leo made a noise that sounded like a snort. "Is that what you think you're doing? I'm being imprisoned."

"Just keep your arms down and stop twisting around."

"I was doing just fine on my own," he insisted.

Lucía gave him a sidelong look. "I beg to differ."

The black fabric clung to his shoulders and biceps as if wrapping him in an unwanted embrace. As Lucía struggled with it, the faint scent of laundry soap wafted from it, underlaid with another, earthier, scent that she was beginning to recognize as his.

Lucía would be lying if she tried to claim that being in such close proximity to him—and the feel of those hard muscles under her hands—didn't arouse a series of thrills like the ones she had felt while lying under him the other night. It was almost disturbing, the way her body seemed to immediately respond to his nearness.

All too aware that she might do something impulsive if she continued to touch him, Lucía hastened to free him from the jacket. One more yank was all it took for it to come off. Unfortunately, it also sent Lucía crashing against the table, hard enough to bruise.

Leo reached out and stabilized her. His hand at the

small of her back made her feel as warm as she had earlier, when she'd soaked in the sun. It felt intimate—and so overwhelming that she couldn't keep herself from jerking out of his grasp.

Letting his hand fall to his side, Leo asked, "Are you all right?"

"Fine," Lucía said, though she couldn't resist rubbing her hip before holding up what remained of the jacket, now split into two. "I can't say the same for this, though."

"I'll buy the cousin an entire new wardrobe as soon as I can access my bank accounts." Leo gave a restless shake of his head. "I should go."

"Go?"

"To ask one of the maids for some ink and paper. I have a great deal of business to take care of."

Resuming her seat, Lucía propped her chin on her palm. "What can you do, at such a distance?"

He shrugged. "I hate to involve Eduardo any more than I already have, but I was hoping he would find a way to smuggle some of my correspondence to San Pedro. I also wanted to compile a list of questions to ask him and his grandfather about things I should know before purchasing another ship. Eduardo didn't seem to think much about the *Caridad*, though it looked perfectly fine to me, and I need to know what he saw that I didn't."

Though he was visibly frustrated about his lack of maritime knowledge, Lucía noticed how much Leo's expression brightened when he spoke about his work. His features grew mobile, and even more striking than they were at rest.

She didn't have to wonder what it was like to live with such passion—for years, she had found a sense of purpose in her music, as well as the satisfaction of witnessing her skills expand and refine. It was a passion that had taken her and her family halfway around the world. And for what? What had all that accomplished, save wasting staggering amounts of money that might have been better spent elsewhere?

The thought filled her with a prickly kind of annoyance that made her say, "Do you ever think of anything that isn't your work?"

Leo's shoulders stiffened. "Why would I?"

"Because there's an entire world out there, full of interesting things to see and experience. Much more interesting than staring at ledgers all day or counting your money or whatever it is you do."

Leo countered her irritated tone with a sharp look. "I don't see you doing much of interest, either. There was a time when I would have sworn that you weren't the type to sit idle all day. I know you don't have your instrument here, but I do remember you writing more than once about spending hours reading sheets of music as if they were novels."

Leo looked like he was about to say more, but he was forced to pause as one of the maids came onto the terrace to refresh the pitcher of ice water and ask if they wanted more coffee. Leo declined and asked for ink and paper instead. He didn't take up the thread of conversation again when the girl left, which left Lucía curiously disappointed underneath the annoyance that still swirled inside her.

Neither Amalia nor Julian had done more than ask a gently probing question or two when they'd noticed that Lucía no longer spent her mornings poring over sheet music or sawing away at her violin. They'd respected her space, and she had appreciated it.

Or maybe they'd just enjoyed not being roused from sleep before the sun had a chance to finish rising because Lucía required three or four hours of practice in the morning.

Leo, she suspected, wouldn't have been so gentle. In fact, he'd looked like he was on the verge of issuing a lecture. And though she wouldn't welcome such an intrusion, exactly, she did admit to feeling curious as to what he would say.

Lucía broke away from her momentary abstraction at the sight of Leo unbuttoning his cuffs. "What are you doing?"

"I thought you wanted to see me in dishabille." His raised eyebrow punctuated the attempt at humor. "Don't worry, I'm not undressing. I just like rolling up my sleeves when I'm working—I see no sense in making my laundress's life more difficult by staining all my cuffs with ink. Since this is not my shirt and the person who will be washing it is not in my employ, I should be even more careful."

"That's kind," Lucía said grudgingly.

The shrug he responded with would look like embarrassment on someone else. On Leo, it didn't take away from the commanding air he projected. "Just efficient—and thrifty. There have been times in my life when I've had to scrimp even on washing soap."

Briskly, he finished folding up the starched white fabric, revealing hard, muscled forearms that were almost as dark a brown as his sun-burnished face. Heat spread over her as she pictured him walking around the mill with his forearms exposed and his necktie loosened.

"What will you do while I'm writing letters?" he asked.

With the tip of her finger, Lucía began to trace the edge of an embroidered leaf on the tablecloth. "I'll think of something," she said, adding after a few seconds, "I might explore the house."

Or the garden—though Lucía was half-afraid that saying so out loud would evoke the confusing tension that had unspooled between them earlier, and she was not keen on revisiting it.

Leo gave her a probing look. "Is there a reason why you're not playing your violin anymore?"

Lucía felt herself growing taut. "How do you know I'm not?"

"You once told me, in one of your letters, that your fingers were becoming calloused from the strings. They're smooth now. On another occasion, you wrote that you had purchased a bottle of perfume to cover up the ever-present scent of rosin."

Surprise curled through her as he all but quoted her own words back at her. She could remember penning them, sitting at her little burled-wood secretary with her favorite piano shawl snug around her shoulders. That he should have remembered…

She swiftly severed the line of thought. It didn't mean anything except that he had a good memory.

"I've been so busy with my travels and my—and all the things I wanted to do," she lied. "I scarcely had enough time to devote to practicing."

"Have you thought of taking up another occupation?"

"I've never been good at needlework," Lucía said, quirking up her lips.

Her attempt at levity was met with an impatient shake of his head.

"I don't mean some sort of genteel pastime. There

are so many things you could be doing, Lucía. So many ways to put your fortune—and your brains—to use. If I had a fraction of your assets…" Leo pulled out the chair and sat on its edge, leaning toward her. "Why not start a new business? Or invest in one?"

Lucía shifted in her seat. He wasn't indirectly asking for money, was he? The man she used to know would have never done such a thing, but he had changed so much that she just couldn't be sure of him anymore. This hard, ambitious man who spoke of business the way he'd once spoken of poetry…

Why wouldn't he be like everyone else?

Oh, she hated this uncertainty—this sickly feeling of never knowing if someone was interested in her for herself, or for what she could do for them.

"I haven't any interest in business," she said flatly.

"The theater, then," he insisted. "Find artists in need of a patroness, or sponsor a play or a concert. Put your money to good use."

Leo wasn't wrong. Lucía *was* aching for something to do, and she had been ever since she had stuffed her sheet music into a trunk and snapped the clasp on her violin case for the last time.

"You seem to be convinced that money can solve everything. It doesn't, you know," she told him. It was one of the first things she had learned after she and Amalia had finally gained control of their own finances. "And I fail to see how much of a difference mine can make beyond the very generous charitable contributions that Amalia makes on our behalf."

"Can't you?" There was a challenge in his gaze, and Lucía didn't know how to answer it. "Women like you need a passion, and a purpose. You won't be happy unless you have both those things."

"It's incredibly presumptuous of you to imply that I'm unhappy, just because I don't choose to spend my life wallowing in greed," Lucía snapped. In the years that she lived with her uncle, Lucía had become practiced at hiding her emotions—particularly her anger. Giving them free rein felt more freeing than she would have thought possible. "And to act like you know me, or my habits, when we have already established that you have no idea who I am, or what I value, or what I even do with my days. It's more than presumptuous—it's—"

She cut herself off, breathing hard, fully expecting him to scowl at her.

But all he did was smile.

"See?" Leo said softly, his eyes alight with triumph. "Passion."

Oh, but this man was *impossible*.

With a strangled exclamation, Lucía pushed her chair back and rose from the table.

She hadn't taken so much as a step away when his hand landed on her arm.

"I know you think I'm greedy," he said, looking up at her, his brown eyes unexpectedly serious. "You may be right. But it's not just about accumulating wealth or counting coins, as you put it. I want to give my mother all the comforts she deserves. After all she sacrificed to raise me, it's the least I can do for her. A large house, with all the modern conveniences, and help enough to keep her from having to toil away her days. But more than that—I want to give her security."

It was the kind of noble sentiment he would express in one of his letters, and it gave Lucía pause. Maybe there was more to this new Leo than she had considered. Maybe the man she had grown to know over months of correspondence wasn't a complete fiction, but a complex, complicated person who had undergone a terrible ordeal and made it through changed.

She didn't blame him for keeping the harder parts of his life from her. After all, hadn't she done the same thing by never telling him about almost being forced into marriage by her greedy uncle? She hadn't done it out of a desire to conceal her history from him, or from fear that he'd think badly of her, but because it had seemed so much easier to let herself glide along in the rush of pretty words and lovely sentiments than to try to find the words to recount what had been the most harrowing moments of her life.

Doing otherwise would have felt like a confrontation of sorts, and for better or worse, Lucía had always shied from confrontations.

A little grudgingly, she moved back to the chair she had been so anxious to vacate a moment before and laid a hand on Leo's bare forearm in an echo of his previous gesture. His skin was startlingly warm, as if he had been sitting in the sun instead of the terrace's mellow shade. Ignoring the impulse to snatch her hand away, Lucía said, "I know that you'll give her all of that and more. You're a good son, Leo. Your mother is lucky to have you."

Lucía saw an unfamiliar gentleness come into his eyes—they were the color of toffee, not his skin, and they were meltingly sweet as he regarded her. He lifted a hand, and Lucía's heart started to thud hard inside her chest when he carefully brushed a stray curl behind her ear.

"I also do it because it's devilishly fun when all those rich old men realize how much better I am at business than they are." His mouth curved into a smile. "I feel I should be honest, lest you give me too much credit."

"I haven't given you enough—and I haven't been altogether fair with you. I think—"

Lucía paused and licked her lips. Without realizing it, she and Leo had both drawn close enough that when he shifted, her knee knocked against his thigh. The thudding of her heart turned into a rapid symphony, and suddenly, Lucía could not remember what she had been about to say.

"I think…"

Her hand was still on Leo's forearm. The dark hairs there were springy under her palm, the muscles below taut with tension and as hard as marble. Every ounce of sense Lucía possessed told her to let go, but her fingers remained tight around him as he flexed his arm.

The slight movement made a rush of heat gather between her thighs. Lucía clutched a handful of the tablecloth with her free hand, feeling her fingers knock into Leo's abandoned coffee cup as she wrenched the fabric tightly in her fist.

"Lucía…" he murmured raggedly. The tip of his tongue darted out over his full lower lip and Lucía's breath caught. She was starting to lean even closer when Leo screwed his eyes shut. "I… I can't. I can't do this."

Her mouth went dry. Even if she had stopped to think at any point within the past couple of minutes, she wouldn't have expected for the sweet earnestness in Leo's expression to translate into a complete change in character. Outright rejection, however, when she'd sworn by the heat in his gaze that his thoughts were running in the same direction as hers...

It was crushing—and all too reminiscent of the grief and heartbreak that had almost overcome her when he had stopped writing.

Even so, it wasn't until a faint squeak brought her attention to the doorway that Lucía reared away from Leo.

She whipped her head around to see the maid from earlier, holding a silver tray that contained a pot of ink and a small sheaf of writing paper. The girl mumbled out a mortified apology, turned and disappeared inside the house.

Abruptly, Leo scraped back his chair and went to stand by the balustrade, averting his face away from her.

No going back.

That was what Lucía had told herself on the ship. Leo had broken her heart once—why would she ever give him the opportunity to do it again?

Being around him inspired all sorts of sensations in her treacherous body, but Lucía should know better than to give in to them.

She should know better than to want to kiss him.

"I should go," Lucía blurted out.

Leo glanced back, looking almost startled to realize that she was still there. "I should offer you my apologies," he said, and Lucía didn't quite know what he was professing to feel apologetic about—having almost kissed her or having not. "I don't usually let myself get so carried—"

She didn't let him finish. Pushing away from the table so quickly her chair almost overturned, Lucía strode quickly off the terrace.

Chapter Eight

Lucía made sure to stay away from Leo for the rest of that day. Her newfound confidence as Luz Robles led her to the kitchen, where she talked the maids into letting her help make the *dulce de coco* they intended to serve for dessert that night. She even had lunch with them, though they had laid the dining table with two place settings for her and Leo.

"He has plenty of work to keep him company," Lucía had told them airily.

Her fascination with their cooking wasn't entirely a pretense—she'd always had a sweet tooth, and after helping grate the coconut and stir the milk and sugar into the steaming pot, she had been given a small saucer full of the still-warm dessert to enjoy before she went upstairs to bathe and dress before dinner.

She breathed a sigh of relief when the group came trooping into the house in the late afternoon. They had been greeted in the downstairs terrace with pitchers of ice water, and they milled around, telling Lucía about their day as they sipped from prettily etched glasses.

Cristina, who hadn't stopped shooting knowing looks

her way, found a quiet moment to sidle up to Lucía and ask how her day had gone.

"It was very quiet," Lucía said firmly, not wanting to encourage her new friend. "I spent most of it in the kitchen."

"Oh," Cristina said, sounding disappointed at the lack of gossip. "Well, it sounds like you're feeling better—maybe you'll be able to join us tomorrow."

"I hope so."

Catching sight of Leo as he talked quietly with Eduardo on the other side of the terrace, Lucía resolved to do whatever it took to keep from spending another day alone with him. To her intense relief, Eduardo greeted her the next morning with the news that she and Leo would be able to join in that day's expedition.

"I'm taking everyone to see an underwater lake—or, rather, four of them," he said, taking her and Leo aside.

Giras campestres were popular pastimes among Lucía's acquaintances—going out to someone's farm and spending the better part of a day in the countryside, playing games and enjoying the taste of food cooked over wood instead of coal. An excursion to an underwater lake sounded positively adventurous to Lucía, like something out of a novel.

Eduardo continued, "We'll be out in the wilderness for most of the day, in and around the caves, and there will be little chance of anyone outside our group catching sight of the two of you. What do you say?"

"I'd love to go," Lucía said quickly.

It would have been much easier for her if Leo had declined the invitation—she half thought he would, given his refusal to mingle with the group—but he gave Eduardo a nod and consented to accompany them. Even though the presence of other people meant that Lucía wouldn't have to interact much with Leo if she didn't want to, knowing that he was coming along suffused her with equal parts trepidation and excitement.

Eduardo's family had not one but two long carriages, each of which held around a dozen people aside from the coachman. The group quickly settled themselves into one of them. The second one, packed with folding chairs and tables and more food than Lucía was sure they needed for a single day's outing, trundled along behind them, carrying also the three members of the household's staff who would help serve lunch.

The sky was perfectly clear as they set out. The tropical almond trees lining the street, which Lucía had glimpsed upon their arrival, met overhead and formed something of a tunnel as they passed several large, beautiful houses. As they turned right at the crumbling remains of a stone gateway, Eduardo, who was sitting beside her, explained they were part of the colonial-era walls that had once surrounded the city.

Another couple of minutes and the sea came into view, brilliantly blue and restless with cresting waves. Lucía, who had her hat's brim drawn low, found herself relaxing as they crossed a bridge and left the city behind.

Though Lucía's uncle had never really allowed her to expand her friendships in any meaningful way, opening up to other people hadn't become difficult until the past few years. Pretending to be someone other than herself allowed her to lower her guard. The elegant simplicity of the white cotton blouse with a subtle window check and the dark brown skirt she had found in her bedroom's wardrobe helped her transform even further into her false persona, and soon she was laughing and chatter-

ing along with Eduardo and Cristina, and twisting back
to laugh at the Fajardos' antics.

Even Leo was deep in conversation with Eduardo's
grandfather, a sprightly septuagenarian with a silver
mustache.

It must have taken a couple of hours to reach their
destination. The early morning sunshine had darkened
into a golden tone when the carriage turned off the main
road and rattled down a dirt path before rolling to a gentle stop in a clearing.

"Are we here?" Lucía asked, peering at the dense fo-
liage surrounding them.

"Almost," Eduardo answered. "We'll have to walk
the rest of the way to the main entrance to the caves."

Lucía was amused to realize that her borrowed wardrobe allowed for so much ease of movement that even
her stride felt different. She was walking more quickly,
and with more purpose, charging ahead with Eduardo
as he led the way.

Well, all right—cowardly as it was, she was mostly
intent on avoiding Leo, who had taken the rear as he
helped haul one of the crates that the housekeeper had
stuffed with food meant for their midday meal. During
their time apart the day before, he had apparently dispatched someone from Eduardo's household to a tailor, and was now wearing a suit that had been cut with
plenty of room to spare around his shoulders and thighs.

Not that Lucía was noticing his shoulders. Or his
thighs.

She did notice, however, that he also seemed to be
keeping his distance from her. It was for the better. Lucía
was not under the illusion that what had almost happened the day before had been anything but a lapse in

judgement on both of their parts. Nor did she think that it had been enough for him to see her in a different light.

A grim thought had followed her into bed the night before. What if, in getting to know her better, all he did was confirm that she really was as frivolous and pampered and demanding as he believed her to be?

No, it was far better for everyone concerned that they stay away from each other. Fortunately, Eduardo's raucous friends were making it easy. One of them was carrying the leather case with Cristina's expensive photographic equipment, and he seemed determined to give her apoplexy as he pretended to drop it every few steps. From Cristina's squeals, Lucía was fairly sure that her friend was enjoying the attention. Still, Lucía made a point of commanding Rafael Fajardo, in laughing, flirtatious tones, to rescue the endangered case.

The Fajardo brothers all seemed to be at least five years older than her, and flirting with them was a harmless endeavor, as they all were inclined to treat her like a younger relation. It certainly was fun, though.

And not only because it seemed to irritate Leo to no end.

The banter—and an impromptu sword fight using fallen branches as weapons—kept them occupied until they reached another, much smaller clearing. The servants wasted no time in setting up the chairs they had brought along on a little handcart. Cristina's mother and Eduardo's grandfather settled into them, while Eduardo beckoned to the rest of the group to follow him.

"My cousins and I came across this place several years ago," he said, holding a kerosene lamp high over his head. He paused to pull aside some dangling vines and thick palm fronds and waved them through, saying,

"Careful on the steps down. There's a rope to the right if you need to hang on to something."

The Fajardos bounded down recklessly, though the steps were no more than uneven grooves worn into the rock. Leo, however, paused to offer Cristina a hand. Before anyone could do the same to Lucía, she scrambled for the rope and made her own way.

She could feel the change in temperature the moment they stepped out of the sunshine and cool, damp air wafted over her face.

"Has this place been surveyed?" asked one of the young men.

"Not yet," Eduardo answered. "We resolved not to let anyone outside the family and a few select friends know about it, save for a local man who acts as guide, though I'm sure we're not the only people who have found it by chance. It's not much to look at from the outside. But when you come around here…"

They reached a small landing and Eduardo used the fire in his lamp to light a second one, which he handed to one of his friends.

Lucía's breath caught. Around her, she could hear similar intakes of breath as the others came to a halt in front of the most brilliant blue waters Lucía had ever seen—a more intense blue than that of even the Caribbean Sea, which looked turquoise in places. Though only illuminated by a shaft of sunlight coming from an opening overhead, the underwater lake was as bright and glittering as a jewel. In the far, shadowy recesses of the cave, stalactites dripped down to meet the crystal-clear water, almost as long as the vines that trailed from the trees above.

The hush that had spread over the gathering was broken by a low murmur that echoed throughout the damp space. It took a moment for Lucía to recognize Leo's voice, made even more resonant by the rock curving around them.

Startled, she glanced over her shoulder to look at him. A glimpse of his face was all it took for her to feel as if she had interrupted an intimate moment. As if feeling her gaze on him, Leo paused abruptly, looking half embarrassed and half annoyed with himself.

"Did you write that?" Lucía asked.

Leo shook his head. "It's a poem by Salomé Ureña de Henríquez."

Lucía had studied the nineteenth-century poet in school, though she had only memorized one of her poems, a sweet one about a bird and a nest. She had no idea that the woman who had written such verses was capable of such strength of feeling.

Or that Leo still had the ability to stir her with words.

The others murmured appreciative comments about the poem and moved on, walking farther down the strip of rock above the glimmering lake. Lucía hesitated, feeling as though she should say something to Leo, though his expression had taken on a forbidding cast. But before she could decide what, he too moved on.

Eduardo pointed into the distance. "Do you see the figures painted on the rock over there?"

Enough sunlight came through an opening for Lucía to make out black-and-red markings on the cave's pale, craggy surface.

"Taino, aren't they?" Leo asked, peering interestedly.

Eduardo nodded. "We think they must have held rituals down here—we found a few clay pots, and figurines, too."

One of the Fajardos crouched down to peer over the rim of the rock and into the pristine water. "Looks like a good place for a swim. Is the water deep enough to jump in? Or is there another way to get down there?"

"My cousins and I let ourselves down on a rope ladder we rigged," Eduardo said, gesturing to where it was fastened, just above a rowboat. "I can't imagine it's entirely safe, but we do have our fun. The water's always cool, even on the hottest day. And the next lake is even colder—there's a little nook in the water we used to chill our champagne."

"How many lakes are there?" someone else asked as Lucía stepped closer to the edge to look for herself. The distance down didn't seem too great, and the water looked so tempting that Lucía could see the appeal in braving the short descent.

"Four of them in total that we know of. We've explored the area fairly thoroughly over the past few years, but you can never be sure if there's another section that was walled off by a rock slide or something like that. The last lake is open to the sky and perfectly round. It's ringed by ferns almost as tall as I am—it all looks positively primeval."

"It sounds incredible," Lucía breathed. "Any chance we'll get to see it?"

"The water isn't deep at all. Anyone who wants to can take the rowboat and paddle around."

Cristina tugged on Eduardo's sleeve to ask him where she could set up her tripod. The two of them moved away and the others wandered off to explore the cave. All but Leo. He was bending down to examine a few traces of red-and-white pigment that was all that remained of the Taino symbols that had once been brushed onto the walls of the cave.

They weren't alone, not really, but Lucía's pulse started to thrum anyway as her gaze lingered on the interested tilt of his head. She couldn't help thinking about the way his face had softened when the poem had come bursting out of him earlier, as if no matter how hard he'd tried to suppress it, his affinity for poetry still lived inside him. If that aspect of his old self still remained, then perhaps others did as well?

The thought made Lucía take a step backward.

Maybe she'd made some sort of noise, or maybe the movement had disturbed the shadows around them. But as she did, Leo straightened and glanced behind him, his eyes meeting Lucía's. Even with the sunshine streaming in through an overhead shaft, it was too dark without the lanterns for her to make out what lurked in the depths of his eyes.

And she didn't exactly want to.

Which was why she did what any sensible woman would do—she went directly for the rope that hung above the rowboat.

"The devil do you think you're doing?" Leo blurted out as Lucía reached for the rope ladder.

Pausing in the act of wrapping her fingers around a fraying segment of rope, she lifted her shoulder in a shrug. "I want to see if the water really is as cold as Eduardo said."

The flippant response incensed him.

"You really are determined to prove me right," he told her. "Or did you not realize that going off on your own is thoughtless as well as reckless—do you know how terrible Eduardo would feel if anything were to happen to you? Or how annoying for his guests to have their outing cut short if you were to hurt yourself because you were too impatient to wait for the others?"

"You were the one who told me to find an occupation, remember?" she fired back. "Maybe I'll take up an interest in natural history. Maybe I'll make a study on Taino cave drawings. Or who knows—I could discover a new kind of plant that revolutionizes the field of botany."

"You'd do all that just to avoid working on your music?"

"I'm not avoiding anything," Lucía said archly, tossing her head. Then, in complete contradiction to her words, she turned her back to him and proceeded to make her way down the makeshift ladder. Nimble as she had been on the descent to the cave, from the way she lowered herself tentatively onto each swaying rung it was evident that she had never climbed one before.

Of course, she hadn't—Leo doubted there were rope ladders in European concert halls.

His chest tight, Leo reached for the ladder to keep it steady, but Lucía attained the bottom without incident. He waited until she dropped lightly onto the craggy rocks below before letting himself down after her.

"No," he said as soon as he had released the rope. "I'm not going to let you row through a series of unfamiliar caves. What if there are more than Eduardo thinks? What if you get lost down there, or the tide rises and you're trapped, or—"

But Lucía wasn't listening to his arguments—she was already stepping into the boat. "Look, there's a lantern down here." She pried open a small tin box and added, "Matches wrapped in oil cloth, too. And the boat looks sound enough."

"Sound enough? How reassuring," Leo muttered. "Lucía, I'm serious. You can't go haring off into a cave without a guide. Wait for Eduardo—I'm sure he'd be more than happy to take you."

Lucía glanced to where Eduardo was still helping Cristina set up her tripod while she poured dark powder into a pan. "He'll be busy for a while."

Leo heaved a noisy sigh and swung a leg over the edge of the rowboat, which bobbed slightly with his weight. "Move over."

"I don't need your help," she said, frowning up at him. "I'm sure there's nothing to rowing that I can't figure out on my own."

"Well, I don't need you getting lost or injured—I'd have your sister to answer to if anything should happen to you, and Eduardo isn't the only one who's terrified of her."

It was a half-truth, but one that Leo didn't feel bad about uttering since there was no way he could tell her that the thought of anything happening to her filled him with such anxiety that he would row her clear across the Atlantic Ocean just to make sure she wouldn't come to harm.

He shucked his new jacket—much more easily than he had the old one—and folded it on the narrow wooden seat beside him. He'd sent his measurements over to a tailor who'd had an almost-finished suit that he could adapt to fit Leo, but it would be days before he received a second one, so he had to keep this one as neat as possible.

Without access to his bank account, he had been forced to get the suit on credit, and though the tailor was happy enough to extend it because the request had come from the Martinez household, Leo wouldn't be at peace until he had paid off his debt.

Another old rope, this one tied around an outcropping of rock, held the boat in place. Leo unhooked it easily before reaching for the oars and pushing away. The muscles in his arms and back stretched pleasantly as he began to guide the craft toward the opening that led to the next lake. After the previous day's inactivity, the exercise felt so good to his stiff body that he was almost able to ignore the frowns Lucía was shooting his way.

With no tides or even waves to exert their influence on the boat, their progress through the shallow waters was smooth.

Lucía's brow, however, wasn't—she was still glowering at him. "I could have done this myself, you know," she said when she noticed him looking.

"Then, you try it." Leo pushed the oars her way. "Go ahead."

A determined expression settled on her face as Lucía seized the oars and began imitating his strokes—or trying to. The oars were heavier than they looked, and it took a great deal of effort just to move the boat, never mind steer in a specific direction.

"Nothing to it," Lucía said through gritted teeth.

Leo reclined on one elbow, watching her with amusement. "Then, I suppose you won't mind rowing us the rest of the way."

She looked momentarily dismayed, but before Leo could retract his words, she hardened her jaw and gave him a brief nod. "I can do it."

To her credit, Lucía did manage to pull the boat along a few meters deeper into the cavern, though anyone who took the merest glance at her could see how much she was straining. After several minutes of hearing her labored breaths, Leo took pity on her.

"I can keep going if you want me to," he told her, gesturing for her to pass him the oars.

She shook her head, refusing to relinquish her hold on them, even though she barely had the breath to spare to say so out loud.

"Have you always been this stubborn?" he demanded.

"Have *you*…always been…this insufferable?"

"You think I'm insufferable just because I'm trying to help you? Or not willing to let you lose your way alone in a series of caverns that have yet to be surveyed and could extend halfway across the island for all you know?"

"You're insufferable—" she panted "—because you keep trying—" another pant "—to push yourself in where you're not wanted."

"It's not like I had a choice in the matter," he said dryly.

Lucía could do nothing in response save huff out a breath.

He shook his head, torn between irritation and amusement. Lucía was being foolishly stubborn—but even Leo had to admit that there was something in the way she was pushing herself that reminded him of…well, of himself and the single-minded drive he applied to his work.

"I don't mean to disparage your rowing abilities. It's just that you won't be able to move your arms tomorrow if you continue for much longer—not because you're not capable, but because you're not used to it."

"Oh, fine."

Reluctantly, she passed him the oars. As she did, Leo caught a glimpse of her palms, which had been rubbed raw by the rope and the rough wood of the oars. He couldn't stop himself from letting out an exclamation. "Your hands!"

Taking them in his, he turned them over to examine the livid marks on her palms.

"It's nothing," Lucía murmured.

Leo whipped his handkerchief out of his pocket and, dipping it into the fresh, cool water, he brushed it over her palms to dislodge bits of dirt and peeling paint. The skin wasn't broken, he was pleased to see as he turned her hands over. Her fingers were slim, and as he had noticed before, devoid of any telltale calluses.

All the self-control that Leo had carefully hoarded from the moment that he had seen her in Don Enrique's store must have been worn away by the events of the past few days. It certainly wasn't because he felt sorry that a woman who had never done a hard day's work in her life was finding out for perhaps the first time what it meant to have her hands ruined by manual labor.

In any case, there was no other explanation for why he ran his thumb over the backs of her fingers.

"No splinters," he said belatedly, after more than a few moments had passed.

The slight caress made her breath hitch audibly, amplified into almost a gasp by the acoustics of the cave and oddly reminiscent of the little moan that had come out when he'd massaged her leg.

Suddenly awash in heat, Leo went still, his eyes darting to her face.

The sight of Lucía always seemed to catch Leo unawares. It wasn't just because she was breathtaking, framed against the vivid blue of the water behind her and with her neatly braided hair coiled at the nape of her neck in a style that made her profile appear almost regal. Warm lantern light, coupled with the otherworldly flicker of sunlight on water, reflected on her features, making her look more like a mirage than ever. But she was here, in the flesh, and her warm hands in his own were proof of it, even if he still couldn't quite believe it.

Or that he had almost kissed her.

The near kiss had haunted his thoughts all through the previous day. Leo tried to tell himself that he would have stopped in time, that reason would have prevailed, but if he was entirely honest, he wasn't completely certain that would have been the case.

He didn't want to want her. But it was undeniable that he felt her nearness like others would sense a live wire—it was impossible to ignore, and necessary that he keep as far away from the danger as possible.

From the way she had tried to avoid him, Leo couldn't help but wonder if she also felt the same way.

Her lips parted. She seemed to be on the verge of saying something, and anticipation gripped Leo fiercely. At the last moment, however, she averted her eyes, pulling her hands out of his grasp and exclaiming, "Oh, look! Is that a fish?"

"A whole school of them," Leo replied, tearing his gaze away from her and looking instead at the water around them. The fish's silvery scales seemed to wink at him as they moved through the clear blue waters around the oar.

He began to row again, pulling them through the entrance to the second cave, his fingers clenched too tightly around the wooden poles.

Lucía reached over the side of the boat, trailing her fingertips in the water. "It feels delightful," she reported. "I wish I had a bathing costume."

Choosing to ignore the mental image that conjured, Leo gazed straight ahead. "Dip your hands into the water—that'll soothe the pain until we get back. I'm sure Eduardo has some sort of salve in that first aid kit everyone was teasing him about."

Lucía acquiesced so readily that Leo suspected she was glad for an excuse not to face him. It was a relief, honestly. If nothing else because it gave him time to gather the remains of his composure.

Once, a very long time ago, Leo had been walking past the firehouse at the center of town when someone up on the lookout had spotted smoke and raised the alarm. The discordant clanging of the bells had been a call to action to the men inside the station, but to Leo, they signaled nothing but disaster.

Sitting across from Lucía in the near dark, Leo felt like the moment should be overlaid with the sound of alarm bells.

The only problem was, he wasn't sure he would heed them.

Chapter Nine

The acoustics inside the cave were like nothing she had experienced before, the slightest noise acquiring a resonance that made music out of ordinary sounds. Lucía experimented with a little humming—she hadn't the voice to be a true singer, but melodies came to her like breathing and it was delightful to hear the cave answer as if it were a living thing.

She could feel Leo's gaze on her, but she was determined not to let him ruin her enjoyment with his disapproval.

"We should turn back," he said when she looked at him.

Lucía didn't bother to hide her disappointment. "So soon? I really wanted to see the last lake."

"The others will be wondering where we've got to," he said, and Lucía was suddenly sorry that she had relinquished control of the oars.

Her palms were sore, but to Lucía, the slight pain was only a reminder that she had done something, or at least attempted to. She only wished she had more such reminders. In fact…

She bent to unbuckle her shoes.

"What the devil are you doing now?" he asked warily as she toed off her shoes and reached for the narrow leather belt around her waist.

"You can turn back if you like—I'm going to swim to the last lake."

"Oh, for—" Clamping his mouth into a straight line, Leo changed courses, steering them easily toward the next cave, which was lighter than the others.

Lucía didn't bother to refasten her shoes. It was a hot day and her feet felt wonderful, freed from the constraining leather.

Leo glanced at her stockinged toes, which were peeking out from under the hem of her skirt, but made no comment. "*Can* you swim?" he asked instead. "I thought genteel young women in San Pedro didn't do something as common as bathe in the sea or the river."

"I learned in Europe, actually. They have a different view on women exercising than we do."

His face was more visible here, and it took a moment for Lucía to realize that it was because this third cave was open to the outside. She twisted around in her seat to watch as Leo rowed them through to the far end.

"It looks shallow there. I don't think I can go farther without getting out and pulling the boat over that ledge."

Lucía gazed out at what she could see of the lake. It appeared to be perfectly round, open to the sky, and ringed with trees and ferns taller than her. It was the kind of sight that would inspire anyone to poetry, but the only poet in her presence seemed content to remain silent.

She hadn't been going to say anything. After telling herself that she didn't need to seek any more answers from Leo, she had been determined never to raise the subject again. But the words burst out of her now, and she couldn't hold them back.

"If we hadn't seen those men sneaking the crates out of the ship…would you really have turned me away?"

She didn't think he was going to answer. He didn't look like he wanted to, at any rate—he was motionless, his gaze averted, like he was contemplating throwing himself into the water to avoid responding to her impulsive question.

"I wanted to," he said after a few moments, surprising a blink out of Lucía. "And I meant to, though I don't know how successful I would have been, considering that you didn't seem inclined to make it easy for me."

"Would I have gotten any answers if I'd persisted?"

"What difference does it make?" he asked, finally meeting her eyes. "What do you think would have happened if we had continued our correspondence? A years-long courtship conducted over letters, at a distance so great it makes my eyes water to think about it, and then what? Marriage?"

Her silence must have said far more than she intended to.

"Would your family ever have accepted me? I saw the notices in the gossip columns when you sailed away—your sister had just married into one of the wealthiest families in the island. What would she and her husband have said if you'd told them you were being courted by a penniless bookkeeper? A penniless bookkeeper who had an ailing mother to support, no less." Leo shook his head. "I would have never passed muster. They would have wanted better for you."

"Amalia and Julian have never cared about things like that. For the longest time after they met, Amalia thought he was a bandit—and she fell in love with him, regardless. If you had fought for me…" Her voice broke. "If you had taken a risk—"

"Taking risks only ever works out in adventure novels," Leo said flatly. "I really don't see the point in rehashing all of this. The past is over and done with, Lucía, and we're both too old to indulge in fantasies."

"I see,"

"What, exactly, do you see?"

Lucía swallowed past the knot in her throat. "That it was only ever a fantasy to you."

"You can't tell me that you believed that the two of us truly had a future together."

She gave a tight little shrug. "To quote you, what difference does it make?"

Scrambling to her feet, Lucía seized the rope that kept the rowboat tethered in place and flung it around an outcropping of rock. Standing cautiously as the boat rocked beneath her, she stepped out onto the ledge and began to undo the buttons on her shirtwaist.

"Dare I ask?" Leo asked from the boat, which was bobbing up and down in the water with the force of her hasty disembarkation.

Lucía shrugged. "This looks like a good place for a swim."

"You cannot be serious," he said. "You haven't a towel, or dry clothes, and it looks like rain, and—"

"Where's your sense of adventure?"

"It doesn't exist," Leo said dryly, but he clambered onto the narrow ledge, too, taking up a shockingly large amount of room with those broad shoulders of his.

He was half turned away from her, making a show of looking out at the lake, as if to spare himself the sight of her undressing. Even so, prickles of awareness were dancing over her exposed skin, turning her earlier frustration into pure, though not uncomplicated, longing.

Lucía gave him a sidelong look. Leo had seen her in less clothing than this the day before, albeit from a distance. He had looked at her like she was a woman then, rather than a problem. And she had liked it.

Her chin swinging up in defiance, she undid the last button and let the shirtwaist fall to the rocky ground.

Her corset cover came off next, and her corset, front laced for her convenience, followed it swiftly.

"You really are going to do this, aren't you?" he asked, resignation written all over his face.

Not bothering to stifle his sigh, he took his watch and a slim bundle of folded banknotes, held together by a silver money clip, out of his pocket and tucked them neatly inside his shoes. Then he folded his necktie on top and began working on his shirt buttons.

Lucía glanced at him without making it too obvious that she was admiring his powerful, athletic body and the way his muscles rippled when he pulled his shirt over his head.

"You aren't worried about what the others will say?" she asked archly. "Or the lack of towels?"

"I can't let you go in the water alone."

"Why not?" Planting herself squarely in front of him, Lucía placed her hands on her hips.

By that point, Lucía had stepped out of her skirt and had successfully hung it from a protruding rock. Her chemise and drawers, made out of thin, supple linen, were sure to grow transparent in the water, but even her newly acquired sense of boldness balked at the thought of removing them.

"I'm not your responsibility, and I would like it if you would stop treating me like—"

He seized her by the waist. Lucía's heart was beating faster now, for an altogether different reason.

"Leo," she began—and that was as far as she got before Leo lifted her in his arms and jumped with her into the water.

The cool shock of it made her breathless. The water here was a little higher than chest deep, and invigoratingly cold.

Caught up in the moment, Lucía let out a shriek of pure exhilaration. Her arms were entwined around Leo's neck and she didn't particularly want to let go just yet, and he was *smiling* at her.

Was this the first genuine smile he had given her since meeting again? It felt almost like a gift—something to be cherished, certainly, if only because she couldn't be sure she would ever see it again.

Sure enough, it vanished within a few moments and his arms slipped away. Lucía released him, too, kicking up a little sand as she swam a short distance through the pristine waters.

"Your letters didn't go astray," he said suddenly.

She glanced at him, lips parting.

"There didn't seem to be much point to answering. I was busy, and then..." He shrugged. "I figured you would have gotten married to some count or duke. I hear Europe is littered with titled men willing to sell their family name for a fresh infusion to their bank accounts."

"Yes, and they're all old and unappealing. And I..."

Lucía looked away. Most, if not all, of the suitors she'd had in Europe had only begun pursuing her when they'd heard that she was an heiress. Shy to begin with, their attention had made Lucía so uncomfortable that she had withdrawn from society with the excuse that she had to focus on her studies. But her violin had been a poor substitute for real companionship, and even with her sister and the impish Julian and their Friday-afternoon tradition of taking dessert in one of Vienna's many cafés, Lucía had often found herself lonely.

"You what?"

Lightly, Lucía tapped the surface of the water with her open hands. "I wasn't interested in anything that distracted me from my music. I suppose I ought to be grateful to you for that."

He didn't reply right away. Lucía was getting used to his short silences, a product of his need to carefully consider what he was about to say. Several moments went by, during which the only sounds that reached her were the chirping of birds and the wind ruffling the branches on the trees overhead.

Finally, Leo said, "There's something you should know. My mother had an apoplexy. The day it happened I was late getting home. I had stopped to write poetry in the sugarcane fields, even though the light was fading. I'd had an idea while working at the mill, and I was deeply resentful about having to spend the day balancing figures instead of giving rein to my imagination. When I finally got home, I found the house dark and my mother sprawled on the floor. Who knows how long she lay there, waiting for me—" Cutting himself off, Leo pressed his lips together for a long moment. "I wasn't there when she needed me."

Lucía's heart ached for him. "Oh, Leo. I'm so sorry. When did it happen?"

A second passed, then Leo glanced away before answering. "Four years ago."

The impact of his words shuddered through Lucía. Four years. That was when he— Was *that* why he had stopped writing?

"Why did you never tell me?" she asked softly. "I'd have—"

"Sent me money?" Leo's expression hardened. "Telegrammed whichever high-class doctor attends to your family and demanded that he treat my mother like a human being?"

"I would have done something. Or tried to. If nothing else, I would have tried to give you comfort. I can't imagine what that must have been like for you, after the way you lost your father."

Leo shook his head. "I didn't need comfort. I needed to put a stop to all that foolish dreaming and do something useful—for my mother's sake, and my own."

"You certainly have done that," Lucía murmured.

She didn't mean it facetiously, but Leo seemed to take it that way.

"And in any case," he said, glancing away from her, "you were so busy and happy with your new life that it felt unfair to burden you with it all."

Lucía hadn't been happy at all. Maybe the first few weeks, when everything was still new and exciting and playing music had still been a simple pleasure.

"It wouldn't have been a burden," she said firmly. "It won't be, if you ever feel the need to confide in me. I'm not as fragile as I look, you know."

He looked as though he were going to add something else, but fell quiet instead.

Lucía prodded him with her toe, finding his muscular

legs closer than she'd realized. "I wish you would stop censoring yourself. What had you been about to say?"

"Nothing, just… Your life seemed so comfortable and beautiful that the last thing I wanted was to fill it with my worries. I suppose I wanted to protect you."

"I really wish everyone would stop trying to protect me," Lucía exclaimed. "I'm not some sort of delicate porcelain doll that needs to be kept in a cupboard. I had enough of that from my uncle."

She broke off, breathing hard.

Leo seemed inexplicably puzzled at her reaction. "Your uncle?"

Lucía shrugged. "You've probably heard the gossip. It was all anyone could talk about for months."

"Believe it or not, there isn't much society gossip to be had at the mill," Leo told her, batting away a leaf that had landed in the water between them. "And I rarely have time to go out socially."

Rumors and gossip had been impossible to quash, but Lucía knew that Julian had exerted his considerable influence to keep the abduction out of the papers. She studied Leo's face. He really did mean it, didn't he? Still, she couldn't help but ask, "Sebastian and Paulina never told you about my uncle?"

Leo's gaze sharpened with curiosity. "I never discussed you or your family with either of them. If they knew we corresponded for a while, they didn't mention it. What makes you think they would have talked to me about your uncle?"

Lucía inhaled, drawing in the rich, green scent of the water and the vegetation around them. "You were the first man I ever kissed."

"And second and third, I suppose," he said flippantly,

as if the memory of those few stolen seconds hadn't loomed as large in his life as they had in hers. "I know."

"But you don't know *why*." Lucía brushed away a droplet that was coursing down her cheek. "I think I told you once that Amalia and I were raised by our uncle after our parents died. He denied us all kinds of things under the guise of protecting us from anyone with bad intentions. But he didn't truly want to protect us," she said bitterly. "All he wanted was to keep us locked up until the time came when we would prove useful to him. A handful of weeks before I met you, my uncle arranged to have me marry a business associate of his. I was never given the opportunity to refuse—or even told what was happening. He had booked passage on a steamer, and before I knew it, I was clear across the island in an unfamiliar town where I knew no one."

She wasn't looking at Leo, but at the patch of rock and greenery just behind his shoulder, so she felt a jolt of surprise at the roiling anger in his voice when he said, "Your uncle *abducted* you?"

"I— He was my guardian, so it wouldn't legally have been considered an abduction. But yes. He did. And even though Amalia rescued me and made our uncle go away, and I knew that she and Julian would do anything in their power to keep that from ever happening again, I wanted—I *needed*—to make sure that if it did, I would at least have a beautiful memory to look back on. A perfect first kiss."

Leo shook his head. His brow had grown progressively more furrowed as Lucía spoke, and the words burst out of him with something akin to violence. "A kiss can't be perfect under that kind of shadow. Not if it never would have happened had you not been abducted and almost coerced into marriage. Not if you didn't kiss me because you wanted me—"

"Kissing you was *my* choice," Lucía told him fiercely. "Just as it would be my choice if I were to kiss you now."

She had no idea why she said that. She hadn't been thinking about kissing Leo, or at least not any more than seemed natural when he was floating in the water across from her, licking droplets from his lips.

The dark, hungry look was back in his eyes. "If I started kissing you, I would never want to stop."

"Would that be such a bad thing?"

Her heartbeat, which had resumed its normal rhythm after the cool shock of plunging into the water, sped up again.

"Days would go by—months, years, maybe millennia— and we would still be in this spot, my lips pressed to yours."

Every time Lucía had seen Leo since her return, his hair had been ruthlessly scraped back and kept in place with pomade. The water must have washed it away, though, because the furrows left behind by his comb had disappeared and his natural curl was reasserting itself. Lucía touched one of the curls grazing his ear, her throat tight.

In response, he lifted a hand out of the water and used the tip of his finger to trace the lines of her lips. Her own hand rose to cover his, to brush it aside, but only to make room for his mouth as it came to find hers.

It was a light, sweet whisper of a kiss, and if Leo's brain had been in working order, he would have kept it that way. But then she tightened her arms around him and recaptured his lips with a voraciousness that was as surprising as it was arousing.

And Leo could no longer ignore how much he had longed for her body.

She arched into his touch. Her undergarments clung wetly to her, revealing more than they covered. Below the water, though, the long, lithe legs he had glimpsed while on the ledge were bare and silky where they touched his. Planting his feet firmly on the muddy sand of the lake's bottom, he pulled her closer to him. Their bodies nestled together as if they were a matched pair, carved for such a purpose.

He couldn't stop thinking of what she had just told him. Lucía had been kidnapped and almost coerced into marriage, and somehow, it was his damn letters she couldn't stop dwelling on. As if Leo had meant something to her.

But he couldn't have. Because if that was the case, it meant that Leo had written them off as an impossible dream when the reality had been much more attainable than he'd realized.

Three days in her presence and everything he had considered a fact was being swept away.

He broke their kiss, needing a moment to catch his breath and yet unable to prevent his fingertips from following the line of her neck and jaw.

She turned into his touch, brushing her lips over his battered knuckles. "Where did you get those scars?"

He flexed his fingers and gave the scars a dispassionate glance. "At the mill."

"I thought you were supposed to be the bookkeeper."

"I was, for the first year. Then Sebastian told me that he wanted to spend more time at home with Paulina and the children, and that he thought I should be trained to take over the running of it. He'd only meant to teach me the business end of things and perhaps a little about the machinery, but I was more aware than most, I think, what a responsibility that was. It had been three years, but my father's death was still fresh in mind." He shrugged. "I made it my mission to learn everything there was to know about each part of the process."

"Something tells me you didn't absorb it from a book."

Leo shook his head, smiling briefly. "I asked the men to teach me. I spent a week cutting cane and helping haul it onto the carts that transported it from the fields to the mill. Another week feeding stalks of cane through the machines that turn it into pulp. By the end of the month, I was sore and battered and cut and burned. But nobody could say I didn't know anything about what it takes to make sugar out of cane—or how to keep the men safe at every step."

"What did Sebastian think of all that?" Lucía asked, toying idly with his fingers.

"He was impressed, I believe. Did you know that his father worked at the mill, like mine? And died in an accident like mine, too."

"I hadn't known that," Lucía said softly.

Leo looked down at her. Droplets were caught in her curls, and in her eyelashes, glimmering in the sunlight like diamonds. His gaze skipped down, to the thin fabric that had molded itself to her breasts.

"Have you ever heard the expression 'his face was a poem'?" Lucía asked teasingly.

Leo's gaze returned to hers. It usually meant that someone's face had been rendered unusually expressive—as his no doubt had been by the sight of her body. "I'm familiar with it."

"Well, yours is an entire epic. A novel."

"A set of encyclopedias?" he suggested dryly.

Lucía locked her fingers around the wet fabric of his shirt. "A song." She pressed her lips to the underside of his jaw. "Every word that ever came to Gustavo Adolfo Bécquer's mind."

Leo blinked. "You like Bécquer's poetry?"

"That," Lucía informed him, "is beside the point."

She wrapped her legs around his waist, drawing him tightly against her. Leo's hands landed on each of her thighs, gripping hard as she began to rub herself against the hard ridge of his arousal.

There was no reticence on her part, only eagerness, a desire to explore and be explored that was reflected in the way she moved her tongue over the seam of his lips.

His hands left her thighs and roamed over her waist until they were spanning her narrow rib cage, his thumbs perfectly positioned to stroke the underside of her breasts, which were buoyant in the water. She made an encouraging noise, arching into his touch, and Leo moved the pad of his thumb over her tight nipple. Briefly, he entertained the notion of helping her back onto the ledge and lying down with her there as they both dried in the sun, basking in the warmth and in each other's bodies.

She brought him back into the moment by closing her teeth over his lower lip before murmuring, "Leandro…"

It was the singularly most breathtaking moment of his life. It was everything he had dreamed of when he'd lain in bed after a long day of staring at figures and a longer night of scratching poems into his battered notebook.

It was…unbearable.

He had to be on guard when it came to his emotions— he couldn't let them get the best of him. Cooler heads had to prevail. And since he couldn't count on Lucía to be sensible, putting a stop to this was entirely up to him.

His chest was suddenly filled with a rumble that felt like thunder. And then he realized—it *was* thunder.

Dark clouds had rolled in with astonishing speed, covering the circle of sky above them.

"We have to get back," he said, and even Lucía couldn't disagree.

They hauled themselves up, dripping, onto the ledge, and hurried into their clothes. Leo shoved his legs into his trousers, more than a little regretfully—part of him was still dwelling on his fantasy of lying down with her on the ledge, now with the addition of curtains of rain falling just outside.

Throwing on his shirt, he reached for his other things—and found his shoe turned on its side, probably knocked carelessly aside as they had come out of or gone into the water.

He must have made some noise of distress, because she glanced at him as she struggled into her corset. "What's wrong?"

"I can't find my money clip." A wild panic was starting to rise in his chest, and he made no attempt to tamp it down as he knelt to scrabble among the plants growing in between the cracks in the rock, even though he could feel her gaze on him.

By the time he glanced at her, she was looking up at the sky with a worried frown. "Is it a great deal of money?"

"No. But money is the only thing I value, remember?" he bit out.

His questing hand brushed aside a *yagrumo* leaf twice

the size of his palm, and there was the clip and its contents, a little muddy but otherwise unharmed.

He had just slid it into his pocket when the clouds broke, and rain started falling in sheets.

Even with their shoes on, the rocks were slippery with the deluge, and Lucía didn't protest too hard when Leo helped her back into the rowboat. Gliding back into the cave was a reprieve from the rain, but not from the thundering roar of it, magnified by the damp stone.

They hurried up the path to where the luncheon table had been laid out. But Eduardo and the others must have taken alarm at the clear signs of an incoming storm, because there was no sign of the tables and chairs that had filled the area an hour before. No sign of people, either.

The others had left without them.

Chapter Ten

Leo was no stranger to tossing and turning. Whenever sleep failed him, though, he'd always had plenty to occupy him—and the desk in a corner of his bedroom at home had always provided him a welcome refuge from his thoughts. He had no desk here, and nothing to read except for an old newspaper he had already scoured from end to end. Including the advertisements.

According to his pocket watch, it was a quarter of an hour past midnight when he gave up trying to quiet down his thoughts. He slipped on a pair of trousers and the shirt he had worn to dinner before venturing downstairs. Eduardo had told them all to help themselves to the contents of the two bookcases in a small parlor just off the main sitting room, explaining that there was a wide variety of reading material behind its glass-fronted doors to suit his family's disparate tastes.

Moonlight fell on the floor tiles as Leo stepped barefoot into the room. Like the rest of the house, this particular sitting room had been decorated for comfort rather than to impress or intimidate—it was furnished with armchairs and love seats made out of wicker, comfortably upholstered chairs surrounding a table that held a chessboard with a game already in place, and there was even a phonograph on a stand in the corner.

The comforting scent of old books and good liquor enveloped Leo as he unlatched one of the shutters, all the better to see without having to light a lamp.

An abundance of plants cascaded from hanging baskets by the window and from brass and clay pots on the side tables. One particular arrangement was so thick that Leo was halfway to the bookcases before he realized that there was someone sitting in the love seat.

"Oh," he said, halting. "I'm sorry—I don't mean to intrude."

The figure shifted, her nightdress a pale smudge in the moonlight. "You're not intruding."

Recognizing Lucía's voice, Leo tensed, ready to make his escape.

"I was just thinking about you, in fact."

"Were you?" he asked warily.

The two of them hadn't exchanged much more than polite pleasantries for the rest of that afternoon. Eduardo had gone back to search for them after making sure his grandfather had gotten safely into the carriage, and between hurrying to join the others and then to change out of their wet clothes once they had reached the house, there had been little time for conversation.

Conversation was not exactly what he had been left craving after their abrupt departure from the water, but there was still much to be said. In the moment, he'd hardly found himself able to react to the news that she had once been abducted by her uncle. He'd had plenty of opportunity to dwell on it since then, and he was still roiling with leftover anger.

"I was looking through the bookcase for something to read and I found a shelf full of sheet music. It felt—" Lucía breathed out something that wasn't quite a laugh "—like unexpectedly coming across an old friend who you've tried desperately hard to keep out of your mind— and realizing that they have been in the back of your thoughts all the while."

Leo's eyes were starting to grow accustomed to the dark, at least enough that he was able to see Lucía clasp her arms around her bent knees. He didn't know how to respond to what she had just said. She had described the jolt he had felt when he'd seen her in Don Enrique's store so precisely that it made him feel vaguely disconcerted.

"You were right when you said that I was avoiding my music," she said quietly.

Leo crossed his arms over his chest. In his bare feet, with his shirtsleeves rolled up, he felt as much in dishabille as Lucía was in her nightdress. "It was presumptuous of me to say anything at all. I had no right to lecture you about running away from your dreams when I've been doing the same thing myself."

Reaching for her hem, Lucía started to fiddle with something too small for Leo to see. A loose thread, perhaps, or a section of stitching that had come undone. "I won't argue with that," she said dryly. "But it doesn't mean you weren't right. I haven't been playing— I haven't touched my violin in weeks, as a matter of fact. I had almost convinced myself that I no longer wished to pursue music. But now…"

"But now?" Leo prompted her, perching on the love seat next to her. The connection that had flared to life between them when they'd kissed in the water hadn't been entirely severed by the change in location, and the hushed intimacy of the dark was too fraught with danger for him to find it altogether comfortable. He reached for the electric lamp on the table next to him, seeking safety in its unwavering glare, but Lucía stopped him with a murmur.

"Don't. I like the dark—it makes me feel braver."

Against his better judgment, Leo sat back. "Brave enough to tell me why you're brooding in the dark?" A brief pause followed his question, which Leo filled by asking another one. "Does it have anything to do with what you told me earlier? About your uncle?"

"Nothing like that. It's not important, really. I…" She made an impatient noise. "How can I ask you to have any sympathy for such a small thing when you have been through so much?"

"You've been through your share of misfortunes. Does that mean you only feel for those who are experiencing major catastrophes?"

"No, I suppose not," she said, adding with a degree of annoyance, "I think I liked you better when your arguments were based on poetry, not logic."

Leo couldn't hold back a smile.

Lucía sighed. "Oh, all right. I give in. It's just that, as I was lying in bed earlier, I couldn't stop thinking that I may have missed my chance altogether at having a musical career. I had the opportunity of a lifetime at the Academy, and I squandered it."

Surely heiresses got more than one opportunity. "Are you sure that's the case? If you wrote to the Academy—"

"I can't. Not after the way I left. It was…well, *abrupt* is one word for it."

Recalling what she had said outside the bank, Leo asked, "Because of your sister's condition?"

Lucía shook her head. "Not entirely. I did use it as an excuse at the time, though Amalia had offered to wait a little longer. You see, I had just been awarded the coveted solo performance at the Academy's next concert. Call it a lack of modesty, but I was so proud of all I had accomplished and I had so many expectations about what it might mean—I could think of nothing better than to be first chair at the philharmonic or even the opera house. I was on the verge of telling Amalia that she and Julian should go on ahead and I would visit them closer to the date of the birth, but then..."

Leo may not have been able to see her face, but it hardly mattered when he could hear so much of what she was feeling in her voice.

"One of the girls who had befriended me when I had first come to the Academy let me know, in no uncertain terms, that the only reason I was given the solo was because the *kapellmeister* was hoping to encourage me to make a sizable donation to the Academy."

"Had he ever solicited you for donations?"

Lucía gave a small pause. "He hadn't."

"So why would you believe her?"

"I... Well, everyone else seemed to agree. All our classmates." Whatever momentary doubt his question had sparked, she had managed to banish it. "It would have been unpardonably naive—or arrogant—of me to think that they were merely jealous that I had gotten the solo."

Anger was beginning to kindle inside him at how unfairly she'd been treated. The question of Lucía's talent aside, which he had no way of judging, it seemed unnecessarily cruel to make anyone doubt themselves. And for it to have come from a friend, and from someone who undoubtedly had seen with her own eyes what Leo had only read about in letters… Though she was supposed to practice for four hours a day, Lucía often devoted six or seven hours to it and pored over compositions in her spare time.

Hard work didn't always translate into showers of accolades and riches. Leo knew that just as well as anyone. But every ounce of logic he possessed had shriveled away to nothing in the face of the overwhelming urge to make sure Lucía never experienced that kind of pain and uncertainty again.

"When we first settled in Vienna, after traveling around Europe for several months, I was so eager to make friends that I didn't waste any time in inviting my classmates to our apartment for coffee and cake. I hadn't thought twice about what it might mean—Julian had found us a lovely place, with high windows and beautiful paneling, but it wasn't ostentatious. You'd have thought it was a palace by the way they talked about it the next day. After that, they made it their business to introduce me to everyone as the exotic heiress from the tropics. It was amusing at first, but after a while, I couldn't help but notice how oddly people behaved around me. It made me wonder if my uncle had been right, after all, when he'd tried to keep us from befriending other people. And that made me feel all the more wretched."

It was a long way from the life of leisure and luxury he had imagined her leading while he toiled over ledgers and pleaded with doctors to take his mother's pain seriously. All his little daydreams about her life in Vienna suddenly seemed like such petty, childish nonsense, particularly after he thought about how it had all come on the heels of his rejection…

Leo had known he was hurting her feelings. It had seemed like a necessary evil—and much less of one, once he'd convinced himself that the depths of her feelings for him did not come close to his for her and that she would find it easy enough to turn her attentions to someone far more suitable.

As necessary as he had known it to be at the time, Leo had never been more ashamed of his callousness.

"I let my friends persuade me that I didn't work as hard as everyone else did," she continued. "And that I wasn't as talented. It was too easy to believe—my uncle had always made it clear to me that he thought I wouldn't amount to much, and that if other people were in any way kind to Amalia and me, it was only because they wanted something from us."

An angry noise burst forcefully from Leo's lips. "Despicable. What he did to you—both of you—was despicable."

"It was," Lucía agreed softly. "I had refused to believe it for most of my life, but everything my classmates were saying just seemed to prove him right. Suddenly, I was doubting my own judgment and questioning whether I had a right to accept the honor of a solo if I didn't truly deserve it. In the end, it seemed easier to remove myself from the situation altogether."

Leo shifted in his seat, restless with the urge to take action against things that had already happened. There was shame in there, too—how was he any different from her uncle or her classmates, and everyone who had decided they knew her without bothering to get to know her?

It was no wonder Lucía had wrapped her new identity around her like a mantle.

Leo must have made a small noise, because Lucía

said, "You have to understand, I don't blame them for believing that I wasn't good enough, or even for telling me so. The fact that I decided to run away instead of proving to them and to myself that they were wrong lies entirely on me. I can tell you one thing," Lucía added with a little of her usual spice. "Luz Robles wouldn't have done it."

"Lucía Troncoso shouldn't have, either." Leo paused. "Is this why you've been so…well, enthusiastic about…?"

"Pretending to be someone else?"

He thought he saw Lucía nod in the dark.

"Luz isn't an heiress," she said simply. "She's no one special. Anyone who enjoys her company does so for her own sake."

Leo was aware of the impulse to cover her hand with his own, in reassurance. He ignored it, limiting himself to words. "You don't have to pretend to be someone else. Not with me."

"You don't seem to like me much when I'm Lucía, either," she said, letting out another half laugh that didn't quite conceal her hurt.

"It's not that I don't like you." Leo rubbed a hand over his face. "I just…"

How to explain to her that the fault had never been with her, exactly, but with the circumstances of his life? He'd thought he was done having these intimate conversations with Lucía, which felt like flaying away the protective layers he'd built around himself.

But Lucía had moved on. "There's a part of me that wishes I had stayed in Vienna and faced them. If I'd gone through with the concert, and if they'd heard me play…" She yanked another loose thread out of her hem. "Or maybe I am just as talentless as they all believed me to be. No way of knowing now."

"You wouldn't consider returning, if only to find out?"

"Even if I were to return to Vienna, it would be impossible to avoid being treated as I was before. And I couldn't leave Amalia now—not to travel to Europe, in any case. It's such a long distance."

Robbed of color by the lack of light, Lucía was nevertheless vivid. He had always found a serene loveliness in her features, and it was just now that he was beginning to realize that it concealed a liveliness of spirit that he found compelling and attractive. There was strength in her, too. More than he would have given her credit for even a few short days before.

"Honestly, I think she never wanted to leave San Pedro in the first place. She only did it for my sake—she and her husband both. It's time for me to return the favor."

Everything Leo had learned about Lucía in the past two days felt like pieces from the jigsaw puzzles he used to pore over on nights like this one when sleep proved elusive. There always came a moment when he had snapped enough of them into place that the picture they were meant to form became clear—and finishing the puzzle so much easier than it had before.

Her controlling uncle. The marriage she had almost been forced into. Her escape to Vienna, where all her hopes for a career had been dashed.

The only thing that became clear was how much he had misjudged her.

She could have used his friendship. And he'd been so absorbed in his own affairs, and so sure that she would never understand what he was going through, that he had never paused to consider what it would mean to her to lose it.

* * *

After hearing mainly German spoken around her for years, except when she was home, Lucía had assumed that it would take a while for her ear to grow accustomed to hearing Spanish again—the staccato beat of its consonants and the bitten off syllables at the end of most words. In fact, it had felt like letting out a breath she hadn't realized she had been holding.

It seemed extraordinary to her that being around Leo could feel so similar.

He was an imposing presence, even in his shirt-sleeves. It wasn't just his broad shoulders, either—Leo had a way of filling up a room with just the low bass of his voice or those smoldering gazes that made Lucía want to do all kinds of things she had never before contemplated doing, just to make him look at her with that oddly appealing mixture of scandalized desire. Like crawl into his lap to see if the rumble in his voice made his chest reverberate…or slide the ribbon-thin straps of her nightdress off her shoulders so that the fabric slid to the cool tiles under her feet.

The window Leo had opened overlooked the court-yard at the center of the house. Lucía went to stand in front of it, hoping for a breeze to cool down her thoughts.

Though the moon was waning, now only a fraction of the fullness and brightness it had held on the night she and Leo had escaped, the courtyard was fairly bright in contrast to the darkened house. There was nothing much in it, save for large terra-cotta pots, filled with fish-tailed palms, and a wrought iron table surrounded by three chairs in the one corner that remained shady even when the sun was directly overhead.

According to Eduardo, that had been his grandfather's preferred spot for sitting in wait whenever one of his children or grandchildren was late getting home from some frolic. Only one of his cousins had ever managed to sneak into her bedroom without being seen, and she'd done it by climbing the trellis outside the window of the bedroom Lucía was occupying.

When Lucía and her sister were younger, Amalia had become an expert in the art of sneaking in and out of the house without attracting their uncle's notice. Lucía had never dared to do it. She wouldn't have climbed the trellis like Eduardo's, either, though of course all she wanted now was to try it.

Leo's voice drifted from behind her. "It hardly seems possible that I've never heard you play."

Lucía turned, but remained by the window, unable to trust herself when every particle of her body seemed to yearn for his touch. "Would you want to?"

She didn't have her violin with her, and there were no musical instruments in the family's private parlor, so it really was more of a question than an offer.

"I would," Leo said. "At the very least, you wouldn't have to worry about me offering any critiques—I don't know much about music."

Even in the half dark—or maybe because of it—his smile was bright. There was an openness to it that she hadn't seen before, and it moved her to ask something she had been wondering since she had realized that he had abandoned his writing in order to focus on his business interests.

"Do you ever regret not following your dreams?"

"Which dreams?" Leo asked, though Lucía was certain he knew what she was talking about.

"In one of your letters, you told me that you wanted

to submit one of your poems to the editor of *La Cuna de América*. You seemed to think there could be no greater achievement than to be published in that magazine."

"Oh, that," he said lightly. "It was a silly, childish notion. To think that I could be a poet, of all things."

"But did you ever try? Did you ever send something in?"

He shook his head. "I tried to make time to write when I got home from the mill in the evenings but was never able to finish anything that felt suitable. And then my mother fell ill, and writing began to feel like such a self-indulgent waste of time that I couldn't, in good conscience, continue trying. So no, I don't regret it. At least," he added, as if honesty compelled him to, "I haven't. Maybe I never will. But sometimes…"

"Sometimes?" she echoed softly.

Leo paused briefly. Then he shook his head again. "Nothing. It's too late for me, Lucía."

He sounded tired. No, not tired—exhausted.

"I don't think it could ever be too late to return to something you once loved," Lucía said, and she wasn't entirely sure that she wasn't speaking about herself and Leo.

It was difficult to tell in the dark, but Lucía thought he glanced away from her. "What would be the point?"

"Hope." Lucía's fingers fluttered at her side with the urge to smooth them over his cheekbone, even though he'd told her that he didn't want her comfort. "Hope is the point."

"I can't afford hope. Dreams, either."

It wasn't the first time Lucía had heard him say something so desperately bleak. "I would think that hopes and dreams are the one thing everyone could afford."

"Not when all it does is expose you to endless disappointment." Standing in one fluid movement, with more grace than a man as bulky as Leo had a right to possess, he strode her way. "It's painful enough when you burn for unattainable things. But when what you desire is so close within your grasp that you fool yourself into thinking that maybe someday it'll be yours... That's when you break your own heart."

He came to a stop on the other side of the window frame, at arm's length from her.

Lucía's heart fluttered inside her chest. "And did you? Break your own heart?"

In spite of all the confidences they were exchanging, Lucía half expected him not to answer. But a moment later, a murmur came curling through the darkness between them.

"I did."

"You broke mine, too." Lucía gripped the edge of the window frame, hardly conscious of the pain on her stinging palms.

"I know that now." Gently, he brushed away a tendril of hair that had come loose from the pinned mass on top of her head. It grazed the bare skin of her shoulder, making her shiver. "And I'm so sorry I did. I wish I could say I didn't know how much I was hurting you."

"I understand why you felt you had to."

Lucía smoothed a palm over her own shoulder. Only a handful of hours had passed since he had laid claim to her breasts and the hollow of her neck. Since she had discovered that she had felt his absence in her body, like a persistent ache she had spent years to ignore. Was she supposed to forget how it had been soothed just by his touch? Was she supposed to let the distance unspool between them again?

After all that had been said and done, Lucía didn't know if that was possible.

But she also couldn't let herself forget the sting of wondering if Leo had stopped writing because he had gotten to know her and found her... Lucía wasn't altogether sure. Too spoiled, too meek, too sheltered from the world?

"To be fair, you weren't the only one to abandon our acquaintance," she said quietly.

"Oh?"

"Hardly any of my friends wrote to me after I left. Three of them even went on a European tour last year and neglected to tell me they would be in Vienna for nearly a month. I only found out because Paulina de Linares had written to Amalia to ask if she could send some sundries back with them."

"Why would they slight you?"

"I can only imagine it had something to do with their families' disapproval over the way Amalia and I handled the affair with our uncle—Amalia rode a horse right into the church as I stood at the altar, brandishing pistols, and tried to kidnap me back. Only Julian's cousin shot her instead. It was all very scandalous."

Even now, after everything that had happened, Lucía couldn't help but grin as she recalled the sight of her sister looking like the most disreputable bandit, as she made one last, desperate effort to save Lucía from a life she would have hated.

"I knew your sister was terrifying. I hadn't realized she was fearless as well," Leo said. "It's a shame your friends don't feel the same way."

"I'm sure they were only trying to look after their reputations."

"And yet you risked yours again by running away with me." Enough moonlight fell on his features for her to see the slight furrow between his brows.

Lucía may not have had a mother, but she couldn't have asked for a fiercer guardian than her older sister. "I'd risk that and more for Amalia. She has spent her entire life rescuing me—she was twelve when our mother died, nowhere near old enough for the responsibility, but she undertook it anyway. I don't know what would have become of me without her."

"She's a good deal older than you, isn't she?"

Lucía nodded. "Almost eight years."

"You were lucky to have her. It must be a comfort to have someone to share in all the worries and the decision-making."

The loneliness of that sentence made Lucía ache to wrap her arms around him. She didn't know if the fiercely independent Leo would welcome such a gesture, so she limited herself to commenting, "Some people would say that's what marriage is for."

The faint moonlight molding over his features moved as he shook his head slowly. "What would I have to offer a wife? I'm nose-deep in work most days, and when I'm not, I'm reviewing ledgers for fun or worrying about my mother's health. It would be unfair to marry someone just to make her shoulder half my burden."

"Well, you do work too much—I won't argue with you there. But I can think of any number of reasons why a woman would gladly offer you her help, and they have nothing to do with your ledgers. You're not unattractive, you know. You know how to use your hands. And if my memory serves me correctly, you do have a very nice…ledger."

Leo sputtered out a laugh. "Are you trying to shock me?"

"Why? Is it working?"

The darkness felt different after Leo stopped laughing. Or maybe it was Lucía who felt different. Lighter. That might have been what led her to ask, "Was that all?"

"What do you mean?"

"Have we finally told each other everything we'd been holding back?"

A cloud scudded over the moon, and the falling darkness prevented her from seeing his eyes. Maybe that was a good thing. Once, she had thought that Leo was the one person who could see all the way down into the deep recesses of her soul. As it turned out, he had only seen as far as she had let him. And the same had gone for her.

Even after all the confidences they had shared that day, Lucía didn't think she was done exploring the depths of Leo's soul. It had only been a start—and maybe that was all it would ever be.

It would have to be enough.

"I damn well hope so," Leo said, with feeling.

"Can we call it a clean slate, then? And be friends again?"

"Friends." Leo said the word as if he were tasting it, and trying to decide if he liked it enough for another bite. "I should like that."

It was only appropriate to seal their truce with a handshake.

And if her lips parted when their hands met, well, it was her own fault for having called forth the memory of how he had played with her breasts like he'd been trying to tease chords out of them.

"I should get back to bed," she said, then felt a wave of heat wash over her at the mental image it conjured. It wasn't the first time she had imagined lying between the sheets next to Leo, but knowing how his body felt against hers lent an accuracy to the fantasy that made her momentarily breathless. "*Buenas noches*, Leo."

"*Buenas noches,*" he echoed, and the warmth in his voice was a caress that followed her all the way back to her bed.

Chapter Eleven

It took a day or two for Leo to arrange it all, but after Eduardo's messenger delivered his letters to Sebastian Linares, Leo finally had access to his own funds. The first thing he did was pay off his debt to the tailor, who had finished a second suit of clothes for him based entirely on the evening attire Leo had worn to Sebastian's party, which had been laundered and pressed to perfection by the Martinez's laundress.

Then he bought Lucía a violin.

Leo had spent most of that morning ensconced in Don Amable's study with the elderly man's team of lawyers. The consensus among them seemed to be that Leo's position was a precarious one, given that he didn't have a good enough reason to have been at the docks that late at night. The messenger who had been dispatched with Leo's correspondence had been charged with procuring from his office every document pertaining to the potential sale of the sloop, though, in the hopes that something among his papers might help him prove his case in court.

"If it comes to that," Eduardo had said, meaning to be reassuring.

From the look he had exchanged with his grandfather, Leo had a good idea of how slight the chances were that it wouldn't.

Dwelling on the matter wouldn't do any good, nor would giving into his fury. Leo had to proceed the best way he knew how—with a great deal of careful planning.

At the top of his list was his mother. In Leo's letter to Sebastian, he had asked for Paulina to find her a nurse and a companion. Steps also had to be taken to ensure her financial well-being should something happen to Leo. He'd opened a bank account in her name years before, and added to it generously every chance he got, but he needed to make sure that she would be well provided for.

As much as he hated the thought of piling more work on Sebastian's plate, when the other man had declared his intentions to take a step back and spend more time with his family, there was also a great deal of business he would have to take care of in Leo's absence.

And then there was Lucía.

The violin was delivered a couple of hours after his meeting with the lawyers had ended. Nestled inside a leather case lined in padded indigo satin that brought out the luster in its curves, it was as beautiful an instrument as the woman it was intended for. The case had been well-made, too, its brass fittings as bright as gold against leather the color of fine brandy.

He had brought it into his bedroom to look over the violin and make sure it was worthy of her. He'd meant to give it to Lucía in private, then thought better about being alone with her and decided, instead, that he had better call one of the maids and ask her to leave the violin in Lucía's bedroom.

After all, it wasn't a token of Leo's devotion, to be

presented to Lucía with flourishes and flowers in the hopes of being rewarded with a kiss or two. It meant nothing more than an offer of friendship. Less than that—it was merely his way of telling her that he believed in her even if she didn't believe in herself.

There was a rap at his half-open door. A moment later, Lucía's head poked through the opening. "Leo? Everyone's ready to go in to dinner. Are you— Oh!"

With no regard for propriety, Lucía opened the door the rest of the way and came into his bedroom, gazing at the violin case on his bed with surprise-rounded eyes.

"Is that…?"

"For you."

"I'd say you shouldn't have, but I'm so glad you did. I— Why did you? Did my sad little story make such an impression on you?"

She said it lightly, teasingly, in the kind of tone she employed when she was being Luz Robles. But the light in her eyes was entirely Lucía.

After snapping open the clasps, she ran her hands lightly over the hourglass shape. "It's beautiful. It might be a better instrument than the one I have at home. Where on earth did you get it? I didn't think the stores here carried instruments of this quality."

"They don't. Eduardo arranged for me to buy it through an art-and-antiques dealer he's acquainted with. There are several books of sheet music inside the case—I didn't know what you liked, so I had him include everything he had. I ordered a stand, too, but it won't come until tomorrow."

Slowly, almost reverently, she lifted the instrument from its satin cradle and notched it between her shoulder and chin in a fluid, graceful movement that spoke of how often she had done it. Her eyelids fluttered closed as she half turned away from him.

Her white gown was severe in its simplicity. It was comprised of a long, slim skirt under a tunic that had been cut in a dramatically angular diagonal across her hips and cinched at her waist with a tasseled sash. Its only ornamentation was a little silver embroidery near the neckline, which skimmed her collarbone in the front and dipped even lower in the back.

The spray of jasmine she had threaded through her hair reminded Leo of the day they had met, when she'd tucked the flowers he'd picked for her into her braids. The hairstyle, and the low back of her gown, left the nape of her long neck bare, save for one, short, trailing curl.

With sudden fierceness, Leo wanted to push the curl aside with the tip of his finger and kiss the delicate skin underneath it. To smooth his hands over her shoulders as his mouth took liberties with her sensitive, vulnerable neck. To hold her flush against him while he kneaded her firm, shapely breasts through the filmy fabric of her evening dress.

Lucía's eyes snapped open, as if she had felt the arousal charging through Leo.

"It feels perfect—like it was made for me. Oh, Leo, I could kiss you."

Leo froze.

"I won't," she added quickly, laughing at his expression. "Really, you needn't act like it would be such a hardship. You do seem to like it when I kiss you—and I do feel like I should thank you in some way."

If she only knew what he'd really been thinking. It was as if all the desire and longing for Lucía that he thought he had suppressed had come bursting forcefully out to the surface after their kiss. Trying to stuff it back down felt like putting back clothes that had once fit into a tightly packed suitcase.

"I didn't do it for thanks, or for kisses," he told her. They were standing too close for comfort, but he didn't move away. "I don't quite know why I did it, really, except that I couldn't stop thinking about what you told me the other night. I never showed my poetry to anyone but you, so I never ran the risk of being made to feel like I wasn't suited to do the thing I loved the most in the world. But you did, Lucía. It must have taken so much strength and courage, and it would be a pity if you went through life without finding out how talented you truly are."

"I could say the same to you." Lucía captured his gaze with her own unwavering one.

"I'd really rather you didn't," he said swiftly. "This is your moment, not mine."

Just because he hadn't seen the point in pursuing his own dreams, it didn't mean that she shouldn't pursue hers.

She dimpled. "You mean you'd rather be the one telling other people what to do with their lives. That's all right—I'll get even one of these days."

. Leo was saved from having to answer by the sound of someone calling both their names.

"Dinner," Lucía said regretfully, returning the violin to its case.

She was snapping the fastenings on the case when the open door swung a little wider and Cristina called out, "José? Have you seen— Oh!"

The eyebrows that Cristina had raised at finding them unexpectedly together returned to their normal positions as she spied the violin case. "Is that yours?" she asked Lucía, who nodded happily. "*Bendito*, I had no idea we had a musician in our midst. You really must play for us."

Lucía's gaze skipped to Leo. "Oh, I…"

"My mother would be delighted if you did," Cristina continued. "Did I tell you that she taught piano when she was younger? She doesn't play much anymore, but she attends concerts every week."

"I haven't practiced in so long." Lucía tried to protest. "And I haven't had a chance to tune the violin yet."

Cristina waved a hand in the air. "I doubt any of us will be able to tell. Come on."

Small though the photographer might be, she was as insistent as a hurricane. Threading her arm through Lucía's, she tugged the taller woman out of Leo's bedroom, barely allowing Lucía the time to seize the violin case by its handle.

Leo trailed after them as they made their way to the downstairs terrace, where Eduardo, his grandfather and his guests had gathered for a round of drinks before dinner. Within minutes, Cristina had commanded the young men to arrange the wicker seats so that they faced the straight-backed chair she had set out for Lucía.

Leo studied Lucía's expression as she fiddled with the pegs holding the strings taut and the amber-colored block that had been in the case. If she had looked the slightest bit unwilling, he wouldn't have hesitated in coming up with a reason to drag her away from her eager audience. As it was, though, all he could make out in her expression was nervous excitement.

The violin seemed to be in tune, at least as far as he could tell. Lucía gave an experimental swipe of the bow across the strings, and even that brief sound made her issue a breath so deep, her chest swelled under the white fabric of her gown.

"I might be rusty," she warned her audience. Leo couldn't be sure if anyone else heard the quiet emotion in her tone, but to him, it was as loud as a church bell. "It's been a long time since I last practiced and—"

"Enough excuses," Leo said as he went to lean against the railing, positioning himself behind the chairs so that no one could see his face. "Show us what Luz Robles can do."

The allusion to her false identity was a challenge, and one Leo knew Lucía wouldn't fail to meet.

Her beautiful mouth curled into a slow smile. And then she began to play.

At first visibly tense, she began to relax when the first few notes rippled into the air. He had told her that he was no judge of music, and he had little experience with it, aside from occasionally escorting his mother to Sunday concerts in the park.

But if there was one thing Leo knew how to recognize, it was passion. And Lucía was brimming with it. There was no mistaking the light in her eyes as her hesitation melted away.

The others had fallen silent as they gave their polite attention to Lucía. Leo, however, felt nothing short of spellbound. Dressed in white, with white flowers tucked into her curls, the fingers of her left hand dancing over the violin's strings like the little yellow butterflies in Don Amable's garden, she looked like a nymph—or one of the Greek muses. Only instead of inspiring musical genius, she embodied it.

Leo was suddenly, fiercely glad that he'd had the foresight to get out of sight from the group. The carefully blank expression he had arranged on his face was no match for the sight of Lucía—or for the wonder that seemed to be making its way into his bloodstream, leaving him overly warm and breathless.

If he were to step up behind her and press his face against the back of her neck, would he be able to feel the rise and fall of the music as it poured out of her? Would he be able to feel her joy?

On the heels of that thought came the disconcerting realization that he had never seen Lucía happy. Not truly. That was what had rattled him when he'd seen her half hanging out the window—not her nightdress or the tantalizing patches of skin it had revealed, but how content she had looked as she basked in the sunlight.

There had been something fragile in her smile when he'd run into her outside the bank. Since then, her smile had gained strength and brightness and some of the shadows had been chased from her eyes. But it wasn't until this very moment that Lucía looked truly, genuinely, blissfully happy. And Leo was at least partially responsible for it.

Leo slid a hand into his pocket and fingered the folded paper held together by his silver clip. Most of it was banknotes, but tucked between them was a thin piece of stationery that he had folded first lengthwise, then across. He hadn't taken it out to read in at least a year or two, though its worn edges attested to how often he used to run a thoughtful finger along its edge.

The last letter he had ever written Lucía, which he'd never sent.

He didn't fool himself into thinking he could make Lucía happy in life. They didn't suit each other, for one. The thread of desire and attraction that bound him to her, though undeniable, would be easily snapped when they returned to their regular lives. It would be a mistake to think that it could lead to anything more lasting than momentary pleasure.

And in any case, Leo had no inclination to risk his heart again. He was certain of that, if not much else.

Still, he ran a finger along the edge of the folded paper in his pocket, and he basked in her radiance, and he hoped that would be enough to sustain him for at least another five years.

One moment Lucía was a person, holding a wooden instrument. There came a moment, though, when she relaxed into the music and the violin became an extension of herself, each individual note dissolving into the other until the melodies came out of her as easy as breathing. Without conscious thought, and without making any sort of plan, she eased from the scales and arpeggios she had been playing and into the first movement of Haydn's violin concerto in G major.

Then Strauss. Schubert. Mendelssohn.

There was a sharp, joyful ache in her chest as she played each measure from memory, the sensation of greeting old, beloved friends even stronger than it had been when she'd come across the music on Don Amable's bookshelves.

And then, feeling herself carried aloft in the notes, she segued into a composition of her own, a melody that began in a soft whisper and slowly transformed into a rollicking tune that had always reminded her of the play of light on water.

When she looked in front of her, it wasn't her audience she saw, seated in wicker chairs and sipping *Jerez.*

Her gaze went directly over their heads to Leo. It didn't seem to matter that there were eight people and a half a room between them—the charge that passed from Lucía to Leo and back again was stunning in its intimacy. Lucía felt herself caught in it, momentarily helpless, like a butterfly ensnared in a net.

Helpless, but not motionless. Her right arm arced with increasing speed and force as Lucía threw herself into the crescendo, trying to show him how much his gift had meant to her. Lucía didn't often improvise while playing, but she did it now, breathing hard as her violin produced notes that swept through the terrace, like wind whistling through sugarcane fields while white herons soared overhead. It was fire and passion and beauty and everything that reminded her of Leo.

When she felt her heart about to burst inside her chest, she slowed the melody into something more gentle and tender, closing her eyes in order to see Leo by moonlight, murmuring low confidences into the warm dark.

She fingered the last note, pianissimo, letting it trail into silence before lifting her bow into the sultry air and finally reopening her eyes. In the hush that followed, reality rushed back into her world and Lucía felt a familiar fluttering in her chest.

Her left hand had been too tense, her tremolo messy, and her vibrato had faltered more than once. It wasn't only due to her recent lack of practice—her instructors had all agreed that she had a bad habit of getting herself a little too carried away in feeling the music and allowing her emotions to overshadow her technique.

She couldn't look at Leo, though she still felt his heated gaze on hers.

Don Amable was the first one to react, crying "Splendid!" a second before a smattering of applause broke the silence. It wasn't the thundering sound of a concert hall full of people, but Lucía's heart felt suddenly so full that she found herself blinking back tears.

"That was extraordinary," one of the Fajardo brothers said.

"You flatter me," she said, flushed and laughing as she lowered her violin. The strings had stilled, but she could still feel their vibrations against her fingertips.

Cristina's mother lowered her glass of Spanish sherry. "*Bendito, nena*, you really are very talented. Where did you say you studied music?"

"Oh, in several places," Lucía said vaguely.

Her gaze kept straying to Leo. He hadn't moved from the railing, though his arms were no longer crossed over his chest and he no longer looked as enthralled as he'd looked while she had been playing. He just looked… happy.

It was as if he'd been holding a shield in front of himself, and though it had slipped in brief, heady moments, this time it felt like he had chosen to drop it in order to let her see into the soft, vulnerable part of himself that he kept so guarded.

Her fingers caressed the deep indentation in the body of the violin, the varnished wood gliding under her fingertips. If she could only have a private moment with Leo to say with words everything she had tried to say through music…

Guiltily, she realized that her attention had wandered along with her gaze, and Cristina was still speaking.

"We'll have to have a concert, of course," Cristina said briskly, leaning forward in her chair. "Eduardo, I'll help you make the arrangements. There's less than a week left until we sail for home, so we haven't any time to waste."

"A concert?" Lucía realized that everyone around her was nodding.

The idea of performing in front of an audience filled Lucía with equal parts excitement and nerves. Her usual reserve had melted away the second she'd begun pretending to be Luz Robles, and Lucía couldn't help but wonder what it would be like to play music under that guise.

If the abandon she had just played with was any indication, it was sure to feel glorious.

"It shouldn't be too difficult to arrange," Cristina continued. "Eduardo, surely you must be acquainted with someone who could be of assistance."

"I can't think of anyone at the moment," he hedged, drumming his fingers against the arm of his chair.

Before Lucía could say anything to rescue him, his grandfather spoke up.

"As it happens, one of my sister's grandsons purchased a theater recently. I'll arrange for him to join us for luncheon in a day or two," Don Amable said. "Why don't we discuss the details over dinner?"

He stood, signaling that it was time to enter the dining room. As the others followed his lead and started to stroll away, Lucía remained behind to return her violin to its case.

What was left of the afternoon was quickly fading into twilight, the shadows so deep and long that Lucía almost confused Leo for one when he came up behind her and touched her elbow.

"What did you think?" she asked him, sliding the bow into the leather straps that held it in place before snapping the case shut.

"I said I would offer no judgment," he said, but there was a smile lurking at the corner of his lips.

"I'll allow you an opinion," Lucía replied in a lofty tone. "Just this once."

Leo stepped closer. "It was…stirring."

The compliment curled around her, as enveloping as the warm, humid evening.

"Weak praise, coming from a poet," she said, not caring if Leo would have rather she appended the word *former* to it. "Shouldn't you be comparing me to, say, a summer's day?"

"I would never." Before she could show her affront, he added, "You defy all comparisons. And metaphors and similes and categorizations. You're—"

"Not made out of ink and paper?"

"In a class of your own. And it's a shame that the world won't be able to see it yet."

It took her a moment to realize that she had misinterpreted his reasons for waiting to approach her—and when she did, she couldn't help but bristle. "Do you mean the concert? Eduardo had nothing to say against Cristina's plan. Neither did Don Amable, who you said has been apprised of our situation."

"They've hardly had time to consider the implications—and they couldn't exactly turn down Cristina's suggestion without a good reason." His gaze softened. "Lucía, you deserve to be on stage, and to have everyone appreciate you as I—as I did. But we are running from the law. Until we find a way to prove our innocence, it's just too much of a risk."

"I hardly think Eduardo will put up a notice in the newspaper or hang posters in the plaza. What harm can it do if a handful of his friends come to listen to me play?"

"I know how much you want this," Leo said in a pleading tone. "But Lucía—"

She didn't let him continue. "In any case, Vargas hasn't found us yet. He might have stopped looking, you know."

"He hasn't," Leo said flatly. "Eduardo has a man in San Pedro who's been reporting on Vargas's doings. He's still looking for us—both of us, though we don't think he's entirely certain of your identity."

"Then, there really is nothing to worry about." Lucía glanced away from the warning etched in his features, trying not to let it dampen her excitement. "You worry too much, Leo."

"Just promise me you'll think about it."

Lucía let a moment go by before saying, reluctantly, "I promise. But Leo—"

"A promise is all I ask," he said, and if he was as aware as Lucía of all the other promises, unspoken and otherwise, between them, he didn't mention them and neither did she.

Chapter Twelve

After another lavish dinner, the group migrated to the wicker chairs that had been moved to the garden, close enough to the ornamental pond for Leo to feel the ribbons of cool dampness the breeze was lifting from the water.

They wouldn't stay out here long. Night had fallen while they were at the table, and the dark was crowded with mosquitos and other insects. Every few seconds, something small and winged bumped into the glass-shaded lanterns that cast their glow over the group, making the light flicker.

The wavering light picked out the silver embroidery on Lucía's gown and brought out the lustrousness in her brown skin. She had been as bright as a new candle all throughout dinner, shining as though with an inner light as she took little sips of her wine and moved the food around her plate. Leo had noticed that she'd only really eaten dessert, a tartly sweet soursop sorbet that had been served in little crystal dishes with gilt rims, for all the world as if she needed no nourishment other than sugar and music.

She had been incandescent. And it was obvious just

from looking at the dimple on the corner of her mouth that she was still filled with excitement and delight.

Eduardo spoke quietly beside him, making Leo start.

Embarrassed to have been caught staring, he turned to his friend, who gave him a knowing smile.

"Magnificent, isn't she?" Eduardo said, with the air of someone who was repeating himself. "She's always been so quiet, almost invisible beside Amalia. Who knew that such a small frame could hold so much fire?"

Leo had known. He almost said so out loud, but managed to catch himself at the last second and offer instead a vague noise.

"But then," Eduardo said, "something tells me that you did."

It was so close to what Leo had been thinking just a moment before that he scraped a hand over his face, wondering just how transparent it was. "I don't know what you mean."

"Give me more credit than that." Eduardo shot him a grin. "I've seen the way you look at each other—or the way you very carefully avoid doing so. It's painfully obvious that you're both engaged in some serious pining."

"I don't think I would call it *pining*, exactly," Leo protested.

Eduardo shrugged. "I've been acquainted with the Troncosos for a long time, though their uncle kept them too isolated from society for anyone to truly get to know them. Even from a distance, I thought there was something a little sad and lonely about Lucía. When she's around you, however…"

Eduardo cast another glance at him, and whatever he saw in Leo's expression made him change the subject. Leo sat there, pretending to listen as Eduardo chatted about a book he had recently read, but all he could think about was what Eduardo had seen in his demeanor to make him think he had been *pining* for Lucía Troncoso.

The Fajardos acted like they had an obligation to tease everyone in their presence and Cristina seemed determined to do something for her new friend, whether that was arranging a concert or at the very least, a match. Eduardo, though… He was the only one who had known Leo and Lucía since before all this happened, and the only one whose opinion Leo trusted.

When she's around you…

Part of Leo wanted to interrupt Eduardo and ask him what he had been about to say.

Cristina and the Fajardos were holding a whispered conference, shooting the occasional glance their way. For one wild moment, Leo thought they had overheard him and Eduardo talking.

But then Cristina sprang up from her seat, fishing out something from under it, and leaped lightly onto the brick rim of the pond.

"*Querido* Eduardo," she said, "on behalf of my mother, the Fajardos and myself, I would like to present you with this symbol of our deep gratitude and friendship."

Looking pleased, Eduardo stood up to receive his gift, a bottle of rum with a bow tied around its neck.

"We were fortunate enough to tour the Bacardí family's warehouses while in Cuba and were so impressed with the quality of their drink that we couldn't let the occasion pass without bringing you back a bottle."

"We've heard good things about the Brugals and their rum," one of the Fajardo brothers added. "So earlier today, I had one of your gardeners go out and purchase a bottle."

"Are you proposing an experiment?" Eduardo asked with a raised eyebrow.

"Rafael has always fancied himself a scientist," another one of the Fajardos said, and the others jumped in with jokes.

Leo sat back, listening with half an ear and quirking up his lips into a semblance of a smile whenever the conversation required it. Eduardo's words were still echoing through his mind. Maybe they each had pined for the other, a long time ago. But not anymore. And thinking about it was like reopening a door that had been slammed and bolted shut.

Murmuring a vague excuse that went unheard, Leo strode away from the gathering. He would have made a clean getaway, but of course, Lucía noticed his absence.

"Where's Leo?" he heard her ask.

"I think he's going back inside," someone answered. "Will you ask him if he wants a glass?"

Leo didn't stop, even though he heard the light patter of footsteps behind him. By the time Lucía caught up with him, he had reached the mango tree on the east side of the yard, close enough to the house that the brick pavers under their feet were bathed in the electric light of the lamps on the terrace.

The branches of the mango tree were so laden with fruit—still green—that while some soared high overhead, others hung so low that Leo was forced to stop and hold them aside so that he, and then Lucía, could pass underneath without having to step off the path and onto the grass.

"Following me again?" he asked as he swung around to face her.

"I was sent to ask if you wanted any rum."

"Not tonight. I need to keep my wits about me," Leo said. And the sight of Lucía was intoxicating enough.

"Why is that?" She cocked her head. "What exactly do you think could happen here? We're safe."

Were they? More to the point, was he? Maybe from external concerns like thieves and murderers and men trying to accuse him of arson. But not from the dangerous sparkle of Lucía's eyes.

"You don't want to know what happens when I lose control."

It wasn't an attempt at flirtation, but Lucía must have thought so because a slow smile spread over her lips as she replied, "Maybe I do."

"I wouldn't be so sure about that."

Without warning, he slid his arms around her waist and pulled her to him sharply—almost roughly. He'd meant to discomfit her enough to make her stop pestering him once and for all. But then her lips parted, and her breath quickened, and the only discomfited one was himself.

A tiny, stiff-petaled blossom had drifted through the mango tree's dark green leaves and fallen on her hair, right next to the slightly larger flowers that he recognized as having come from the trellis outside her window. The heady scent of jasmine and sugar mingled with the garden's green earthiness, and Leo wanted nothing more than to bury his face in her neck and breathe her in.

"Well?" She tilted her head. Not coquettishly as she had done on the day they'd arrived here, when he'd accused her of not acting like herself, but as if it were her turn to issue him a challenge. "Aren't you going to kiss me? You did say I needed passion in my life."

A sweet little smile was lurking in the corner of her lips, just waiting for his own to draw it out.

Leo was helpless to resist. One by one, his inhibitions came crashing down and he felt himself bowing under a wave of passion so strong it bordered on despair.

He sank into her chest, feeling her silky, hot skin with his lips, nipping at the swell of her breasts. Her lightly boned corset was stiff and unyielding under the froth of her dress, preventing him from feeling the suppleness of her torso. But lower, where her corset ended just below her hips…

His eager hands traced a rounded swell before finding purchase on the back of her thighs and wrenching her higher in a sharp jerk that dragged a gasp from her lips.

He held her up. Her white dress would show the slightest mark, so he couldn't press her against a wall or the trunk of the mango tree. It didn't matter. She was so slight that it didn't take much effort to keep her aloft while he explored the hollow of her throat with his tongue until she grew languid in his arms.

Even as all those practical considerations crossed his mind, his need for her overrode all other thoughts. For years on end, Leo had tried desperately to do the right thing. The practical thing. The logical thing. He never took unnecessary risks—and he never indulged in anything that might prove a distraction from his goals.

Lucía, warm and eager in his arms as she cradled his head against her chest, was more than an indulgence.

It would have been so easy to let himself get carried away. To ruck up her skirt and slide a hand between her thighs and tease her with his fingers until she was trembling and pliant in his arms. To lead her upstairs by the hand and undress her delicately and watch her lay back among his pillows while he kissed and caressed all the slopes and valleys that made up her body and discovered what made her beg for more. To ply her with roses and poetry and promises of days drenched in sunlight and evenings on bedsheets silvered with moonlight.

To worship her with every part of his body and soul.

But he couldn't give in to the urge—not again.

He hadn't been lying when he'd told her that if he started kissing her, he wouldn't be able to stop. The magnetic pull drawing him to her was just too irresistible. The divot above her upper lip too enchanting. The gleam of her eyes, devastating.

And they had both been devastated enough. Why on earth would they risk it happening again?

It was one of the most difficult things Leo had ever done, but he lowered her down to the brick pavers. Struggling for breath, he kept his hands on her waist for a moment, but the inquiry in her upturned face made him snatch them away and take a step backward.

"We really need to stop doing this," he muttered.

"Any particular reason why? I didn't have any complaints with how things were proceeding."

"You don't understand. I can't form any emotional attachments. I won't. I have too much I still need to do, and no time to spare. And I refuse to offer you anything less than…well, than everything you deserve."

"I'm not a spoiled heiress making unreasonable demands of you, Leandro."

The quiet reproach in her voice dug into his chest like a splinter. Leo didn't trust himself to answer, though it didn't seem to matter as Lucía clearly still had more to say.

"It's only been a handful of days since you told me I needed passion in my life to be happy. You weren't wrong. But Leo, you need it, too."

He shook his head. "Not with you," he said, his words coming out more harshly than he'd intended them to. "I could show you passion, Lucía, but it wouldn't come with affection or marriage or any of the things you would have a right to expect from me. You're better off with a man like Eduardo, or one of the Fajardos—someone who could give you everything you want."

"You don't know what I want."

The trunk of the mango tree was rough under his palm. Leo felt his lips compressing into an obstinate line. "I can't give you anything at all."

"Then, it's a good thing I want nothing from you," she told him, and walked away.

Leo disappeared for the rest of the evening. Although Lucía laughed and talked and sipped rum with the others, she was painfully aware of his absence.

And how alive her body still felt after their interlude behind the mango tree.

She couldn't help contrasting it to the last time he had kissed her. His kisses then had been like pearls on a string, delicate and precious little drops, each one ending where the other began.

As if he'd had to temper his desire. As if he'd been holding back.

What she had felt tonight, however, had been raw and unguarded and explosive—and frustratingly brief.

Left aching for release, Lucía took a deep, cooling

draft of her ice water. And then another and another until Don Amable and Cristina's mother started dropping hints that they thought the group should retire for the night.

Leo still hadn't reappeared. She glanced at his bedroom door on her way past, but no light escaped from behind it.

Closing her own door slowly, Lucía leaned against it for a long moment before starting to undress. She had barely started on the concealed buttons at the side of her white gown when she heard a light rap.

Her heart gave a curious little leap, and she hurried to open the door, feeling almost nervous.

But the only person on the other side was a maid in a starched apron and head wrap. She was holding a small silver tray lined with a lace cloth, on which rested a bowl full of something that smelled slightly like coconut oil and herbs. At Lucía's curious expression, the woman told her it was from Leo. "He asked the cook to make a salve for you, miss. Said you would need it for your hands."

Lucía should have been moved. But all she felt was a deep weariness. As thoughtful and caring as Leo could be, the wall he had built between himself and the world was impossible to breach. Not that she wanted to.

If he'd allowed her to get a word in edgewise, she would have told him that she had formed no expectations with regard to any emotional commitment between them. In fact, she was decidedly against it—she could never let herself grow attached to someone who considered love an inconvenience and used the people he cared for as an excuse to keep from venturing outside the safe confines of the course he had charted for himself.

Lucía would be damned if she would let anyone use her as an excuse.

After a restless night, she was the first one at the breakfast table the next morning. She paused on her way from fetching a plate of fruit to glance down at the garden from the upstairs terrace, expecting to see Leo on one of his walks, and instead saw Don Amable conferring with a gardener. On the other side of the brick-paved pathway, one of the kitchen maids was taking a moment's respite behind a bush.

Lucía chose a seat and sat scowling at the embroidered napkin on the place setting in front of her. She had been in Santo Domingo less than a week and already she had grown used to seeing Leo's face across the table from her at mealtimes. She had thus far resisted the urge to think about what would happen when all this was over and they returned home, but it was clear that nothing would.

However drawn they were to each other, Lucía knew in her heart that there was no future for her and Leo.

"Buenos días."

She turned to see Eduardo striding into the room, freshly shaven and hatless. Tilting her head to kiss his cheek, Lucía caught sight of the thin envelope in his hand.

"The messenger I sent to San Pedro with Leo's correspondence returned earlier," he explained. "Leo's in Abuelo's study reading the replies to his letters, but he sent this for you."

He turned the envelope over so that Lucía could see her own name written across its back in her sister's characteristic scrawl.

Eduardo didn't hide his grin as Lucía cried out and

took the envelope from his hands. He pulled out a chair for her, then busied himself pouring her a cup of coffee while she tore open the envelope and found a sheet of stationery scented with the perfume Amalia had purchased in Paris.

Dear Lu,

I suppose you were overdue for a little rebellion, though for the life of me I can't understand what possessed you to run off with Leandro Díaz, of all people. I was able to persuade his mother to spend a fortnight with us, though she is as puzzled as I am as to why the two of you should be so impulsive. You didn't elope, did you?

I don't think you did, though I know as well as anyone that impetuous decisions run in the family, particularly when it comes to love. The only other alternative for your disappearance is a worrying one, considering some of the things Julian and I have heard about a man whose ship burned down on the night you left.

Rumor has it that the esteemed gentleman has left town, possibly on the run from his creditors. Even so, Julian and I agree that it was a good thing that you and Leo have decided to take our friend up on the offer he so kindly extended at Sebastian's party. I'm only sorry I can't join you.

I'm in good health and so is the baby, but Julian is as impossible as ever and would drive us all to distraction if not for Leo's mother and her saintly patience. I'm tempted to hire a real bandit to kidnap me and take me far, far away from all his fussing.

*The rogue, who is reading over my shoulder,
bids me to tell you that would only result in him
chasing after me and that at thirty-three he is too
ancient to jump in or out of moving trains, so I
had better stay put.*
I love you. Be safe.

Several inches down the page was a postscript.

Just wait until I get my hands on you!

Even as she breathed out a laugh, a sharp longing
for home and for her sister filled Lucía's chest. If not
for Amalia, Lucía would at this very moment be married to Julian's vile cousin. Lucía had never really let
herself dwell on it for too long. She'd had the displea-
sure of meeting Victor only two or three times—one
of which was at the altar at their own wedding, which
Amalia had cut short—but what little she had seen of
him was enough to know that she would be desperately
unhappy at his side.

He'd been scornful about her music, uninterested in
anything she had to say and clearly determined to marry
her only for the access to her inheritance. The cruel
streak that had led him to play all kinds of horrible tricks
on Julian had lived on his face in the form of an arrogant sneer. Lucía couldn't imagine having to face that
expression day in and day out, without even the solace
of music to turn to.

Music had been Lucía's one escape during the years
she'd been forced to meekly follow all her uncle's rules.
When she'd played the day before, however, it hadn't felt
like escaping as much as finding herself.

That decided her. She had to say yes to the concert.

"Eduardo," she began, lowering the letter.

Eduardo, who had fixed himself a cup of coffee and had unfolded a newspaper, glanced at her. "Everything all right at home?"

"Amalia's fine. I was just thinking about the concert that Cristina mentioned last night."

"Are you sure?" Eduardo asked. "Given your situation? And Leo didn't seem to think it was a good idea."

"Leo doesn't have a say in everything that concerns me," Lucía said, a little more sharply than she'd intended. She drew in a deep breath and extended the letter across the table so that Eduardo could see the paragraph she was pointing out. "According to Amalia, Vargas left San Pedro. He must have finally given up searching for us."

"Maybe," Eduardo said noncommittally, though he did look thoughtful as he read Amalia's words.

Lucía persisted. "I understand the need to be circumspect, and I won't insist if it's truly too dangerous. It needn't be a big affair—we wouldn't want Leo to have the vapors—but I would appreciate if *something* could be arranged. We wouldn't have to use my real name—Luz Robles would do. I could wear a mask or play behind a screen, or…"

Eduardo must have seen how much the notion of a concert meant to Lucía, because he nodded, saying simply, "I'll see what I can do. If nothing else, we could always hold it here—set out chairs in the garden and have a stage built by the pond. I know the acoustics aren't the same as in a theater, but…"

"I would play in a chicken coop with a sack over my head if I had to." Impulsively, Lucía reached across the table and squeezed Eduardo's hand. "Thank you, Eduardo."

She sprang up, ignoring the coffee she hadn't even begun to sip.

Eduardo gave her a bemused glance. "Where are you going?"

She tossed her answer over her shoulder, already halfway to the door. "To practice!"

She added a quick hello as the others started to straggle into the terrace but didn't let their presence stop her from hurrying to her bedroom and snapping open her violin case.

Whoever had come in to make the bed and straighten the room while Lucía had gone to breakfast had thrown open the shutters. The room was suffused with golden morning light as Lucía lifted the violin from its bed of indigo satin and found a little booklet with music by a Cuban composer.

How many years had Lucía devoted to waiting? Waiting for her uncle to give her permission to take music lessons. For other people to acknowledge her hard work. For someone to ask her to dance. Waiting, even, for Leo to write.

Now, for the first time in her entire life, Lucía felt like she was truly in charge of herself. The concert would just be the first of many steps forward.

Chapter Thirteen

It rained the next day.

The heat and humidity had intensified so much the night before that it was a relief when the clouds finally broke open before breakfast, though it spoiled Eduardo's plans. The visitors from Puerto Rico were to be joined by some local friends of Eduardo's on a jaunt up and down the Ozama River, which meant that Lucía and Leo would not have been able to join them.

As much as she would have liked to go on Eduardo's sailboat, Lucía was so busy practicing and making up a list of possible songs to perform at the concert that she wouldn't have been too devastated at having to miss it. As it was, she was able to practice for an hour or two before joining the others.

The torrential downpour didn't cede all morning. Following a breakfast of hot chocolate and buns in the dining room—where the chandelier had been lit against the gloom and the shutters closed to prevent the rain from blowing in—Eduardo led the group to the family's private sitting room.

"There's baccarat, chess, plenty of reading material—

Cristina, there's a book of photographs you might be interested in—and the desk in the corner is stocked with paper, pens and ink if anyone needs to catch up on their correspondence. There should be stamps in there as well."

But no one seemed to be in the mood for letter writing. A crisis at the offices of his shipping company had forced Don Amable to brave the rain. With Cristina's mother in bed with a humidity-induced headache, the group was rowdier than usual.

Rafael Fajardo had draped a tablecloth around his shoulders in imitation of Cristina's lace shawl. He had the group in stitches with his theatrics as he transformed himself first into a fist-shaking crone and then into a winged creature and pretended to dive at Cristina, just to make her shriek. Lucía couldn't remember the last time she'd laughed so much.

Even Leo, stiff-backed at an armchair with a stack of papers balanced on one knee, looked faintly amused.

"You should have a career on the stage," Cristina told the young man as he breathlessly tossed the tablecloth over a chair.

The man *was* a born performer. "I thought his greatest desire was to be a scientist," Lucía said.

"I'm a man of many talents, my dear mademoiselle." He made her an elaborate bow to accompany his atrocious French accent. "There's really nothing I can't do, except make music." With a wink at Lucía, he added, "It's a good thing we have a celebrated violinist in our midst. Tell the truth—how many of the great symphony orchestras have written, begging you to join them?"

Lucía felt her smile tightening.

She hadn't thought much about it at first, but as the days passed and acquaintanceship turned into what felt like a real friendship, Lucía felt more and more uncomfortable concealing the truth of her identity from Cristina and the Fajardos. Still, her memories of Vienna were too sharp for her to feel altogether comfortable revealing most details about her life.

She didn't think that Cristina and the Fajardos would treat her any differently if they knew she was an heiress, and one pursued by family scandal at that.

But then, she hadn't thought her friends in Vienna would have, either.

So when Cristina asked Rafael to perform a monologue he had memorized after hearing it at a theatrical performance in Havana and he replied by saying that he would, if only Mademoiselle the Violinist could be persuaded to provide the musical accompaniment, Lucía agreed at once. She did need the practice, and as long as she was playing, she could ignore any uncomfortable questions that came her way.

The patter of rain on the shutters filled the house as she ran lightly up the stairs, thinking dreamily about how she might make use of the sound to fill out one of her own compositions. She bounded eagerly past Leo's bedroom and toward her own—and found to her dismay that the porcelain doorknob wouldn't turn under her hand.

A brief consultation with the maid who was mopping up a puddle at the end of the hallway revealed that the housekeeper had been given the day off with the understanding that most of the occupants would be out for the day, and that the only other people with access to the keys were Eduardo and his grandfather.

Lucía hurried back to the small sitting room.

"Eduardo, would you—"

She paused, blinking as she looked around the room. Leo had moved to the desk and was annotating the correspondence he had received while the others were squabbling good-naturedly about a play they had all attended in Havana. Their host was nowhere to be seen. "Where's Eduardo?"

"He left—said something about taking advantage of the break in the rain to take some document or another to his grandfather," Cristina reported from her place on the love seat. "If you ask me, I think he's worried about the old man taking a spill in this rain."

"Is it too late to catch him?" Lucía glanced over her shoulder, as if expecting Eduardo to suddenly materialize behind her.

"You could try," Cristina said doubtfully. "But he seemed to be in a terrible hurry."

"Anything the matter?" Rafael had gotten ahold of Cristina's shawl and was idly grazing her forearm with its silk fringe. Cristina batted his hand away with a quelling look.

"Nothing, save that my door is locked and Eduardo and his grandfather are the only ones with keys to the bedrooms."

"Looks like you'll have to climb in through the window."

Rafael couldn't have meant it as anything more than a joke, but Lucía hadn't abandoned the notion of trying to climb the trellis outside her window, and if it meant avoiding a return to the avenue of conversation Rafael and Cristina had embarked on earlier…

"Maybe I will," she said musingly. "And the rain *has* slowed." She snuck a glance at Leo, who appeared to be too absorbed in his papers to interfere with her plans. "I'll do it."

Two of the Fajardos were busy setting up the chessboard, while the eldest alternated between making suggestions and jokes, so only Cristina and Rafael followed her outside.

Her heels sank into the mud as soon as she stepped out of the brick pavers. It had rained so hard and for so long that Don Amable's garden was half-flooded, the flower beds waterlogged and the miniature grove of lime trees as battered as if they had survived a hurricane.

The trellis didn't look *too* daunting. The diamond-shaped crevices would provide perfectly adequate foot and handholds, and the whole thing only extended as far as Lucía's second-floor window. The rope ladder at the cave had been almost as long and she'd managed *that* without too much trouble.

Rafael and Cristina arranged themselves on a bench as if they were spectators at a particularly thrilling theatrical performance. Aware of their gazes on her, Lucía waded over to the trellis and grabbed it with both hands.

And immediately released it when Leo spoke just behind her.

"Are you really considering climbing up there?" He had left his jacket inside and his sleeves were rolled partway up his forearms, which were crossed over his thick chest.

"I'm not considering it, no," Lucía said calmly, more determined now than ever. "I'm going to do it."

"You'll break your neck."

"Oh, for heaven's sake. The trellis is not so very high, and it's solidly built."

"I don't care about the trellis—I care about you."

"Well, I'm not breakable," she said fiercely. "I'm not a piece of fine china to keep in a cabinet nor the kind of porcelain dolls that little girls are forbidden to play with lest they break. Honestly L—José. You're behaving exactly like my uncle." She didn't mean it as harshly as it came out, but the ripple that went over Leo's expression made Lucía soften her tone. "You think you mean well, and maybe you do. But don't you see that there are things I have to do? Not out of defiance or for the sole purpose of giving you gray hairs, but because I will never find out what I'm capable of if everyone around me insists on coddling me."

"Please," he said, and she could tell that he was struggling to contain his emotions. "Can you be sensible for once?"

"No," Lucía replied promptly. "I've done nothing but be sensible for years, and I'm very tired of it."

"There must be something else you can do to prove how capable you are."

"I imagine so," Lucía said, shrugging. "But this is what I've chosen to do right now. I can't relinquish the first scrap of freedom I've ever had just to make you feel better."

He drew in a breath. "If this is because of what I said the other night…"

"This has nothing to do with you." She tilted her head, giving him a curious look. "If it had been Cristina who'd proposed to climb the trellis, would you be trying to forbid her?"

The way Leo's brow instantly furrowed into a frown told Lucía that she had hit a nerve. "It's not the same thing—"

"I don't need you to take care of me. I can take care of myself."

Fitting the tip of her shoe into one of the spaces on the lattice, Lucía began to climb.

Maneuvering around the jasmine's thick stems was a little more difficult than she expected, and her arms and thighs were burning with the effort of hauling herself higher and higher. Once she had cleared the windows on the lower floor, however, the burning subsided and the climb felt easier.

When she got home, she was going to overhaul her entire wardrobe—she would never have been able to do this in her regular clothes. Her skirts were too modishly narrow to allow for much movement, and the lace and soutache that embellished them would have snagged on the jasmine. The skirt she was wearing that morning was the one she had worn on the outing to the caves— the laundress had done a beautiful job of getting the mud out of its dark hem—and the concealed pleat down its front allowed her to raise her knees high enough to climb without fear that those below would see anything they shouldn't.

There really was nothing to it once she got used to it—with the trellis fixed solidly to the house's exterior wall, climbing it was even easier than ascending the rope ladder at the caves.

Once she had reached high enough that the window to her bedroom was at arm's length, Lucía paused for a second to bask in triumph.

The rain had slowed, but the breeze hadn't—it was picking strands of hair out of the tidy coil at the base of her neck and making them flutter around her face. Lucía couldn't help but feel reminded of the moment when she'd sat at the table aboard the *Leonor* as the wind played with her collar and it had dawned on her that, for the first time in her life, she had the freedom to be someone other than herself.

And the thrill that had coursed through her when Leo had wrapped his arms around her and jumped into the lake.

This was what performing felt like—exhilarating to the point of nerve-racking. Lucía had always tied herself into knots before every performance, but when the time came to start playing, deep breaths were all it took for her fear to dissolve.

On his tour of the gardens, Don Amable had told them that the plant winding up the trellis was an Arabian jasmine, planted by his wife when they had first built the house half a century before. Lucía paused to break off a tiny bloom by the stem. Clinging one-handed to the trellis, she tucked the jasmine into her hair—partly because she liked how the white flowers had looked against her dark hair the previous night, but also to show off a little for those gathered below.

She cast a flirtatious glance over her shoulder, which was answered with raucous applause, as if she really were on stage. The noise was loud enough that she almost didn't hear the ominous crack…right before the wood began to give way under her feet.

For the first time in years, Leo was feeling the one emotion he'd sought to evade for years—he felt helpless.

And it was thanks to Lucía.

With slow deliberation, Leo drew in one breath, and then another. If Lucía was determined to break her own neck in order to prove something to herself, so be it. He didn't have to stand around and watch it happen.

Leo had only walked a step or two away from the trellis when the terrible sound of splintering wood reached his ears. Whirling around with his heart in his mouth and his pulse racing like a locomotive, he was just in time to catch Lucía as she came tumbling down.

Gasps and curses pierced the air, but Leo hadn't a scrap of breath left to make any sound.

Lucía fell hard into his outstretched arms—the force of it made Leo's knees buckle and bend, though he managed to stay upright.

"You were saying?" he asked.

His words might have been flippant, but Leo was inwardly livid, a product of the undiluted panic that was coursing through him at the thought of what would have happened if he had gone just a little farther.

The others had rushed over from their bench and were crowding around Leo, pelting Lucía with questions. Lucía only seemed to have eyes for Leo. She was looking up at him with the oddest twist to her lip, as if she had found her fall such an exhilarating adventure that she couldn't wait to do it again.

"You're like a hero in a storybook," she told him, her eyes sparkling. "Always there to catch me when I fall." Her smile faded as she took in Leo's narrowed eyes. "I'd ask what was wrong with you, but I'm sure there are too many things to name just one."

"What's wrong with *me*?" For once, Leo's extensive vocabulary failed to provide him with an appropriate response, so he had to settle for a growl. "Could it have something to do with the fact that I just watched you nearly plummet to your death?"

She glared at him. "Plummet to my death? Really, what an outrageous exaggeration. The trellis barely reaches the second story. I'm completely unharmed. I just had the wind knocked out of me—by your absurdly hard arms, I may add."

"I saw your ankle turn when the trellis gave out from under you," he snapped. "Your hands are a ruin, you just narrowly avoided breaking your back, and don't think I have forgotten about your cramped legs. Are you intentionally trying to make me collapse or are you just the most reckless—"

"Lovely, another insult to add to the collection. Let's see, I'm reckless, thoughtless, entitled… Am I forgetting something?"

"Infuriating," Leo said through gritted teeth. "Provoking. I'll write you a list if you want me to."

Just as soon as he found a doctor to conduct a thorough inventory of her body to make sure she wasn't downplaying her injuries.

Leo turned to Rafael Fajardo. "Will you ask one of the maids to fetch a doctor?"

Lucía let out a sound of protest. "There's no need for that. I'm perfectly fine."

Cristina whipped out her handkerchief and began to clean a long streak of dirt off Lucía's arm, looking shaken and contrite. As well she would—none of this would have happened if she had helped him talk some sense into Lucía. "Maybe it would be a good idea. It did look like you turned your ankle."

"It doesn't hurt in the slightest," Lucía claimed, wearing the same expression she had on the rowboat when she'd tried to tell Leo that the oars weren't hurting her hands. "And it would be cruel to make a man go out into the streets in weather like this for something so trivial. Le—that is, José, you can put me down."

"Why, so you can pitch yourself headfirst off something else?"

Ignoring her, he carried her carefully over the wet path and laid her on a bench on one side of the terrace.

His heart was still racing. Seeing her fall had been far more effective than the cold water he had doused himself with after their moment behind the mango tree the other night. Lucía wasn't a mirage—she was a menace. To his peace of mind, if nothing else.

Lucía sat up immediately. When she attempted to stand up, however, she wasn't able to hold back a wince. "Maybe my foot does twinge a little," she admitted. "But there really is no need to fetch a doctor."

"Ice, then," Leo said, glancing at Rafael, who nodded. "Wrapped in a clean towel, if you please."

He waited for Lucía's nod of permission before easing her mud-caked shoe off and trying to feel her ankle through her stocking. There was no swelling that he could tell, but it was impossible to know for certain without removing her stockings—and the memory of massaging the cramp from her leg was still too fresh in his mind for him to be altogether comfortable with the idea of lifting the hem of her skirt more than a couple of centimeters.

"Well," Cristina said with a faltering smile as Leo rose from where he'd been crouching in front of the bench, "we can be grateful you didn't injure one of your arms, or we would've had to cancel the concert."

"Concert?" Leo echoed, turning to look at Lucía. "I thought you had decided against it. You promised—"

"I promised you I would think about it. Cristina,

would you be so kind as to get me a glass of water?"
Lucía asked her friend. When the other woman nodded
and hurried off, Lucía glanced over Leo's shoulder as if
to satisfy herself that they were alone. "I'm prepared to
take every precaution. I suggested to Eduardo that we
could make it a masked affair, to be even more certain
that no one will recognize me."

"Masks?" Leo asked in a furious whisper. "It would
take much more than a scrap of fabric across your eyes
to make you unrecognizable. We—" He cut himself off
swiftly when he noticed a brownish smear along her
midsection. "Is that blood?"

"Blood?"

Lucía glanced down at her white shirtwaist, now
streaked with dirt from the trellis—and something else.
As she spread her arms, Leo caught sight of a long scrape
across her right forearm, just below the torn edge of
her sleeve.

"It's nothing," Lucía said dismissively, following his
gaze. "Only a scrape."

"Scrapes can get infected."

Scowling, he jerked his handkerchief out of his pocket
and moistened it with some of the raindrops that were
beginning to fall again. As gently as he could, he patted her skin clean and removed the two splinters that
were digging into her tender flesh. One of them was
long enough that she flinched as he pulled it out, the
skin around her eyes tightening with pain.

She didn't say a word, or make a single sound, though
he was sure her restraint was costing her. Leo was often
called upon to administer first aid to the men at the sugar
mill, and Lucía had born the pain with as much forti-
tude as any of them.

Cristina returned just then, along with a fresh glass of ice water and all four of the Fajardos. One of them offered Leo his own handkerchief—along with a quip. Accepting the handkerchief gratefully and limiting himself to a bland smile at the smart remark, Leo tried not to pay too much attention to the young men as they gathered around him and Lucía, holding clinking glasses of lime juice and getting in the way of the maid who was carrying out a tray with a bowl of the ice Leo had requested and a pile of small, clean towels.

Swiftly, Leo bound a handful of ice chips into a handkerchief-sized towel and placed it gently on Lucía's ankle.

"If it doesn't feel better soon," he said gruffly, "we *will* send for a doctor. As for the other matter…" He glanced at the brothers, who were squabbling over whether a wrenched ankle should be plied with warm compresses or ice. "We'll discuss it later."

"There's nothing to discuss," Lucía said with a smile that was as sweet as it was insincere. Plucking the ice off her ankle, she rose from her reclining position and swung her legs down as if in preparation for standing—or walking away from a potential argument.

Leo stifled a sigh. "I wouldn't put any weight on that ankle just yet. Why don't you lie down for the rest of the afternoon?"

"Maybe you should take a little rest yourself," she suggested with exaggerated politeness. "Your nerves seem overset."

Now there was a wicked curve to her lips, and Leo had no choice but to admit defeat. For the moment— he may not be able to speak his mind in front of their avid spectators, but he could certainly give her a piece of it later.

Lucía looked almost cheerful as Leo muttered something about having work to do and retreated to the safety of his correspondence, discretion being the better part of valor and all that.

Fetching his papers from the family parlor, he set up a makeshift office in the empty dining room, where the prosaic scent of beeswax rose from the polished table and banished the faint sweetness that had transferred from Lucía's clothes to his own. He could still feel the weight of her in his arms, and the wild, breathless panic of seeing her fall through the air was something he was certain would follow him into his dreams.

The more time he spent around her, the more he was convinced that being around Lucía Troncoso was not merely inconvenient, or even irritating.

It was unbearable.

Chapter Fourteen

Eduardo and Don Amable didn't return until the afternoon. Rain had begun falling again, though with far less intensity than it had in the morning. From his spot at the dining table, which he had turned into a makeshift desk, Leo watched through the window as Eduardo carefully helped his grandfather out of the carriage and into the house.

Several moments later, Eduardo was striding through the archway that led into the dining room. "The maids told me I would find you here. There's another parcel for you from San Pedro."

Leo accepted it gratefully and laid it next to the papers spread out on the polished mahogany.

"I can't thank you enough for the use of your messenger, Eduardo. And I apologize for the mess." Eduardo waved off his apology as Leo continued. "I hate to ask Sebastian to take on too much when his wife is so close to her time. And with our deal with Vargas gone up in flames—" his lips twisted in a wry smile "—I find myself in the need of finding another ship to purchase. Which won't be easy now that half of San Pedro thinks

I'm an arsonist. I'd appreciate any advice you might have on that regard."

Eduardo took a seat across from Leo. "I may be able to do more than offer advice. My cousin and I have been taking on more of the business to give Abuelo a rest, and we both agree that we should diversify our investments. If you're willing to wait until he returns next week, we should be able to work something out."

Thoughtfully, Leo rubbed a drop of ink off the nib of his pen with a rag the maids had provided for that purpose. While he would have preferred not to share the profits with anyone but Sebastian, going into business with the Martinez family meant being backed by their power and influence. The risk was reduced, too—no one knew more about shipping than Eduardo's family, who had built the bulk of their fortune on importing luxury goods onto the island.

It was not the outcome he'd hoped for, but it might prove even more beneficial than his original plan.

"I'd have to discuss it with Sebastian, of course, but I think he'll be as pleased as I am at the notion of a partnership," he told Eduardo, setting down the pen.

Eduardo nodded. "In the meantime, I wanted to introduce you to a business acquaintance of ours who is looking to purchase some of your surplus bagasse to mix into his livestock feed. Can you meet with him tomorrow? I can ask him to come to the house—and rest assured, he's the soul of discretion."

Leo should have said no, but the promise of another avenue for profit was too tempting for him to resist. Not because selling a little leftover pulped sugarcane would represent such a great change in his income, but because if he wasn't exonerated soon, he was going to hire a damn nurse and send his mother out of the country to take a rest cure in a European spa town where she wouldn't be followed by the shadow of Vargas's threats.

He only wished he could do the same with Lucía—but she would never let him get her out of the way.

He agreed quickly to the meeting, then added, "Any news of Vargas?"

Eduardo's brow furrowed. "Well, word is that he left town, possibly to escape whatever creditors haven't yet been satisfied. Before he did, he was still making noise about having you arrested the moment you turn up. I made some discreet inquiries and was able to find out that he did receive a disbursement from an insurance company. I was hoping that would quiet him, but he appears to be even more determined to pin the blame on you. You're sure he doesn't hold a grudge against you for some reason?"

"I couldn't think of a reason why he would—as far as I remember, I hadn't met him before I started looking into the sale of the ship, and that was less than a month ago. Sebastian thinks that Vargas may be receiving pressure from the insurance company to produce the culprit—maybe they mean to extract the price of the settlement from the guilty party." Leo nudged the pencil on the table. "Or maybe it's the Americans."

It had been three years since the country's customs revenue had been pledged to the United States government in order to repay what Leo understood to be a massive debt. Not content to trust the Dominicans, the Americans had dispatched their own customs inspectors, none of whom would let a situation like this go by without close scrutiny.

Eduardo's frown deepened. "If only we could find

where he stored the goods he removed from the ship…
That would go a long way toward helping disprove his
claim."

"If he hasn't disposed of it all by now." Leo rubbed a
hand over his face. When he reopened his eyes, it was
to find Eduardo looking uneasy. "There's more?"

Eduardo nodded slowly. "There's a possibility that
Vargas might have identified Lucía."

Leo drew in a sharp breath. "I had hoped that it had
been too dark or he'd been too far away to see her clearly.
It was busy in the docks, and dark, save for the flames."

"He remembered her by the gown she was wearing
that night. It seems that he'd been asking idly about the
pretty young woman in the sparkling rose gown, making it seem as though he was interested in seeking her
out because he'd found her attractive. An unwitting acquaintance who'd been at Sebastian's party gave him
her name."

Leo swore under his breath. "She can't go through
with the damned concert now."

"It may be unwise to do anything that brings attention to her," Eduardo admitted. "Though it *is* a shame—
Abuelo's grand-nephew invited us all to his house for
luncheon tomorrow and it's too late to decline his invitation. Lucía will be so disappointed when she hears it
will have been for nothing."

Leo was perhaps the one person in the world who
knew just how devastated Lucía would be at the news.
"I'd rather see her disappointed than accused of arson—
or worse."

"You're a far stronger man than I am, my friend. One
more pleading look from her and I would've agreed to
hand over my firstborn."

Leo couldn't blame Eduardo for caving in—all the blame rested solely on Leo himself. After all, Lucía wouldn't have been embroiled in this if it hadn't been for him. If he hadn't been so eager to rush into a business deal with Vargas, or to escape Lucía's questions…

If he hadn't started writing to her in the first place.

Before his thoughts could spiral too far, a housemaid entered holding what looked like a folded tablecloth and a towering pile of freshly starched napkins.

It must have been later than Leo realized if the table was about to be set for dinner.

"Excuse me, Don Eduardo," she said, not completely able to hide her dismay as she took in the mess strewn over the polished surface of the table. "I didn't realize anyone was in here. I'll come back later."

"No, it's all right," Leo said, and started to gather his papers into a neat pile. "I'll get out of your way." In a lower voice meant for Eduardo, he added, "I'll go speak with Lucía about all this."

"And I'll see about hiring a guard for you both." Eduardo looked as grim as Leo felt. "I'd rather not take any chances where Vargas is concerned."

The men parted on that grim note. After stopping by his bedroom to put away his documents and writing implements, Leo went to see Lucía.

The past several days had been crammed with so many unusual events that visiting a young woman in her bedroom didn't seem as scandalous as it should have. He'd asked one of the housemaids about her, and he'd been told that after the housekeeper's ring of keys had been discovered hanging from the woman's door, Lucía had gone up to her bedroom for a nap.

He rapped softly at the door, which opened under

his knuckles. As high-ceilinged as all the rooms in the house, this bedroom was on the small side. Directly across from the door were two tall, shuttered windows—the ones he had seen her leaning out of on their first day in Santo Domingo. The rain-darkened afternoon, which was swiftly fading into evening, sent only a suffused gray light through the slats of the closed shutters.

A mahogany wardrobe with mirrors set into its paneled door took up most of the whitewashed wall to the left. To the right was the bed, a large one with four carved posts and a crocheted coverlet. Lucía was lying under it, eyes closed, her long lashes casting crescent shadows on her delicately molded cheekbones.

As hard as she'd protested earlier, she must have been more overcome by the fall than she'd let on.

Leo started to withdraw, but the light that had come in through the open door must have awoken her, because her eyes fluttered open.

"Hola," she murmured as she caught sight of him.

"Hola," Leo echoed. "I just wanted to know if you wanted anything from downstairs. It's almost dinner time."

"Some hot chocolate," she said weakly, her voice so low that Leo was forced to venture farther into the room in order to hear her. "Or maybe tea? I don't feel…"

Alarm blazed inside Leo as her voice trailed off and she slumped back against the pillow. He reached her bedside in another step and took hold of her limp hand, setting his fingers to her wrist as he'd seen countless doctors and nurses do. But it was impossible to feel her pulse over the roar of his own.

Frantically, he cupped her face with his free hand,

moving it gently out of the shadows and toward the hint of gray light coming in through the shutters.

With a jolt, Leo realized that Lucía's large, expressive eyes were open—and they were full of mischief.

"Are you laughing at me?" he demanded.

"I can't help it. You're so serious all the time." The crocheted coverlet and the embroidered blanket under it fell away as Lucía sat up, revealing that she had changed out of her grimy clothes. "And as you seemed so determined to think I was on my deathbed, I decided I might as well go along with it."

The panic that had been surging through him was beginning to recede in the wake of his relief, but he still felt a powerful desire to crush her to his chest and make sure she really was all right. "You little rogue."

"Am I?" she asked, looking a little too pleased with herself.

Leo wanted to groan. "Don't get any ideas." He stepped away from the bed. "I should leave you to get some rest."

She pushed the covers aside and swung her legs off the bed. "I'll come downstairs with you. My ankle is perfectly fine."

In illustration, or perhaps in the spirit of further annoying him, Lucía gave a little pirouette. Only her ankle must not have been quite as perfectly fine as she claimed, because she stumbled and crashed into him.

Acting on reflex, Leo seized her by the waist. How many times had he done so over the past handful of days? It was as if even gravity were conspiring against his need to hold Lucía at bay.

Leo tried to summon up an appropriate amount of outrage, but it was almost impossible when his entire body was straining to absorb the sensation of Lucía pulled flush against him.

It may not be the first time he'd had to save her from falling, but each time he did, Leo was struck anew with how well her slight frame fit against his. Everything about her was so delicate. From her narrow shoulders and hips to the gentle slopes of her features and her dainty wrists and fingers. Holding her felt like holding a live butterfly and feeling its wings fluttering inside his hand.

He could have stood like that for hours.

"I suppose I ought to be grateful that you're so very steady," Lucía grumbled, holding onto his biceps though her hands only spanned a fraction of their girth. Her grip loosened, but instead of releasing him, she began gently tracing the contours of his arms and shoulders.

Leo's absurd instinct was to flex, though he was wearing a jacket and he doubted Lucía could feel much through the fabric.

"I'll catch you as many times as you need me to," Leo told her. "But I wouldn't need to if you took better care of yourself."

"That would make me boring as well as bored. And it would deprive you of the opportunity to play the hero, which I can't help but think you enjoy more than you're letting on."

"If you think I enjoy seeing you in peril, you don't know me at all."

"In peril?" Lucía scoffed.

One of her curls, grown riotous in the humidity, escaped the pins that held her hair back. Leo brushed it behind her ear, letting his fingers linger on her temple for a moment as he felt the heat of her skin.

Lucía's eyes narrowed. "Are you checking me for fever? *Por amor al cielo...*"

Wriggling out of his arms, she went to the small dressing table and began releasing her hair from its pins.

"I'll have someone bring you your dinner." Leo averted his gaze as she picked up the hairbrush that had been lying next to the porcelain water jug and began running it through her curls. He knew he should leave her to tidy up in peace—being present while she made her toilet seemed improper, if not outright transgressive. He knew it, and yet he found himself dawdling at the doorway. "You really should stay in bed."

"And you should stop trying to order me about. Or at the very least, explain your reasons for believing that I would listen to anything you had to say in the matter."

In spite of himself, Leo was amused. He crossed his arms over his chest, trying not to show it. "Have you always been this insolent?"

"No. And that," Lucía told him, glancing backward briefly, "is precisely my problem. Maybe if I'd been less preoccupied with being so quiet and polite and eager to please, my life would have turned out much differently."

"So now, instead, you have to try my patience?"

"A woman's got to have *some* amusements. You should consider yourself lucky—my sister's husband raises racehorses and he's dying to teach me how to stand on the saddle. He once leapt into a moving locomotive— and then out of it—so I have a lot to live up to."

Leo let out a groan.

Lucía's nimble fingers made quick work out of rearranging her locks into a tidy coil at the back of her neck and smoothing out the creases in her dress. As futile as he knew it was, Leo couldn't help but wonder what it would be like to lean against the bedposts as he watched Lucía complete the entire ritual of dressing for the day— or undressing at the end of it.

Did she fling her clothes every which way in her haste to move on to the next activity? Did she strip slowly, humming Bach sonatas under her breath?

Leo would never know. The thought filled him with a disappointment that was not exactly obscure, or unexpected. Such intimacy was a luxury he couldn't afford. Not just yet—and with Lucía, perhaps never.

Slipping into a pair of beaded evening shoes with low heels that didn't seem to pain her too much, she crossed the small bedroom with an almost unnoticeable limp. She hadn't paid much attention to him as she had freshened up, but as she came toward him now, the small smile hovering at the corners of her lips let him know that she hadn't minded the attention.

"Ready to go down?" she asked lightly, as if Leo hadn't just crossed every line of propriety.

Or as if she had enjoyed his doing so.

He nodded his assent and held the door for her, but as she began walking past, he stopped her with a brush of his fingers. "I don't want to be like your uncle. Believe it or not, I get no pleasure from scolding you. It's just that the thought of seeing you get hurt fills me with…"

With more fury and terror than he could even express, but he couldn't quite bring himself to say so out loud. Lucía seemed to understand, however.

"There's more than one way of getting hurt, Leo." Lucía studied him, her thickly fringed eyes serious at long last. "I'd rather have my leg broken than my spirit. You do understand that, don't you?"

"I'm afraid I don't," he told her ruefully. "I can't imagine anything worse than someone I care about being injured or ill."

From the sympathy in her expression, Leo realized she must have thought he meant his parents. With a little start, he realized that he hadn't been thinking about them, not just then. That Lucía had joined them on the short list of people he allowed himself to care for…

It gave him pause.

"I know," she said softly. "The thing is, Leo, I want adventure and romance and excitement. You want to wrap yourself and everyone around you in cotton batting."

Leo didn't reply right away. He looked down at Lucía's face, half turned away from him. It hadn't undergone too many changes in the past five years, so it was somewhat surprising to see how many the past several days had wrought. Her inherent sweetness and serenity were still there, it was just that they were made stronger and lovelier by her newfound confidence.

"Do you know what else you are?" He waited for her to lift her gaze to his before answering his own question. "You're extraordinary. And I wish that everyone who ever snubbed you could see it as clearly as I do."

As easily as Leo could lose command of himself while around Lucía, it was with full awareness of what he was doing that he took her hand and laid a kiss on her open palm, which she then pressed briefly to his jaw.

"They'll be waiting for us," she said, and some of the tautness had eased from her voice.

It wasn't until he was lying in his own bed, late that night, that Leo remembered that he'd never told Lucía about Vargas knowing her identity.

Chapter Fifteen

The sun was blazing so strongly the next morning that not even a puddle remained as evidence of the previous day's torrential rain. A long scrape along Lucía's arm and a leftover twinge in her ankle were the only reminders of her brief dalliance with the trellis.

Eduardo and Don Amable had received the news of the broken trellis with touching concern about her well-being and reassurances that the wooden structure should have been pulled down a long time ago—that if not for Don Amable's fondness for the jasmine, which had been his wife's favorite, it certainly would have been.

Leo certainly hadn't argued with the notion. In fact, he'd made a point of raising his eyebrows at her from across the dinner table, looking so smug that she'd burst into giggles and almost choked on her wine.

Innocent though the exchange may have been, it had Cristina and the Fajardos gleefully nudging each other. They had teased Lucía mercilessly the day before—Leo had been spared only because he had left to attend to his work—and though she enjoyed feeling like she was part of the group, their gentle ribbing had brought such an ache to her chest that she'd been forced to make her escape by pretending that she did need a nap after all.

She had fallen so quickly that she hadn't had time to feel afraid before she was landing in Leo's arms. It hadn't surprised her that he'd caught her—in fact, it had seemed like the most natural thing to have found herself in his arms.

It was more than a little worrying. When had Leo become someone she could rely on?

She didn't bother trying to find an answer as she poured a stream of hot, dark coffee into her cup and followed it with a generous splash of milk. Leo nudged the silver sugar cellar closer to her without her having to ask for it.

Dimly, she heard Don Amable ask where the group intended to pass the day—he and Cristina's mother had accepted an invitation for luncheon at a friend's house, and it was plain that they were looking forward to a restful day.

"Eduardo promised to take us to see the old colonial-era ruins." Cristina might have outwardly appeared composed, but earlier she had confessed to Lucía that she was looking forward to a morning without her chaperone. "I'm very eager to photograph them. Luz, I wonder if it might be a good place for that portrait of you that we discussed. If your ankle doesn't pain you today, of course."

Lucía's twisted ankle would provide the perfect excuse to stay at the Martinez's again—but Lucía had had enough of excuses. And in any case, her ankle felt perfectly fine.

Disapproval furrowed Leo's brow at the suggestion, and Eduardo looked like he was trying to think of a way to change the subject. Before Lucía could reply to Cristina, Don Amable folded his newspaper and set it down, asking blandly, "Do you know the history of the old hospital?"

Not waiting for anyone's reply, Don Amable launched into a comprehensive account of sixteenth-century building practices, which Lucía only heard with half an ear as she speared a piece of papaya from among the sliced bananas and mangoes in her bowl of fruit.

She felt like the strings on a violin that had been strung too tautly and were on the verge of breaking. She did want to see the old ruins. She wanted to see much more of the world than elegant cafés and private ballrooms.

She had lost far too much time—to tyrannical uncles, to worried sisters, to classmates with easily ruffled feathers. And most of all, to her own fear.

With Vargas on the run from his creditors, what was keeping her indoors?

As soon as breakfast was over, Lucía ran up the stairs to fetch a hat. After a moment's thought, she grabbed her violin case as well.

She'd expected Leo to have tucked himself away somewhere quiet with his ink pots and papers, but he was standing by the front door, deep in conversation with Eduardo. He looked up as Lucía started to sail past, his quick gaze instantly taking in her hat and violin case.

With a single glance at the thunderclouds gathering on Leo's brow, Eduardo scurried out the door.

Leo hardly seemed to notice. "You can't mean to go with them."

"I was planning on it, yes," Lucía said lightly.

Urgency colored Leo's voice as he glanced around him

to make sure they were alone in the entranceway. "We need to exercise caution now, more than ever. Vargas—"

"Can't talk now," she interrupted him in a breezy tone that made his eyes narrow. "I'm going busking by the ruins of the old hospital."

"Busking?"

"I always wanted to do it in Vienna—some of the girls at the Academy did every now and then—but I was never brave enough."

At the sound of the carriage rolling into the front drive, she gave Leo a little smile and wave and started to saunter toward the open door. "Time to leave!"

"But—"

"Why not come along?" She turned around for the sole purpose of looking critically up and down his solid, athletic frame. To look at Leo, one would never guess that he had been dressing every day from a vastly reduced wardrobe—every garment he wore was impeccable. "If you ask me, you really could use some time away from your work. A little sunshine and fresh air ought to help with those stooped shoulders and that unhealthy pallor."

Leo looked as though he didn't know whether to laugh or despair—the reddish tint he had acquired over the bridge of his nose and his cheekbones from long mornings spent striding around Don Amable's garden belied her words as much as his straight posture.

"All right, then," he said unexpectedly. "I'll go."

Lucía blinked. "You will?"

"Someone has to keep you out of trouble."

Eduardo's eyes widened when he saw the two of them emerge from the house and climb into the awaiting carriage, but he didn't offer any remarks, and neither did he try to talk them out of going. Leo could stand to learn a thing or two from him.

Lucía settled into a seat next to Cristina, who greeted her with pleased surprise. It was impossible not to notice that Leo took the seat behind them, particularly when he leaned forward and whispered, in a voice just loud enough to be heard over the rattle of the carriage's wheels, "When I called you insolent yesterday, it wasn't a compliment. Or a suggestion to continue behaving that way."

His warm breath touched the back of her neck, like a caress.

"Is that so?" Lucía murmured without turning around—and without giving in to the urge to shiver. "I was under the impression that you liked it."

Cristina had her head turned away from Lucía as she admired the view on her side of the carriage, and Lucía was reasonably sure that neither she nor anyone else was able to hear Leo's response.

"Are you so very certain that you know what I like?"

Something in his voice made heat rush over her skin in a prickling wave.

Lucía had been pleased to find out that she could disarm him with a single remark, which she thought was only fair, considering that he could make her quiver just by lowering his voice like that as he let his words out with slow deliberation.

She pressed her thighs tightly together, but that did little to stem the tide of desire rushing over her.

"I don't just know what you like. I know *you*," she said softly. "The real you. Every version of you. And all the better parts of you that you've inexplicably tried to hide from the world."

They were words that Lucía didn't know if she would dare say in private, and they were met with charged silence.

Certain that she would turn around and see Leo looking outraged, Lucía was startled by the desire in his gaze.

Startled and intrigued.

Leaning forward in his seat, Leo was close enough that it wouldn't have taken too much effort to brush her lips against his. The sunlight that poured in through the open sides of the long carriage made his brown eyes look more like toffee than ever.

"You have always seen all the way into my soul."

There wasn't time for much more. They arrived at the ruins in a matter of minutes, and Lucía found herself unable to respond in the flurry of disembarking from the carriage and shaking the creases out of her skirt.

Cristina set out immediately with her little valise full of photographic instruments, accompanied by Rafael, while the other Fajardos and Eduardo flocked toward a woman selling *empanadas* out of a basket. Lucía didn't know how they could all eat again so soon after their large breakfast, but the men were wolfing down the fried pastries with the enthusiasm of people who had gone without eating for a month or more.

For his part, Leo had evidently meant what he'd said about keeping her out of trouble, because he remained closely by her side.

She still felt slightly out of balance from the remark he had made in the carriage. Leo had a way of making ordinary sentences feel like proclamations, and this one had been delivered with so much conviction that Lucía couldn't help but believe him.

"If you're going to play nursemaid, you might as well make yourself useful," she told him, handing him the violin case as she scouted for a spot that was shady enough to keep them from broiling in the sun.

The ruins of what was once a sixteenth-century hospital were far better preserved than Lucía would expect after hundreds of years' worth of earthquakes and hurricanes. It was midmorning, and the sun was so strong overhead already that everyone seemed to be keeping to the shade, of which there was precious little among the soaring arches and half-crumbling walls.

"I thought busking required an audience," Leo said.

Save for the few pigeons that were pecking among the stones and the *empanada* seller, who had probably just been passing by when she'd been accosted by the men, the area around the ruin was empty.

Perching on a pile of stone, Lucía beckoned to him to bring the violin case within reach. "You can be my audience."

She began running scales, doing her best to put Leo out of her mind even though he had sat down nearby, within full view of her, and was watching her with so much intensity that she could feel his gaze on her even with her eyes closed. Eventually, however, she managed to lose herself in the music, the way she always did, until all that existed was the melody and the warm breeze that wafted over her.

She had no way of knowing how much time had passed when she finally lowered her bow and stretched her neck. The sun had moved so that the stones she leaned against were no longer in the shade and the back of her neck felt scorched above her collar. Eduardo and the three brothers were in the distance, shouting and

laughing as they played ball with a ragtag group of little boys. Cristina and her companion were nowhere to
be seen. And Leo...

Leo was sitting in the same spot, the leather case on
his lap to keep it from getting scratched or dirty on the
ancient floor. His shoulders were set in the same solid
lines as always, but sometime during the past few days,
Leo had stopped holding himself so rigidly. In fact, he
looked almost relaxed as he gazed up at her, a small
smile playing over his lips.

He looked so much like the Leo Lucía had expected
to find when she came back from Europe that her heart
and her stomach and everything inside her seized. There
was no defensiveness or irritation in his eyes, just...
appreciation.

Playing had undone all the knots in her stomach, and
one look at Leo had knotted them again, more tightly
than before.

If it was true that she could see deep into his soul,
what did he see when he looked at her? Not Luz Robles,
that was for certain. Not the carefree, pampered, incon-
siderate heiress still, surely. So what, then?

Could it be possible that he actually saw *her*?

She wanted him to with a longing so sharp it took
her breath away.

"You were right," she said abruptly when she noticed
he was still looking at her, his eyebrows slightly raised
in inquiry. "It's no fun busking without an audience.
Maybe I ought to go exploring instead."

She sprang up from her seat and thrust her violin
and bow at Leo, trusting that in the time it took him to
return them to their proper places within the case, she
would be able to get away.

The ruins of the old hospital were not as extensive as the Martinez's property—or her own home for that matter—but a few moments' worth of trampling around the nooks among the half-fallen walls and caved-in archways were enough to restore her equanimity.

Pausing behind a pile of stones, she readjusted the belt around her waist even though neither it nor her lightly boned corset were the ones responsible for her lack of breath. She had finished threading the thin leather through the buckle when a soft noise made her cautiously peer around the pile of stones to see Cristina and Rafael Fajardo, lost in a passionate kiss.

Hiding a smile, Lucía tried to soundlessly back away from the sight, only to tread on somebody's foot. Leo's naturally—he really was acting like a nursemaid, which put Lucía in the disgruntling position of feeling like the nursemaid's charge.

He didn't see *her*. All he saw was someone to keep out of trouble.

She cut off his irritated "Lu—" by pressing her fingers to his mouth.

Another morning out in the sun had added an attractive reddish glaze to the bridge of his nose and the top of his toffee-colored cheekbones, making him look more delicious than ever. The sharp intake of breath as her fingers collided with his full lips sounded loud among the echoing stones.

Grasping him by the arm, she led him to the other side of the ancient hospital.

She'd been reasonably sure that he hadn't seen the couple, but after several moments, he asked, "Was that—"

"Yes."

"And they were—"

Lucía made herself grin. "You really hadn't noticed? Really Leo, I thought you were more observant than that. They've been making eyes at each other—and more—from the moment they boarded the *Leonor*."

"I've had my hands full with you," he told her. "And full *of* you. Maybe if you stopped trying to give me gray hairs, I'd have more time to catch up on my gossip."

"Don't blame me for your lack of observation."

Something pale and white fluttered in the breeze, catching Lucía's attention. "Are those camellias? I didn't know they grew in the wild."

The bush was growing at the very top of a pile of stones and dirt, looking so picturesque that Lucía couldn't resist scrambling onto the stones. It wasn't just that the flowers were pretty, though they were. She knew that nothing could replace Don Amable's prized jasmine, which had grown so entangled with the trellis that it would have to come down along with what remained of the wood, but maybe she could present him with a cutting from this bush to show her regret for causing the trellis to give way…

"This is hardly the wild. I'm sure someone planted those. Lucía…" The wariness in Leo's voice was starting to become delightfully familiar. "I thought you had learned your lesson when it came to climbing things."

"I thought you weren't going to cast any more aspersions on my predilection for climbing things."

"You'll turn your ankle again," Leo said, sounding scandalized. "Or worse."

"I'm not afraid of falling, because I know that you're always there to catch me," she said teasingly.

"I wouldn't care to bet on that," Leo muttered, but he *was* hovering below her, his head roughly level with her ankles.

"I wonder what the gossips back in San Pedro would think if they saw me now."

"They'd think that you're being incredibly foolish," he said sharply.

By this time, Lucía had plenty of practice in the art of pretending she hadn't heard him. She struck a pose, holding an imaginary violin and bow, and sawing at the air. "This would be a good spot for a concert—better than any stage."

"*Please* get down from there. Lucía, I'm serious."

"When aren't you serious?" She looked tauntingly down at him. "If you want me to come down, you'll have to come fetch me."

Whatever Leo may have thought of her, Lucía was not entirely a fool. Neither was she completely reckless. She'd only meant to scare him a little, as she had when she'd pretended to swoon.

But though she had seen the flowers, she had failed to spot the nest tucked behind the camellia bush. As her hand neared it, a full-grown bird exploded out of it.

She was too startled to cry out. Throwing up her arms to shield her face from the bird's assault, Lucía felt its wings beat against her forearm. She tried to step back, but her perch atop the pile of dirt and ancient stone was too precarious, and her feet began to slide out from under her.

Grasping wildly for something to hold on to, Lucía seized one of the sturdy branches protruding from the camellia bush. She held on to it gratefully—but her relief was short lived as her weight pulled the bush's roots out of the ground.

The dirt and stones under her feet, so stable a moment before, turned into a miniature landslide that she was forced to ride until she fetched up against another partially crumbled wall, hard enough to bruise.

She fell on one knee, and was still struggling to get to her feet when Leo reached her.

"Are you all right?" he asked frantically, checking her over for injuries.

Leaning heavily against Leo, she was so shaken she could only nod. He was reassuringly solid against her— as steady as the world had felt a moment before it had started to move out from under her.

Leo was cold.

He was standing on a patch of sunshine, Lucía in his arms, and although he should have been perspiring, all Leo could feel was a freezing numbness inching along his limbs.

Unable to move, he stood there for a moment, struggling to control his anger.

No, not anger. Emotions. Too many of them to pick out from the snarl in his chest. The only thing he was certain of was that he couldn't do this anymore.

As much as he sympathized with Lucía's desperate need to prove herself, he couldn't stand around while she continued to put herself in danger. If it hadn't been evident before, it was now. He had watched her career past him, dread in the pit of his stomach, knowing that he would have leaped off a cliff if he had to in order to save her, and yet unable to do a single thing to stop her from slamming against the wall opposite.

She was thoroughly unharmed—he had made sure of that. But she might not be the next time, and with the way Lucía was acting, he had no doubt that there would be a next time. And another and another, until Leo was nothing more than a bundle of frayed nerves.

There was a limit, and he had reached it, and he found that he had very little to say save "I have to go."

Lucía looked startled. "Back to the house, you mean? But we're going to the luncheon."

"I have a great deal of work I need to do," Leo said, because it was an easy enough excuse to toss out. He'd talk to her, later, when he'd had the opportunity to sort out his thoughts from the teeming mass of emotions in his chest.

When he could explain to her, in clear, concise tones, that even though he would never attempt to tell her what to do—which would in any case be futile, as she would never deign herself to listen to him—it wasn't fair to expect him to watch this happen over and over again.

The two worst moments of his life had been entirely preventable. If not in their entirety, at least in part. His father wouldn't have died if the machinery at the mill had been working correctly. His mother needn't have lain alone for hours before he found her. Letting Lucía be a part of his life, in any capacity, meant risking a third time.

And that was one more risk Leo wasn't willing to take.

"Work?" Lucía crossed her arms over her chest. "Are you really going to hide behind that old excuse? You're clearly upset."

"Can you blame me?" he asked wryly. "Look, Lucía, I know you won't let me protect you. But—"

"I thought we'd already had this conversation," she said flatly.

"If we have, it hasn't seemed to have taken us anywhere."

Lucía sighed impatiently. "What else is there to say? I'm tired of feeling like a useless heiress who's only good at being decorative. I'm tired of no one ever seeing me as anything but quiet and weak. I don't want to feel like that person anymore. And if that's all I am to you… I'd just as soon not be *anything* to you."

"Is it that no one ever sees you, or that you don't allow yourself to be seen? From what I've witnessed these last few days, it seems like the latter."

That brought her up short. "What do you mean?"

"All this time that we've been here, you've been telling me that you want to take risks and find adventure, but Lucía, have you told any of your new friends a single thing about yourself? Have you gone through a single conversation without changing the subject, or pretending to flirt, or putting yourself in danger just to avoid answering a question about your life?"

Her drawn eyebrows told him that he had hit the mark.

"You have exchanged confidences with me only because you think I'm safe—the kind of person who has nothing better to do than to stand around waiting to catch you if you fall. Well, I can't be that person for you."

She answered him in two brief words that sliced through him. "Then, don't."

Leo's chest heaved up and down with ragged breaths. "If that's the way it is…"

"It is," she said promptly.

This was it. Leo had reached the limits of his tolerance.

"I walked away from you once. I can walk away from you again."

It wasn't a threat, just a reminder to himself. He had lived through leaving her before, and he could do so again.

If Lucía was like a butterfly, and holding her too close would only crush her wings, then he would just have to let her go. For her own sake, as well as his.

He gave a hard, sharp nod. And then he started to walk away.

"This has nothing to do with me," she called after him.

Leo turned. "Pardon me?"

"You couldn't save your father. And you couldn't prevent your mother from falling ill. But Leo, being an overprotective, overbearing oaf won't make it so that none of those things happened. The challenge of caring for others lies entirely in defying your fears and caring anyway."

He didn't answer. How could he? What could he possibly have to say to something that absurd?

"In any case," Lucía continued, "you won't need to worry about me for much longer. Cristina and the Fajardos are going to extend their trip for another few weeks in order to visit Curaçao, and they've asked me to join them."

She would find no argument from him there. The Dutch island was far enough away from Vargas's reach—and his influence—that Leo would have gladly paid for her steamer passage himself. The guard Eduardo intended to hire could have the damn near impossible task of keeping safe until then.

"I hope you have a safe journey," Leo said, with icy politeness that widened the yawning abyss between them that he had never known how to cross.

There was a time when he could have learned how

to, when he would have built them bridges out of words and caresses and hope. But Leo no longer had any of those things left.

He hadn't dared let himself hope. But he'd allowed himself to want, and that was almost worse. Because Lucía wasn't a fire alarm—she was the blaze itself. And Leo had come too close to being burned.

Chapter Sixteen

If there were tears prickling Lucía's eyes, they had nothing to do with Leo's retreating figure. Her palms smarted, as did the long scrape along her right forearm. She had wrenched her ankle again, and it bothered her as much as the dull throbbing on her knee.

But what hurt the most was a memory that she had spent five years trying to get out of her mind.

Lucía had been quiet in the carriage on the way home from the gathering at Paulina de Linares's house. Amalia and Julian had been going over some of the details concerning their departure the following morning—they were setting out early, and there was still a long list of instructions that needed to be drawn out for the staff that was remaining at the house. Lucía had been content to let the soothing sound of their voices wash over her as she sat back and thought about the beautiful young man she had met that day.

The carriage had rolled past the open iron grille that separated their property from the street, and as Julian held out a hand to help her down from the carriage, Lucía had contemplated rushing up to her sister and asking her to delay their departure.

Not forever, only for a few months.

Just long enough for her to explore the feelings that had started bursting like fireworks inside her chest the moment her ball had collided with Leandro Díaz.

She would have denied it had anyone thought to ask, but she'd done it on purpose. Not out of any desire to hurt him, but because he'd looked so lost in thought standing there in the shade of the mango tree that she'd just had to get his attention.

And then he'd turned around and she'd received the full impact of it. Even at eighteen, Leo had been intense and serious, though back then, those qualities had been tempered by an appealingly boyish earnestness. Lucía had known, even at that moment, he was exactly the kind of man who would love her for herself, not for what he could get through her.

She only got as far as saying, "Amalia," before her sister turned around with a smile on her lips and Lucía lost her nerve.

She always lost her nerve. And the fact was that climbing trellises and exploring caves and teasing Leo wouldn't make up for her lack of courage. Nothing would.

Gripping her violin case by its handle, Lucía slowly went to rejoin the men. Their game had ended and the little boys they'd been playing with had left. Three of the brothers were lying on a patch of grass in their shirt-sleeves, red-faced and sweat-soaked. Eduardo had evidently gone to get them something to drink—he returned now with a pair of bottles, a young boy trailing after him with his hands full of tin mugs.

After the cool water had been distributed—and in the case of one of the brothers, poured over his head and shaken off in the manner of a rambunctious puppy—

Eduardo went over to the patch of shade where Lucía was standing.

"Where did Leo go?"

"Off to work," she bit off. "Where else? That's all he cares about."

"Are you certain that's the case?" Eduardo asked quietly.

"What do you mean?"

"I'd arranged an important meeting for him this morning, with an acquaintance of mine who wished to enter into a business deal with the mill. Leo chose not to go in order to come here with you instead."

Lucía blinked up at Eduardo. "But he—"

"He cares about you," Eduardo told her. "More than he wants to admit. I don't understand why he's so damn reluctant to show it—it's none of my business, frankly— but his every thought through this entire ordeal has been for you. He could have left, you know."

"Left? After all his admonishments about so much as poking a toe out of your property?"

"He had a telegraph from Sebastian early this morning— he may have found the warehouse where Vargas stashed all the goods that were supposedly burned in the fire. If what's in the crates matches the inventory given to the customs officials and the insurance company, it'd be enough to call Vargas's accusations into question. Leo could have been out of the house before any of us had finished our breakfast and well on his way toward proving his innocence. And yet he stayed. For you."

"Only because he wants to keep an eye on me," Lucía muttered obstinately, even though she was inwardly reeling.

Was that why he had been in such a good mood that morning? Why hadn't he *told* her?

Granted, she hadn't given him the opportunity to say much of anything.

Eduardo was looking at her. "He stayed because he cares for you and doesn't want to see you hurt. Is it such a bad thing to have someone looking out for you?"

Was it, indeed?

This entire time, Lucía had been railing against his overprotectiveness, seeing it as a form of control because that was how her uncle had used it. But Leo had never made her feel incapable, and when he'd urged her to be careful, it was because he truly wanted her to come to no harm.

Cristina and Rafael, looking rumpled and flushed in a way that indicated to Lucía that they had both enjoyed the freedom from Cristina's chaperone, came around a pile of stones. The smile lurking on Cristina's lips faded when she caught sight of Lucía's miserable expression.

"What's wrong? Did you and José argue?" she asked sympathetically.

"No, I— He had an appointment. And I have a dreadful headache."

The concern on Cristina's face would be touching if Lucía hadn't just piled one more lie on top of the stack of falsehoods she had told her new friends. *Friends*— could she really call them that when they didn't even know who she really was? When they probably wouldn't like her if they did?

"I'd hate to cut your day short. I'll ask the coachman to take me back to the house—if that's all right with you, Eduardo."

"We'll be here a little longer," Eduardo said, glancing at the others. "And afterwards, we're dining with Abuelo's grand-nephew. Are you sure you won't want to join us?"

Lucía had to rebuff several more insistent offers before she was free to climb alone into the long, empty carriage, turning away from the driver's curious gaze.

The ride back to the Martinez's house was not a long one, but in her restlessness, Lucía found herself clasping and unclasping her violin case. She had just unclasped it when the wheels went into a pothole and in the ensuing jolt, the booklets of sheet music cascaded to the floor of the carriage.

Lucía bent to scoop them up, smoothing bent pages and closing booklets that had fallen face down. That was when she saw it—a note written on the paper cover of a collection of arrangements and compositions for the violin and pianoforte, in a hand she recognized as Leo's.

I'll believe in you, even when you don't believe in yourself.

Tears came to her eyes as Lucía stuffed the sheet music back into the violin case, just in time to leap down from the carriage as it arrived at the house and rush past a wide-eyed housemaid.

She didn't get far. Another maid stopped her before she reached the stairs to tell her, "You've a visitor in the front parlor. From San Pedro, he said to tell you."

It had to be Julian. Amalia must have sent him to bring her home.

Lucía had had enough of Santo Domingo and of being Luz Robles—and most of all, of lying to herself. She wasn't brave and bold and independent, and it wasn't only for her sake that she'd been pretending to be all those things.

She was almost running by the time she reached the archway, ignoring the sharp pain in her ankle and knee. "Ju—"

Her exclamation died on her lips as she saw the man sitting in Don Amable's armchair, idly pulling leaves out of one of the cuttings Eduardo's grandfather had been propagating that morning.

The one and only time she had seen that face, it had been lit by roaring flames and contorted in anger. And though he looked almost placid at the moment, there was no mistaking who he was, or what he wanted.

Ignacio Vargas had found them.

The look on Lucía's face followed Leo all the way to his meeting with Eduardo's cattle-rancher friend and then back to the Martinez's house, and so did the heaviness that had installed itself in his chest the moment they had parted.

As much as he and Lucía had squabbled since being reunited, there had been a finality to their argument at the ruins that unsettled Leo.

But he couldn't let it distract him. He had a lot to get done and Lucía had distracted him enough as it was. He had expenses to authorize, instructions to give his clerks, and one devilishly important and therefore also devilishly hard-to-find piece of machinery to replace.

There was Sebastian's telegram to consider, too, crinkling in his pocket where he had folded it among the other important things held together by his clip. It was a strong lead, the only good news he had received since this damned mess started. Under any other circumstances, he would dash back to San Pedro rather than let someone else sort it out for him, but with Lucía doing her damnedest to break her neck…

Sighing, Leo opened the gate that led to the Martinez's property and strode up the drive.

The notion that he might soon be able to return to his regular life wasn't as welcome as it would have been even two or three days before. Leo was surprised at how conflicted he felt about it.

It wasn't just that he was worried about what Lucía would get up to without him. He would genuinely miss her—he could admit that much to himself. He had grown used to seeing her face across from him every morning, and not seeing her every day would take some readjustment.

But he *would* readjust. It wasn't that difficult—he'd done it once before. And it was certainly easier than watching her put herself in danger over and over again.

The long walk had calmed him down enough for him to stop by the table in the entranceway and retrieve the documents he had left there that morning, pinned down by a small glass ink pot and his pen. He meant to take them all into the dining room, taking advantage of the fact that everyone was taking their midday meal elsewhere that day, and put in several hours of hard work.

Or maybe not everyone—there were voices coming from the front room.

It was none of his concern and not a bother. He could take his papers to the upstairs terrace where the family breakfasted. There was no lack of tables in this palace of a house.

He gathered up all the papers, pausing only to hear something over the rustling. He thought he heard Lucía's voice drifting through the open archway, but even if she had gotten tired of performing acrobatics around the ruins, surely she would never miss meeting the theater owner.

The voice came again. Her words were indistinct, but her tone was very clearly distraught.

Irritation surged over him. Trust Lucía to have gotten into trouble the moment he had turned his back.

Dropping the documents back on the table, because in spite of all his declarations earlier, *of course* he wasn't about to let her fall without at least trying to catch her, Leo went to the sitting room.

There was Lucía all right. And what was worse, Ignacio Vargas was with her.

She stood close to the entrance, facing Vargas, fingers gripping the back of a chair. A couple of strides put Leo at her side, close enough that he hoped she felt reassured by his bulk.

Vargas was sitting in the comfortable armchair normally reserved for Don Amable, legs stretched out and crossed at the ankle as if he were in the privacy of his own damned parlor. There were visible signs of exhaustion on his sharp face. Leo would have been stirred to compassion, if Vargas hadn't been trying to ruin his life. As it was, he hoped that the man's creditors were giving him hell.

Previous to their encounter on the night of the fire, Leo had only met with Vargas a handful of times. He'd gotten the sense that the man was a competent enough businessman, if not particularly diligent.

Of all the things he had expected of Vargas—and there had been time to do a great deal of thinking in the past week—he had never thought that Vargas was the kind of man to do his own dirty work. And yet here he was, lolling in the Martinez's formal parlor as if he owned it.

Over the years, Leo had learned how to intimidate other men with his bulk, finding that the promise of violence helped him avert fights when reasoning didn't. He tried it now, puffing out his chest and lowering his voice into a threatening growl as he asked, "What the devil are you doing here?"

His intent was not lost on Vargas.

"I wouldn't, if I were you. I have friends outside," he explained, gesturing out the open window at the two carriages full of guardsmen that were rolling up the drive. "They agreed to let me have a private word with you before coming in to arrest you—as a courtesy, you see, because I have been so very baffled as to why someone I held in such high regard would do what you did."

"I thought you told them I was a business rival," Leo said, dropping the pose. "Listen, Vargas. It's not too late to say that you made a mistake—at least regarding Lucía. I can make it worth your while."

It was something he'd been considering for the past several days. If Vargas's financial troubles were so great that he had burned his own ship as a way out of them, chances were he would be responsive to the idea of a bribe, especially if it was enough to pay back whatever he owed.

Leo didn't think he had nearly enough money to tempt the man, but Lucía did and he wasn't about to let her continue to be in danger for the sake of his pride.

Vargas cocked his head. "You're an ambitious young man. Surely you can understand that a small bribe pales in comparison to what I stand to lose if the truth of what happened that night comes out into the light."

"Who said anything about it being small?" Leo said dryly. He wasn't touching Lucía, but he was close enough to feel the tension radiating from her. He glanced down at her. "Are you all right?"

"He hasn't touched me, if that's what you mean," she said tightly. "Or done much of anything but sit there, looking smug."

Leo couldn't hold back a smile at her glorious insolence. Vargas, on the other hand, didn't look nearly as amused.

"Would you have rather I come in here with pistols blazing?" he demanded, sitting up.

"Of course not," Leo replied. "Clearly, you brought your pet guardsmen for that. Will you tell us why you *have* come, or are we required to guess?"

Irritation flashed over Vargas's features. "I'm having you arrested," he told Leo, "for arson and destruction of property."

"That you and I both know I didn't commit. I thought as much. Why are *you* here, though? I can't imagine the Civil Guard felt the need to call upon your assistance to arrest one man."

He felt surprisingly calm, and it wasn't entirely due to the telegram in his pocket. Even if Sebastian's find was proven to be genuine, it wasn't likely to happen for another day or two, and in the meantime, Leo could find himself spending a nasty couple of days in prison. And that wasn't even considering all the ways in which Vargas might choose to silence him.

"I'm here to make you an offer."

Chapter Seventeen

It was surely a response to what Lucía had once lived through, but she *had* expected pistols and threats and perhaps even a little fistfight or two, not…an offer of employment.

Vargas gave Leo a smile that was clearly intended to be conciliatory, though it didn't quite arrive at the mark. "I'm prepared to make you my partner."

"Your accomplice, you mean," Leo observed. Vargas opened his mouth, possibly to make some sort of denial, but Leo continued. "Why would you concede such a great honor on me?"

Vargas spread his hands. "It's in our best interests to cooperate with each other. I've heard a great deal about your genius for business—with my connections, you and I stand to make a fortune."

Recalling what Julian had said about Vargas being denied loans by all of his connections, Lucía was hard pressed to keep from snorting.

Leo gave him a skeptical glance. "And if I should decline?"

"Are you aware of how fickle fire is? And how easily

it spreads in a place like a sugar mill, with all that bagasse providing the perfect fuel? I hear sugarcane fields are remarkably flammable, too."

Ah, that was more like it. Lucía was filled with an overwhelming and inexplicable and, quite frankly, inappropriate urge to burst into giggles. What did it say about her that she found the threat almost comfortingly familiar? She was no Amalia to meet them with the tenaciousness and audacity of a small locomotive.

The mere thought of it must have made Leo feel faint, however, because he grabbed the back of the chair. The last thing Lucía wanted was to call attention to it by putting her hand over his, so instead she placed a hand on her hip. "You'd really cost dozens of men their living— and potentially their lives—just to avoid facing the consequences of what you did?"

"Do you really think I have a choice in the matter?" Vargas spat out. "I was promised that the fire would be enough. One little blaze and all my troubles would be over. Only you had to choose that night to have an assignation on the docks. And now I'm left with a devil of a mess in my hands."

Lucía was careful not to exchanges glances with Leo, though she desperately wanted to.

Letting Leo get arrested meant a trial, and a trial would give him a platform to say, under oath, everything he knew about what Vargas was doing that night. His and Lucía's testimony wouldn't just implicate Vargas in a crime—it might shine a light on whoever had persuaded Vargas to set his own ship on fire.

A government official, perhaps. Or someone with enough power as to make such a thing a decidedly unattractive prospect. Vargas didn't say as much, but Lucía thought it would explain why he hadn't taken Leo's offer of money and run.

The man looked like he hadn't had a good night's sleep in weeks—funny, considering how well rested she felt—and it didn't seem like it would take much to cause him to unravel. The question was, would he do it in a way she and Leo could take advantage of?

Leo's thoughts must have been running along the same lines, because he was nodding as if he hadn't heard Vargas's slip.

"Leo," Lucía hissed in alarm. "You aren't truly considering accepting his offer?"

Particularly now that he'd gotten that telegram and exoneration was so close.

"I may have no choice," he said, not bothering to lower his voice. "I can't let any harm come to anyone at the mill. Or you, for that matter. And as our friend here said, I *am* an ambitious man."

A week before, she would have easily believed that of him. Lucía knew him better now.

"Sebastian has been too wrapped up with his family to be a satisfactory partner—I've been saddled with more than my fair share of the work," Leo said resentfully, and Lucía almost gave him away by snorting out loud.

The day Leo complained about having too much work was the day she would run for cover because the sky would surely come crashing down around them. Lucía knew it, and Leo knew that she knew it, and therefore must have meant it as some kind of covert reassurance.

"I could be persuaded to tell the magistrate that I set the fire over a business dispute that we've since resolved. But I'd want seventy-five percent of your business, not half."

Vargas took this as an affront. "You greedy bastard. I'm offering to get you out of a tight spot—"

"That I wouldn't have been in if it weren't for you," Leo replied. "Seventy-five percent."

"Sixty," Vargas said mulishly. "Or I should be forced to ask some pointed questions about what the girl—" this said with a raised eyebrow in Lucía's direction "—was doing at the docks with you that night. Or what *you* were doing with her." He shrugged.

Leo gripped the chair so tightly that Lucía was afraid his fingers would puncture the woven cane stretched over its back. "I'd need her unharmed and her reputation pristine if this arrangement is going to work."

Vargas grunted. "The gossips already have plenty to say about her. You might have picked elsewhere if it was respectability you wanted."

Leo made a warning noise, to which Vargas replied with an impatient wave of his hand.

"The girl is your affair. I'll keep her out of it if that's what you want. So. Do we have a deal? Can I call off the guardsmen?"

"Not just yet," Leo said, to Vargas's intense frustration. The more the other man's patience wavered, however, the more unruffled Leo seemed to become. Lucía wasn't sure she would be quite so calm in his position. "First, I'd like to review what we just discussed. Just so there aren't any misunderstandings later, you know."

"What's there to misunderstand? You take the blame for the fire, I retract my accusation against you, and in exchange, you get sixty percent of my business."

"Seventy," Leo countered. "Seventy percent to forget that I saw your men taking the crates out of the ship before the blaze even started."

"Fine," Vargas snapped. "It's a deal—so long as word never gets out about what I did."

"And if any accidents should befall Lucía, or the mill, or anyone in it, or even anyone I have the most passing of acquaintances with, I will tell the entire world that you're a liar, a fraudster—and working on behalf of someone whose name I don't dare mention lest your guardsmen friends overhear it through the open window."

Lucía didn't think that Leo knew who that was any more than she did, but Vargas responded to the threat by giving him a glare that was nothing short of malevolent. "Keep your mouth shut about that," he snarled, rising swiftly and stalking forward, as if he meant to strike Leo.

"I wouldn't do that if I were you," Leo said, a faint smile hovering on his lips. "I have friends, too, you know."

Vargas turned wildly and even Lucía felt her knees weaken when she followed Leo's gaze to the louvered doors that led out to the terrace and saw Eduardo and Cristina and the Fajardos standing there.

Leo had seen flashes of movement in the terrace out of the corner of his eye, but he couldn't be sure of just how much Eduardo and his guests had heard. Most of it, he hoped. Or at least enough to back him up if it came to providing testimony against Vargas.

"Eduardo," Lucía exclaimed. "I thought you were all going to luncheon. Why are you here?"

Eduardo hadn't taken his eyes off Vargas, and Leo suspected that he was right to treat the other man like a wild creature that might attack at any moment. "Cristina felt terrible about leaving you alone when you were so clearly upset. We meant to drop her off, but I saw the guardsmen swarming the front of the house and told the driver to take us around back."

"Luz?" Cristina said in bewilderment. "Are you and José in some sort of trouble?"

Vargas had been watching the exchange closely.

"Luz? This woman is Lucía Troncoso, and her accomplice is Leandro Díaz. Your friends have been lying to you," he announced. "They've been posing as respectable people, but the truth of the matter is that they're hardened criminals—arsonists and thieves. I wouldn't be surprised if they've been trying to gain your trust in order to defraud you of all your possessions."

"Luz, is that true?" Cristina asked, her gaze steady on Lucía.

Lucía gave a short, miserable nod. "The part about my name being Lucía Troncoso is. I feel terrible for lying to you, but…"

"Well, this explains a lot." Cristina broke off from the group and came inside the parlor, smiling wryly. "All those headaches. I did wonder if there was more to them than an excuse to be alone with J— What did you say your name was, again?"

Leo cleared his throat. "Leandro Díaz. Leo."

Cristina nodded. "Pleased to meet you again."

Vargas was looking at them all with an air of aggrieved hostility, as if he couldn't believe that they were no longer paying attention to him. "They're criminals," he tried again. "Fraudsters. The guardsmen outside—"

"It's over, Vargas," Eduardo said flatly. "There are too many witnesses for you to bribe or threaten."

"Wait a minute," Rafael Fajardo interjected. "If you must know, I'm very amenable to bribes. What exactly was he offering?"

Cristina dug an elbow into his side. "What he means is, we won't listen to any slander about our friends. I don't know what your quarrel is with them, but I know for a fact that they are good, honorable people. And we won't let you bully them, even if we have to sign statements testifying to what we all just heard."

"And what did you hear? Leandro Díaz trying to work out a deal to save his own hide? If anything, I could sue him for attempting to coerce me."

Vargas's attempt at a bluff wasn't very successful. Desperation was starting to show on his face, which didn't bode well for anyone—a man with nothing to lose might decide to make his problem everyone else's problem, and Vargas looked belligerent enough as it was.

Eduardo didn't bother to hide his dislike of the man. "Since you're so eager to resort to legal action, I suppose I should tell you that our friend Rafael here is an attorney. One of the most brilliant legal minds in Ponce, as it happens."

An attorney? Leo would swear the man was a professional clown.

"I'd hate to make you work during your holiday, Rafael," Eduardo continued, "but would you be amenable to putting together something to help our friends? I have a feeling that Vargas will oblige us with his signature. There's pen and paper in the desk through there."

"It'd be my pleasure," Rafael said, sauntering to the archway that separated the formal parlor from the intimate sitting room.

Leo was still planted solidly between Vargas and the archway that led to the entrance of the house. Without appearing like they were taking too much trouble about it, the Fajardos were nevertheless blocking the other exits. Leo kept a careful eye on Vargas as the other man's gaze darted around, taking all this in.

Vargas was acting like a cornered beast, and cornered beasts always—

He lunged.

Not at Lucía, and definitely not at Leo, but at Cristina, who was the one standing closest to him. She let out a cry as Vargas wrenched her arm in his haste to pull her toward him, eyes wild.

Leo sprang into action, and so did all the other men in the room, but Lucía was faster than them.

"I'll go with you," she told Vargas pleadingly, standing between the men and Vargas. Her back was to Leo, so he couldn't see her face, but all the insolence had drained out of her voice. "I'll do whatever you want. Just please don't hurt my friend."

"Lucía," Leo said loudly. "What the devil are you playing at?"

She shot a single, fierce look at Leo, silently willing him to trust her.

Leo could have easily overpowered Vargas. Leo had noticed the growth of bristles on the other man's jaw, as well as the deep indentations under his eyes. Desperation might give Vargas strength, but his exhaustion would count against him. And, in any case, Vargas was not nearly as broad through the shoulders as Leo, or likely to have done as much manual labor as Leo was accustomed to. He could get her to safety—and she would never trust him again.

He had to let her save herself. And, perhaps more importantly than that, he had to prove to her that he believed in her.

There was no logic in his thought process, just faith.

Still, he subsided, giving Eduardo and the Fajardos a hard stare, and they must have thought that Leo had something in mind, because they didn't move save to grab Cristina when Vargas flung her at them and grabbed Lucía.

Anyone who looked at Lucía in the moment would see a small, delicate, meek woman allowing herself to be roughly steered out of the room by the grim-faced Vargas. They passed the armchair, so close to where Leo was standing that his hands clenched into fists with the effort of remaining motionless.

All the irritation he had felt toward Lucía for acting reckless paled in comparison to the sheer rage making its way through his limbs as he fought to keep himself from reaching out for her. Leo was not a violent person, but in that moment, he could have cheerfully seized Vargas by the collar and—

Lucía stumbled.

Or pretended to—she knocked into Vargas, who lost his balance, making it easier for Lucía to shove him directly at Leo, who had reflexively reached out. It wasn't Lucía he caught this time, however, but Vargas.

In the time it took for the man to realize what was happening, Leo had him in a tight grip and Lucía was looping her narrow leather belt tightly around his wrists.

Between the two of them, they didn't have too much trouble holding Vargas back as he strained to get free. He only stopped struggling—and cursing—when he spotted the uniformed man at the archway.

Eduardo stepped forward, sounding delighted. "Ignacio Vargas, may I introduce you to our neighbor, Manuel de Jesús Tejera—your friends outside might recognize him as the captain of the Guardia Republicana. I had my driver fetch him while we made your acquaintance. I think he'll be very interested in hearing how you inveigled half a dozen members of the guard into trespassing on my grandfather's property and grievously assaulting my guests."

The captain directed a general greeting at the group, his brow furrowed. Given the hour, Leo could only assume he had been removed from his midday meal and was none too pleased about it. But the man's irritated expression vanished when he glanced down at the belt cinched around Vargas's wrists.

"I've been trying to raise four hundred pesos from the government for the purchase of several sets of handcuffs," he said ruefully as he beckoned to one of the guardsmen who had come in behind him. "If anyone hears about this, they'll turn down my request and tell me to buy belts instead."

Next to Leo, Lucía stifled a giggle. Leo didn't think he could produce a sound past his tight throat, at least not just yet.

Cristina was rubbing her arm where Vargas had twisted it. "Captain, I wish to make a complaint against this man."

"I believe you'll have to wait your turn," Leo put in, half-surprised that he was able to speak after all, and that was what finally broke the tension.

Everyone was still roaring with laughter when Rafael returned from the other room to present—with a characteristic flourish—a document for Vargas to sign. Shortly thereafter, Vargas was led away by a disgruntled guardsman, who had evidently gotten a dressing-down from his superior and must be expecting some kind of repercussion, when he returned to San Pedro, for haring off with Vargas.

It was the best outcome Leo could have hoped for—no bloodshed, no injuries to anything but Vargas's pride, and most importantly of all, nothing had been set on fire.

It was over.

He should have been relieved. He should have been *ecstatic*. And yet all he could feel was a vague ache in his chest, as if it had suddenly become hollow.

He started to go toward Lucía, but the others had swarmed around her, filling the air with exclamations. She resisted an attempt to press her back into a chair, but she gladly took a glass of brandy when it was offered to her, smiling so widely that she was barely able to sip from it.

Backing away to lean against the wall, Leo shook his head to decline the glass Eduardo was extending his way. Vargas was gone, and with the threat of prison no longer hanging over his head, Leo didn't have to waste any time in returning home and resuming his regular life. Back to the mill, never again to see Lucía over breakfast every morning and watch with amazement as she piled spoonful after spoonful of sugar into her coffee and smiled that shimmering smile of hers.

She *was* reckless. And stubborn and infuriating. But she was also more resourceful than he had given her credit for.

And she was damned strong.

How was it possible that he had once found her delicate and fragile? It shouldn't have taken a closer inspection to see the steel running through her veins.

Leo had left San Pedro thinking that his business and his reputation were at stake. He couldn't have been more wrong. It was his heart that was on the line.

Chapter Eighteen

Lucía had never felt so competent in her life. She took a sip of brandy, relishing in the taste and the sensation of having saved herself, for once.

"Have you any idea who that vile man's conspirators are?" Cristina asked, after Lucía had explained everything to the group.

"I don't know," Eduardo said, grimacing, "and I don't relish opening up that particular can of worms. It's up to Leo and Lucía whether or not they want to find more answers."

Lucía wrapped her arms around herself. "I think I've had enough answers for now," she said, and turned around to see if Leo agreed, only to be met with his absence. "Where's Leo?"

"Le— Oh," Cristina said. "I suppose it'll take me a while to get used to your new names. Your true names, I mean. I believe I saw him leave the room several minutes ago."

That was it, then. The dispute with Vargas was over and Leo was so eager to go home that he hadn't even waited until the end of their little celebration.

For a moment, when he'd stood back to let her deal with Vargas herself, Lucía had almost thought... Her mouth firmed.

Eduardo was proposing a toast, which the Fajardos were seconding with enthusiasm as they refreshed their brandies. Lucía accepted another tiny splash of the drink, already a little lightheaded.

Leo hadn't reappeared by the time the decanter had been emptied and a housemaid had come in—twice—to tell them that luncheon was on the table. Upon hearing that the group had returned much earlier than expected, the Martinez's cook had whipped up a quick meal, which was a good thing because they were all famished. To hear Eduardo and the Fajardos, in fact, one would think that it had been decades since the empanadas they'd had at the ruins.

If Leo was going hungry because he just couldn't stand to be a part of the group, that was his problem.

Lucía didn't care, truly she didn't. She'd already decided that there was no future for her and Leo. Nothing had changed just because Vargas would no longer be troubling them and their sole reason for remaining at the Martinez's house was gone.

Cristina, her mother and the Fajardos would be leaving in three days, and Lucía meant to join them. It would be the start of her new, adventurous life.

Still grimy and perspiring from their outing to the ruins, everyone agreed with Lucía when she proposed freshening up before heading to the dining room.

In Lucía's case, that meant changing into an entirely different ensemble. Quickly stripping down to her underthings, she hurried to the washstand and poured a stream of water into the porcelain bowl. She had just finished wiping down her body with a clean square of cotton when a rustle made by something far larger than a bird made her glance sharply at the window.

She set the washcloth down and went to investigate, her heart in her throat. Vargas might have escaped, or he might've had an accomplice or—

"Leo?"

His strong fingers were clinging to what was left of the trellis, and the top of his head, which was beaded with water, was almost even with the low windowsill.

"I thought Don Amable was having the trellis taken down."

"He wants to find a way to preserve the jasmine first," Leo said, and finished heaving himself into Lucía's bedroom. The room felt suddenly full—with his bulk, with the faint scent of soap and with Lucía's unreasonable hopes. "One side of it was rotted almost through, but some of the wood was still in good enough— *Oh*. I can come back after you've dressed."

"And let you plummet to your death, climbing that thing again?" she said, and she managed to make it sound teasing even though her pulse was racing.

"Well, I'd use the door the second time. I don't think my knees can take that climb again."

Lucía gestured for him to sit in the armchair. He glanced at the clothes she had folded over its back, his lips twitching into a mystifying smile.

"Why *did* you make that climb? Feeling a little adventurous after everything that happened?"

"I can't let you take *all* the risks, can I?" Leo said lightly. Lucía waited as a serious expression settled on his face, charmed by the slight dip between his eyebrows. "I was feeling brave, actually."

"So happy to hear you admit that climbing the trellis was an act of courage, not foolhardiness."

"You know what really takes courage? Opening your heart to someone else."

Lucía forgot to breathe for a second.

"There's something I want to show you. And something I need to tell you."

Apprehension shivered through her. "Do you need me to close the shutters? We seem to have our best conversations in the dark."

"No," Leo said, standing up. "I need to see you."

Heat flared over her, though she didn't think Leo meant it lasciviously. Not that she would have minded if he had—her skin was aching for his touch, and had been ever since he had whispered those words to her in the carriage earlier that morning.

Leo was in his shirtsleeves, the latter rolled up almost to the elbow, because he was the kind of man who was considerate of laundresses even while climbing trellises like a prince in a fairy tale.

He reached into his pocket with his free hand and pulled out some folded banknotes held together by a silver clip—the one he was so upset about losing at the lake. Lucía couldn't begin to speculate as to why it was so important to Leo that she see it. Unless…

She crossed her arms over her chest. "Are you about to tell me that the clip was given to you by a former sweetheart and it has dawned on you that you want to rekindle your romance?"

Blinking, Leo glanced down at the clip in his hand. "No, I bought that at Don Enrique's store. What I wanted to show you was this."

Easing the banknotes out of their holder, he unfolded

them to show her a small piece of paper, likewise folded, tucked inside them. Her heart began to pound as she spotted part of an address scribbled across the top, which she recognized as that of the apartment she had shared with Amalia and Julian in Vienna.

"The reason why I tried so hard to avoid answering your question is because I did write to you—I just never posted that last letter. I kept it in my pocket for five years as a reminder of how useless dreaming is."

"How flattering," she said with forced lightness. "Is there a reason you're telling me this now?"

"I realized some things today. The first time we met— the first instant—I thought I had fallen in love with you. I know now that was just infatuation."

An exasperated sigh exploded out of Lucía and she started to turn back to the washstand. She was sore and hungry and she didn't have time for—

He caught her wrist, and she glanced back at him in spite of herself. "The reason I know that is because it pales in comparison to what I feel for you now. How could I have truly loved you back then, when I didn't know the fierceness and strength and bravery in your heart? Or that your kisses could make my own heart take flight. I was just a boy when wet met—I know so much better now."

"Is that so?" she asked tartly. "Might I remind you that a week ago, you were telling me in no uncertain terms—and on a public street, no less—that you were disinclined to renew our acquaintance?"

Leo's lips spread into a broad smile. "I've grown a great deal since then—thanks to you, mostly. Lucía, when I stopped writing to you, it wasn't only because I was too busy taking care of my mother. The hope I needed to envision a future with you was in dangerously short supply. Hoping and dreaming were risks I wasn't willing to take. These days with you have given it back to me. You were right. It doesn't matter how much wealth or power or influence I accumulate. I have nothing without you. I *am* nothing with you."

He was still holding on to her wrist, and that single point of contact—or maybe it was his nearness and the fact that she was in her underthings—was making her nipples tighten with wild, unrestrained longing for his touch.

"Leo..."

Leo's thumb stroked the delicate skin on the inside of her wrist. "I thought that being away from you all those years would make it easier to forget that I had ever cared for you. But all I had to do was lay eyes on you and, suddenly, I wanted you more than I ever had. And that I missed you as surely as if I had carved away a piece of myself and tried to pretend like it didn't matter."

"You might have let me know just a tiny bit sooner," Lucía couldn't resist saying. "Maybe then we wouldn't have spent so much time running from each other."

"I'm ready to stop running. Are you?"

Lucía bit her lip. "I don't know."

It wasn't entirely accurate to say that Leo's heart stopped, as he was still standing in Lucía's bedroom, but it felt like a near thing.

"I wouldn't be the kind of wife who knits quietly or spends her afternoons in a rocking chair, watching the world pass her by," she said, her eyes flashing with defiance.

"Lucía." He perched on the armchair, his pulse roaring in his ears. "I wouldn't want you to be anything other than who you are."

"You say that now," she said, and began pacing along the length of the room. "But what will happen when I decide that I want to walk home in the rain? Or when I burn myself trying to cook a meal? You can say that you won't be overprotective, and I'd appreciate it, but how can I know that you'll always mean it?"

"You can't, I suppose," Leo said, his heart splintering as he recognized that she made a fair point. "And I know I don't have the right to ask that you believe me when I tell you that I'm going to try my best. Loving you is the biggest risk I could think of undertaking. You could devastate me with a single look. Bring me to my knees with a word. You see, it wasn't you I'd been trying to protect this whole time—it was myself."

She paused at that, turning to give him a censorious look. "You did a terrible job of that."

"I know," he confessed. "It made me wretchedly unhappy. And it's taken me this long to realize that I can't protect myself from my feelings. And even though watching you put yourself in danger is almost torture, I can't protect you from your feelings, either."

Lucía nodded slowly. "There's something else," she said, and there went Leo's heart again. "I've been thinking about writing to my old instructors in Vienna. Even if the Academy won't take me back, they may have some idea of where I could go instead. I want to be serious about my music again—I have to."

Lucía sounded like she was trying to convince herself… and like it was an argument against herself that she had already lost.

He started to smile at her.

"You're too devoted to your work to want to follow me to Europe," she told him, frowning. "And you had all these plans about purchasing your mother a new house."

"That is true." Leo looked down at his hands. "If I have to, I will give up my share of the business and everything I have built over the past five years if it means finding a place at your side, wherever you might happen to be. As for my mother… I think it's time I finally asked her what she wants and what will make her happy, instead of trying to impose my own ideas on her. I told you I wanted to give her security, but the truth is that I'm the one who's been craving it. I know now it can't be found in a company or a bank account or even in a large house."

She stood stock-still, staring down at him. "Really? You would do that for me?"

"Lucía, you have no idea how many wild, impossible, risky, impractical things I would do for you."

"Why, Leandro Díaz." A bright, shimmering smile was breaking like dawn over Lucía's lips. She stepped in between his legs and captured his face between both her hands. "You really have changed, haven't you?"

Leo placed his hands on her hips, feeling the heat of her skin through the thin fabric of her drawers. "I'm trying to. I imagine there will be plenty of times through the years when I might need to be reminded of everything I just professed," he said dryly. "But I hope I will never be too stubborn to listen."

Lucía yielded to the hint of pressure he applied to her hips and perched on his thigh, twining her arm around his neck. "You might find it comforting to know that you're not the only one who has been remarkably foolish.

I have made it my business to take all kinds of risks—except for the most obvious one."

She was fiddling with the back of his collar, her nails grazing the skin just above it. "Oh?"

"Trusting you with my heart. The truth is, Leo, you have seen and appreciated me for myself from the moment we met. You didn't know who I was when I struck you with the ball that afternoon at Sebastian and Paulina's, and it didn't seem to matter. When I think about spending the rest of my life with you…well, it doesn't sound like such a great risk after all."

She crushed her lips to his, her need as fathomless as his own.

And this time there was no stick between his shoulder blades—just a slow dawning, like sunlight warming to its full strength from the paleness of dawn.

Leo had been right every time he'd told himself that he hadn't really fallen in love with Lucía under the mango tree. He knew that now, with a swift, fierce certainty.

It hadn't been love because *this* was.

Chapter Nineteen

They had five years to make up for.

Sitting on Leo's lap, her body surrounded by his thick arms, Lucía dove in for one slow, lingering kiss after another, letting him feel all her longing and all her passion. After a while, she realized that all he was doing was holding her, and giving her the freedom to explore his mouth with her own.

He didn't even protest when her fingers threaded into his hair, washed free of the pomade that had ruthlessly held his curls back. Lucía knew that she wouldn't hold Leo to his offer of giving up his business. It had become as important a part of him as poetry had once been, and it was clear that he enjoyed applying his quick mind to solving all kinds of problems, not just ones that involved meter and rhyme. But she could take the businessman, as long as this earnest, tousle-haired dreamer also came along.

They had to stop kissing in order for Leo to carry her over to the bed, because walking the two or three steps there was beyond Lucía at the moment.

He laid her gently on the covers, using the tip of his finger to circle the large bruise that was still forming on her kneecap. "That's going to hurt like the devil tomorrow."

Lucía drew in a breath to say something impertinent, but it turned into a gasp as Leo's mouth met the inside of her knee.

"That…"

"…was good?" he guessed, amusement in his voice as he continued to nuzzle the inside of her knee.

She released a shuddering breath, letting her legs part. "Inconceivably good."

"And if I were to kiss you here?" His mouth found a tender spot on her calf that she hadn't gotten around to noticing.

One by one, as if he had a mental map, Leo found each of the small injuries the past several days had inflicted on her, and he soothed them all with his lips and the tip of his tongue.

"I do love you," he murmured. "Looking at you makes me despair of the Spanish language, for being too clumsy to do you justice."

Lucía ran her fingers over the curls at his temples. "There's my poet. I missed you, you know."

"I think I missed myself." Leo lay next to her, gathering her into his arms as he ran his hands over the curves made by her waist and hips. "But I'm back for good. And I'm yours for good."

There were things that needed to be said in the bright, clear light of day. Lucía laid a hand on his chest, where she thought his heart might be. "I never stopped loving you."

His large, warm hand trailed over her waist, and when she arched her back invitingly he knew to slide it higher until it covered her breast. She let out a sigh of satisfaction and let her body melt into his, learning the ways in which they fit together. His thighs snug between hers, her torso against his, their lips perfectly notched.

"I want to look at you," he murmured.

With his help, it was easy enough to dispose of her chemise so that he could continue languidly stroking the outline of her body, with occasional ventures over her breasts.

"What do you see when you look at me?"

She couldn't help asking it, any less than she could help the soft moan that escaped her when his thumb and forefinger closed gently over the tight bud of her nipple.

He pulled away just enough to look into her eyes. "You," he said, as if it were really that simple. "I see you."

She took Leo's wandering hand and guided it between her thighs. One of his fingers burrowed softly past the split in her drawers and lingered there, stroking her.

Lucía tensed. This was it—the moment when he would turn away from her, leave her throbbing with want, telling her it was for her own good.

But all he did was pause long enough to ask, "Do you like that?"

She gave him her answer in encouraging thrusts of her hips. "Keep going. I want more of you. I want *all* of you."

"You already have all of me."

It was hard to believe that she had found climbing a trellis so thrilling. *This* was real excitement. *This* was what she had been longing for.

Lucía ignored the impulse to let her eyes close, choosing instead to keep her gaze trained on Leo's as his fingers traced languid circles over her heated flesh, until her breath was coming in shuddery bursts that he drank in with long, lingering kisses.

He had looked at her with hunger before, but now he did much more than look, as his mouth ranged over her neck and collarbone before finding the impossibly sensitive skin of her breasts. Her legs parted and her breasts exposed to his merciless mouth, Lucía felt a little wild and a little wanton. But most of all, she felt…right.

When she touched him, it was as if he were another instrument that she knew how to play. And his kisses fell on her skin like rain, washing away all the fallow years.

He touched her with care. Not because he thought she would break, but because he thought he might.

When she helped him off with his clothes, it was as if she was stripping off all the protective layers he had built over himself through the years, but she was gentle with his newly vulnerable self as she ran appreciative hands over his arms and shoulders and the hard ridges of his stomach.

Her hand ventured lower, and found him hard and ready for her.

Lucía kissed the underside of his jaw. "We let five years pass by when we could have been doing this all along?"

Leo breathed out a laugh. "It makes me weep to think of how much time we've wasted."

"You don't really think it was wasted, do you?"

"No." He located her dimple with the tip of his finger and stroked the slight divot. "I think we needed time to grow into the people we were supposed to be. Now that we have, though, I don't intend to let so much as another week go by without having you in my bed—and at my breakfast table. You will marry me when we return home to San Pedro, won't you?"

It wasn't the kind of marriage proposal Leo had ever envisioned himself making, but Lucía must not have been too bothered about the lack of poetry in it. Her lips found his. "I couldn't think of anything I'd like better."

He ran his palm over her silky thigh, hitching it over his hip. There was music in the little moans she made as he slid into her in slow, careful strokes that grew less and less controlled as her enveloping heat and her eager mouth on his own drove him far past the point of control.

And the satisfied sigh she gave when she finally stopped trembling was an entire symphony all on its own.

Through the haze of his own climax, Leo thought he heard applause, which would be a fitting conclusion for that particular duet. Then he realized that the sound wasn't in his head, but coming from downstairs, where the rest of the household was no doubt still celebrating their triumph over Vargas.

"Do you think they're cheering for us?" Lucía asked, stifling a sudden flurry of giggles.

Leo gave her a horrified look. "I wasn't that loud, was I?"

"You were perfect," she said, nudging his nose with hers. "The perfect first kiss. And second and third and…"

Chapter Twenty

Don Amable's garden was the most crowded Lucía had ever seen it, his spectacular plants almost overshadowed by the glossy display made by his guests. Opulently beaded evening gowns competed against the flowers, and the painted fans that were being used to stir the dense evening air reminded Lucía of butterflies.

There'd been no time to commission a new gown for the occasion, so Lucía had come downstairs in the white frock. Instead of adorning it with jasmine flowers, however, she had elected to wear the ruby-and-white-gold necklace she'd worn on the night they escaped San Pedro, and which Eduardo had been keeping safe for her. This blend of Lucía and Luz felt as comfortable as wearing clothes she could move in.

There was no longer any need to conceal the fact that she was an heiress, but Lucía still felt a twinge when she came across Cristina and she felt her friend's gaze fall on the necklace.

But all the young woman said was "White suits you. You ought to wear it more often."

"I— Thank you."

Briskly, Cristina fanned herself. "It's hard to believe we're setting off tomorrow. This has to be the most exciting house party I ever attended."

"In more than one way, I hope," Lucía said teasingly.

"If you mean Rafael…" Cristina's tone was matter-of-fact, but a faint red tinge was spreading over her pale cheekbones. "I hope that we'll have news to share once we're home. We both agree that any questions regarding our futures should be posed in the presence of our families. If I'm not mistaken, you and J—Leo will have similar news of your own."

They had more than news—they had plans, and plenty of them. Leo had snuck into her bedroom on the past two nights, though he'd declined to use the trellis again, and hours had slipped by while they lay entangled in the sheets, discussing their future and their past and everything in between.

They seemed to have little need for sleep. But when they did fall asleep, and Lucía awoke in Leo's arms with his legs notched into hers, it was like being reunited all over again.

A pleasantly warm flush spread over Lucía as she thought about it now. "Is it that obvious?"

"To everyone but yourselves," Cristina said, smiling. "May I assume that you won't be coming to Curaçao with us?"

Lucía shook her head regretfully. "I'll have to join you on another occasion. I think it's time that I went home."

"You're too late," someone said from behind her. "Home has decided it had better come to you."

Lucía whirled around. "Julian? *Amalia?*"

There they were, standing behind her, Julian looking rakish in his evening suit and Amalia in a new green silk with panels to accommodate the small but definite bump at her midsection. Lucía flung her arms around them, pulling away only to make introductions to Cristina, who kissed their cheeks and immediately slipped away, murmuring tactful excuses.

Lucía was still holding on to her sister's small hand. Amalia was half a head shorter than Lucía but so filled with vigor that Lucía often forgot their difference in height. "What in the world are you doing here?"

Amalia glanced at her husband. "Leo Díaz wired Sebastian to tell him what had happened, and he had the courtesy of asking that Julian and I also be filled in. I can't believe you would have let me miss all the excitement— or your very first concert!" There was no rebuke in her face, just leftover worry mingled with relief.

Lucía squeezed her again. "I thought I could have a turn being the impetuous one, for a change."

"Change is right," Julian remarked. Amalia leaned against him and he automatically began to knead the small of her back. "You look different."

"I *feel* different. In the very best way."

"That's only because I haven't given you nearly as many gray hairs as you have me," Leo said.

He wasn't alone. Striding alongside him was a beautiful woman in her forties with deep brown skin and eyes the same color as Leo's.

"Lucía, may I present to you my mother?"

A pleasantly powdery perfume filled Lucía's nose as she leaned in to kiss the woman's cheek.

Leo's mother hung on to her hand for a moment after they parted. "It hardly feels possible that we're meeting for the first time, after everything I've heard about you."

Lucía's eyes skipped to Leo's. "I shudder to think what your son had to say about me."

"Oh, I make it a habit to listen to less than half of the things he says," Leo's mother said airily, and Lucía could suddenly see where he got his dry humor from. She had a feeling she was going to like the other woman. "I'm just happy you found each other again."

Leo held out a hand and Lucía linked their fingers together.

"So am I," she said softly, keeping her gaze trained on him as he raised their tangled fingers to his lips.

Before the conversation got much further, Eduardo came to tell them that it was time for the concert to start. After Amalia helped her smooth back her hair, Leo escorted Lucía to the small, high stage that had been built on one side of the garden. Dozens of chairs, already starting to be filled with the party's glamorous attendees, faced the wooden structure.

The side of the stage that had steps leading up to it was screened by a hibiscus hedge. Lucía was able to hear, but not see, her audience as she and Leo paused behind it.

"How do you feel?" Leo murmured, holding her loosely so as not to wrinkle her gown.

"A little terrified," she admitted. "But mostly excited—and incredibly fortunate to have friends willing to go to so much trouble for my sake. I know how much work it must have taken to put all this together with such short notice."

"You're worth the effort," he said promptly. "If you come away with nothing else from this entire situation, I hope it's the certainty that you, Lucía Troncoso, are worth it."

"Nothing else?" she asked tartly.

"Aside from my heart. I thought that went without saying."

Lucía ran her fingers through his loose curls. She had tossed out his pomade at the first opportunity, and he'd allowed her to silence his grumbles with a kiss. "I like it when you say it."

Leo pulled her closer, bending so that his whispers wafted directly into her ear. "I and my heart are entirely yours. For now and for always."

Lucía captured his lower lip, drinking in the taste of him. He was solid and steady, and he was hers.

Up on the stage, Don Amable finished introducing her. With one final brush of lips, Lucía disentangled herself from Leo and went to join the older gentleman.

A wooden arch crowded with ferns and roses provided the stage's backdrop. There was nothing else on the wooden platform save a stand for her music and her violin. Taking it into her arms as she waited for the polite applause to quiet down, Lucía savored the anticipation.

She raised her bow. A second went by as she drank in the rich, expectant silence. Then she began to play.

This time, she didn't close her eyes—they remained open, trained on Leo as he waited for her offstage.

This was the best she had ever played. She moved her bow in confident strokes, no longer hesitant and half-afraid of what those around her would say. She had run from the law and faced down a villain, and perhaps most importantly of all, she had faced what was in her own heart.

There was no hesitation, no agonizing over her technique—there was only her and the music, flowing together as she and Leo had.

Epilogue

Several months later

She might be a scant few days old, but the infant wriggling in Lucía's arms was as much a hoyden as Amalia ever was.

"She looks more and more like you every day," Lucía informed her sister, who was sitting in a rocking chair next to Julian, looking exhausted and desperately happy. "And I can see she'll soon start acting like you, too."

"We'll have our hands full when that happens," Julian said, grinning.

Amalia nudged him. "She's half yours, so it was always obvious that she was going to be a handful."

Sebastian, who was holding an infant of his own while his wife wiped sticky fruit juice from the faces of their other two children, let out a laugh. "Just as long as he doesn't try to teach her how to stand on her saddle—I still haven't recovered from seeing Carlitos treating his pony like a circus animal."

The five-year-old boy in question looked intrigued, but his mother instantly popped a piece of pineapple into his mouth to quell any forthcoming demands.

Julian's smile broadened—already friendly with Sebastian, the two men had grown closer as they had worked together to find Vargas's cache of goods. "Disparage my skills all you like, but you'll find that having a few bandits in the family comes in handy every now and then."

Lucía hoisted the baby higher onto the embroidered cloth on her shoulder as someone pressed in close next to her and laid a hand on the small of her back. Turning slightly so that Leo could stroke the baby's velvety cheek, she gazed at the people who had gathered on Amalia's terrace.

Leo's mother had chosen to remain at Amalia's after their return from Santo Domingo. She'd claimed that she couldn't bear to be separated from Amalia until the baby was born, but Lucía suspected it was only an attempt to give them a little privacy, as they had married almost as soon as they reached San Pedro.

Paulina had lent her home for the reception, since Amalia's house was still in shambles. Lucía and Leo had both insisted on a small, outdoor affair, all the better to kiss beneath the mango tree.

Leo and Lucía were not the only newlyweds—Cristina and Rafael had been married recently, too, and had returned to San Pedro on their honeymoon. They were standing by the railing with Eduardo, deep in conversation as they planned an excursion for the next day.

The sight of them all filled Lucía with fierce satisfaction. These were the people who knew her and loved her, because and in spite of who she was.

The baby extended a tiny hand toward Leo, and he took her into his arms with a quiet murmur. Lucía smiled at them.

And who understood her, down to the very depths of her soul.

Leaning against Leo, she called for the attention of her friends and family. "I finally received a reply to the letter I wrote to the Academy." An expectant hush fell over the gathering. "I'm pleased to tell you all that they have consented to take me back."

The terrace erupted in cheers as everyone congratulated her. Even the baby in Leo's arms contributed a short wail.

Sebastian patted his baby's diaper. "Leo, are you sure you want to go with her? There's no sugarcane in Europe for you to hack away at when you're upset."

Leo grinned. "I'm sure I'll find a good alternative." He took a deep breath. "I hope I'm not leaving you in the lurch. We've time for me to train one of the clerks before we go, and with Eduardo as a partner and in charge of overseeing the shipping, the mill will be in good hands." Leo turned to his mother. "And you needn't worry that I'd abandon you, either. I've already made plans to hire you a nurse and purchase you a new house and I'll write every day. Unless you'd prefer to come with us, or take a rest cure at a spa, or—"

Sebastian and Leo's mother exchanged a glance before bursting into laughter.

"What?" Leo asked, baffled. "What did I say?"

"Nothing, *mi hijo*." His mother patted him on the arm. "It's just that you can be the tiniest bit inclined to hovering."

Leo started to protest, but his mother raised a hand. "In any case, Amalia and Julian have asked me to stay here with them indefinitely and I would like to agree."

"But—the house—"

"The house has always been your idea," she said gently. "All I have wanted is family. And I have that now." She gestured at all the people around them. "I have everything I could need here—at least until the pair of you give me a grandchild or three."

"Three?" Lucía yelped, relaxing into a smile as she noticed her mother-in-law's grin. "I see negotiations are in order."

An hour and several rounds of celebratory champagne later, Lucía managed to steal her husband away from the gathering.

Amalia's garden was nowhere as interesting as Don Amable's, but Lucía and Leo liked to ramble around it. Sometimes they slipped through the carriage gate at the back and walked until they reached the mango tree in Paulina and Sebastian's backyard.

By unspoken but mutual agreement, they headed there now, walking with their hands clasped together. As soon as they reached the tree, Leo tugged her behind it, so that they were out of sight from the house, and pulled her into his arms to kiss the side of her neck.

"We'll be seen," she protested, but she was laughing.

Leo laid a kiss on the hollow of her throat before adjusting the butterfly-shaped pendant that hung just below it. It had been his wedding gift to her, and though it was fairly simple as jewelry went, the gold filigree, inlaid with a pearl and several small topaz stones, was exquisitely delicate. "I thought you wanted adventure and romance and excitement."

"Being ravished in the privacy and comfort of our own bedroom is exciting enough," she told him, nipping at his lower lip.

Still holding on to his hands, Lucía leaned back to gaze up at the branches.

"Planning how to scale it?" Leo asked wryly.

"I might," Lucía leaned against him, letting out a sound of contentment when he wrapped his arm around her and laid a kiss on her temple. "Would you give me a boost to the lowest branch?"

Leo's dismay was not altogether genuine. "I will if you really want me to."

"That's good to know—for the future. For now, I rather like it down here with you."

"I'm pleased, because I have a confession to make. I didn't bring you here to ravish you."

"Disappointing," she said lightly. "What business do you have with me, then?"

"There's something I'd like to show you." He dug into his pocket for his silver clip, which now held more scraps of paper than banknotes. "I got a response from the editors of *La Cuna de América* about the poem I sent in."

"Well, what does it say?"

"That they'll be pleased to include it in the next issue." Leo's excitement was palpable, almost pulsing through Lucía as she squeezed him. "And that's not all—they want me to submit more poems, and they're making space in the paper for a column by their new European correspondent."

"I had no idea the editors of *La Cuna de América* had such excellent taste," Lucía said. "I'm so proud of you."

"I wouldn't have had the courage to send it in without your relentless badgering—"

Leo burst into laughter as Lucía gave him a playful shove before returning to the comfort of his arms.

"The truth is," he said, once he had found his composure, "you've shown me what true bravery is. When I think of all the things I'd stopped myself from doing—all the dreams I forced myself to put away…"

Lucía rose up on her tiptoes and kissed him, breathing in his scent. "That's all in the past. We're living all our dreams now."

* * * * *

*If you enjoyed this story,
then make sure to read
Lydia San Andres's
other brilliant stories*

Compromised into a Scandalous Marriage
Alliance with His Stolen Heiress

COMING NEXT MONTH FROM

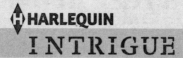

INTRIGUE

#2199 A PLACE TO HIDE
Lookout Mountain Mysteries • by Debra Webb
Two and a half years ago, Grace Myers, infant son in tow, escaped a serial killer. Now, she'll have to trust Deputy Robert Vaughn to safeguard their identities and lives. The culprit is still on the loose and determined to get even...

#2200 WETLANDS INVESTIGATION
The Swamp Slayings • by Carla Cassidy
Investigator Nick Cain is in the small town of Black Bayou for one reason—to catch a serial killer. But between his unwanted attraction to his partner Officer Sarah Beauregard and all the deadly town secrets he uncovers, will his plan to catch the killer implode?

#2201 K-9 DETECTION
New Mexico Guard Dogs • by Nichole Severn
Jocelyn Carville knows a dangerous cartel is responsible for the Alpine Valley PD station bombing. But convincing Captain Baker Halsey is harder than uncovering the cartel's motive. Until the syndicate's next attack makes their risky partnership inevitable...

#2202 SWIFTWATER ENEMIES
Big Sky Search and Rescue • by Danica Winters
When Aspen Stevens and Detective Leo West meet at a crime scene, they instantly dislike each other. But uncovering the truth about their victim means combining search and rescue expertise and acknowledging the fine line between love and hate even as they risk their lives...

#2203 THE PERFECT WITNESS
Secure One • by Katie Mettner
Security expert Cal Newfellow knows safety is an illusion. But when he's tasked with protecting Marlise, a prosecutor's star witness against an infamous trafficker and murderer, he'll do everything in his power to keep the danger—and his heart—away from her.

#2204 MURDER IN THE BLUE RIDGE MOUNTAINS
The Lynleys of Law Enforcement • by R. Barri Flowers
After a body is discovered in the mountains, special agent Garrett Sneed returns home to work the case with his ex, law enforcement ranger Madison Lynley. Before long, their attraction is heating up...until another homicide reveals a possible link to his mother's unsolved murder. And then the killer sets his sights on Madison...

HICNM0124

Get 3 FREE REWARDS!

We'll send you 2 FREE Books plus a FREE Mystery Gift.

FREE
Value Over
$20

Both the **Harlequin® Historical** and **Harlequin® Romance** series feature compelling novels filled with emotion and simmering romance.